Other Books by John D Carter

Shane's Coma

Banny's Boys

Belle Islet Lady

Crazy Cousins

Cape Lazo

Intelligence and Attention

Intimacy in Cocktail Lounges

Cliff's Mayne Therapy Dog

by

John D. Carter

Book and cover design: Vladimir Verano, VertVolta Design

Cover photograph: © SawitreeLyaon, via istockphoto

print ISBN: 978-1-7383629-0-5
ebook ISBN: 978-1-7383629-1-2

Author contact: Belle.Islet@gmail.com

Published by
John D. Carter

He only likes to count his troubles, but he does not count his joys.

~Fyodor Dostoevsky (1821-1881)

Not everything that can be counted counts and not everything that counts can be counted.

~Albert Einstein (1879 – 1955)

Family Ancestral Math*

(Biology differs from Sociology ~ for a theoretical family)
To be born you need:
2 parents

4 grandparents

8 great-grandparents

16 great-great-grandparents

32 third great-grandparents

64 fourth great-grandparents

128 fifth great-grandparents

256 sixth great-grandparents

512 seventh great-grandparents

1024 eighth great-grandparents

2048 ninth great-grandparents

Being born today from twelve previous generations, you needed a total of at least 4,096 ancestors over the last 400 years.

400 hundred years or four centuries – ancestors

(*original author unknown)

TABLE OF CONTENTS

Part One

Clifford

The Car Crash

My mother and sister were killed in a car crash. Some stupid man in a truck didn't stop for the red light. He T-boned mum's Toyota at full speed.

They were trying to get to my sister's ballet recital. It was a basic rainy Saturday morning. I never liked playing soccer in the rain, but I did it because dad likes to watch the games. He's more of a cheerleader than coach. We have two official coaches. Some soccer parents are problematic. Dad's reasonable. He's a lawyer in regular life.

Weather doesn't matter much to dad. Rain, sunshine, wind, whatever, the game goes on. Me, personally, I'm not all that fond of the rain. The field can get slippery, even with my fancy junior league approved plastic cleat soccer shoes. I definitely don't like cold weather, either.

Dad and I were at the Dunbar Beach Soccer Pitch when two plainclothes police people, and another one in uniform, off to the side, came to the sidelines to talk to him. It wasn't good. Dad doesn't do well with bad news. I could definitely see from mid-field, something big was gone wrong. Bad vibes everywhere. Coach waved me in.

I was nine years old. My mother was a document translator of some sort, and my dad had been baseball player. Then he became a lawyer. Both of my parents seemed to have expectations and hopes that I should be a bit more athletic than what I was displaying to that point. Soccer was easier because of social loafing principles. All I had to do was run around and kick the ball every now and then when it came my way. Baseball, on the other hand, three strikes and you are out. Unless the ball hits you, then you're on base. But that hurts.

My older sister, Sandy, was a shining star. She could sing, dance, and school was easy. She was thirteen. She's the smartest person I've ever known. Sandy knew how the world worked. She always helped me with *everything*.

Sandy didn't die right away. All in all, it took a few days. Dad brought me to the hospital to *see* Sandy. After some discussions, dad told the hospital people it was okay to pull the plug and let Sandy leave *life support*. It wasn't good, dad cried a lot. Sandy was brain-dead, but the machines had kept her alive. She wasn't coming back. It was over. Sandy was gone. She became an organ donor.

Mum died at the car crash scene. She was DOA (dead on arrival) at the hospital. I never saw her again until the day of the funeral. They put her in a box with the lid open. I was a little freaked out because that person in the box didn't look like my mum. She looked different. They had two wooden boxes side by side with mum in one and Sandy in the other. Dad said he thought the mortician undertaker team had done a good job on both mum and Sandy. "They look good."

I disagreed. But what did I know about these things? Besides, I was still trying to get along with dad. I did not want to set him off into a mood or anything. Dad's quite fragile. He has mood swings. Mostly he cries quite a bit.

Mum and Sandy were cremated. Then we went out on Uncle Julian's boat and threw their ashes into the Pacific Ocean. Dad didn't do very well on the water. He had to go below deck to get himself together. Cousin Katy and I got to goof around up front on the boat's bow. Usually there are a lot of rules on the boat. Not that day. We got to do whatever we wanted. My cousin is kinda crazy, she's hyper, but I like her. She has no fear. I'm somewhat skittish given all the things going on around me these days.

Before the accident, dad and I never really got along that well to begin with. He doesn't have too much patience and I always do things the hard way. I'm left-handed, and he is not. In the past it wasn't that bad because my mum handled *everything*. Mum was left-handed. When she showed me how to do something, like tying shoes, cutting stuff, or using tools, she showed me the left-handed method.

The girls ran the house. Now that mum and Sandy are gone, life with dad is a lot more difficult. He's always doing quite a bit of crying in his bedroom. Sometimes I knock on the door and ask if he wants some water. He usually says no, he just needs space, and quiet time.

The school people became nicer to me, much nicer. I could hear them whispering, "That's Sandra's little brother." The school principal brought in a bunch of grief counsellors to talk to Sandy's classmates. They cleaned out her desk and locker, put the stuff in a box, and gave the box to me to take home. The vice principal drove me home. I put the box in her bedroom. Seemed like it belongs there. Dad said it didn't matter to him and I should put the box wherever I wished.

Dad's definitely not a *morning person*. Never has been. So, I would get myself out of bed in the morning. Eat some cereal while watching morning television cartoons and then get ready for school. Recently, Sandy said she thought I was getting too old for morning cartoons. "Clifford you should spend your time watching something more meaningful."

Mum said, "Don't worry about it. Cliffie's just fine. Leave him be. Nine-year olds like cartoons."

"That's true – they do." I nodded my head in agreement. "Cartoons are cool!"

Usually, I'd ride my bike to school and back home at the end of the day. I started to suspect that dad wasn't doing too well because he was sleeping when I left for school and sleeping when I got home. These days he's always sleeping. He gets up in the middle of the night and messes up the kitchen. I don't know if he quit his job or what, but he wasn't leaving the bedroom during the day very often.

Dad's behaviour didn't bother me, or make me unhappy, or anything. A couple years ago when we had the first COVID-19 wave crisis, dad worked from home a lot. *Everyone* stayed at home all the time. We were on lock down. Mum bought groceries online. I sort of liked it, but Sandy said not to go around saying such stuff because lots and lots of people were dying from the pandemic virus. "Don't say you like the pandemic, it's a bad look to wear. You don't want to look like that."

Our cousin in Calgary caught the virus and *died*. They didn't know how she got it. Mum said the funeral was not happening because of the restrictions on gatherings. "Difficult times for families."

*

Uncle Julian is married to dad's sister, Esmae. She is a lawyer, just like dad. But they do different types of lawyer work. I don't really know what they do. Uncle Jules is some kind of investor finance person. He likes cars, motorcycles, and boats. He has three boats. One for basic pleasure sailing, one for racing, and a powerboat to go fast. Their daughter, Katy, is unusually loud, and you never know what she's going to do. Katy is the opposite of my sister. But we like Katy, Sandy says, "Katy has a good soul."

Yesterday, I was riding my bike home from school and saw Uncle Jules' shiny white minivan parked in our driveway. At first, I thought that this was going to be a good thing. In the end, it wasn't.

I pedalled faster, got home, put my bike away, and went inside.

I looked through the window, Uncle Jules was sitting at the kitchen table with his little microcomputer gadget doing something, but not video games. He doesn't do games. He's a serious guy. Auntie E was fussing about the place, cleaning and putting away empty cans and stale old food that I'd left lying around. I could see Auntie E's in a *mood*.

"Hi there," I said loudly as came through the door throwing my backpack to the floor. "Sorry, we would have cleaned up the place if we knew you were coming over."

Uncle Jules gave me a small smile, and a three-finger salute, "No problem, Cliff." He came over, picked me up with a bear hug and twirled me about. "How are you doing?"

"Good, thanks, I'm great," I said with a small smile, "I'll go get dad. He's probably still sleeping upstairs."

Auntie E pivoted drew a sour face, pointed to the table, "Clifford, your father is not upstairs. Let's sit down at the table and talk."

"Okay." I knew not to argue when someone was so stern faced. Even though this is *my* house not hers, I thought about saying, "You are not the boss of me!" But sister Sandy sits on my shoulder nowadays whispering in my ear: "Don't be rude. No need for drama."

For a few years I went *everywhere* with my favourite blanket, accompanied by my invisible best friend, Arthur. Last year, Sandy said it was time to stop *both* blanket and Artie. I listened, but I didn't really want to let either of them go. However, I did. The blanket went to storage and Artie went to the land of ether.

"Growing up is not easy." Sandy suggested, "You're a big boy now."

Did I mention, nowadays Sandy sits on my shoulder giving advice all the time. I don't need Artie anymore. Sometimes I miss the blanket. It was warm and comforting.

Auntie E pointed at me and said, "Clifford, *please*, just sit down. We have some things to talk about."

And that's when the wheels fell off the bus. Raffi's song didn't take long to start spinning in my head before everything went wrong. Really wrong.

Uncle Jules took over. He let out a heavy sigh, "We got a phone call this morning from your father," Uncle J's face became a frown, "and that's why we are here now."

"Okay." I gave them a nod.

I knew this discussion was going south now, fast. Wish my mum or Sandy were here in person they were both good with sour stuff. My mum was a no-nonsense woman. She was strong. I'm a bit of a pushover with the grownups. Sandy was not a pushover. She's able stand up to stuff. "You are not the boss of me." She'd say with forcefulness.

"Clifford, you know your dad has not been doing very well since losing your mother and Sandra?"

"Yes," I wobbled my head and shoulder shrugged, "it's not the same now they are gone."

And just like that, Auntie E starts crying with big gushing tears, "Your father is in the hospital," she shrieked.

"What happened?" I asked. "I saw him this morning. He seemed okay then."

Uncle Jules continued to take over the convo because auntie was overboard drowning with the tears. "Your father ate a bottle of sleeping pills and took some other medications. He called us because he didn't want you to find him like that when you got home from school."

"Okay." I raised my eyebrows. I didn't really know what was happening exactly, but I knew they were going to tell me. And I likely was not going to like it.

"We got here as fast as we could," Jules started rubbing auntie's back.

"He was still shallow breathing when the ambulance got here," auntie blurted.

"So, how is he now?" I asked.

"We don't know," Uncle J said softly, "he's in the ICU."

"ICU," I snorted, "what's that?"

"The Intensive Care Unit in Vancouver General Hospital."

"Well, let's go see him," I said with some nine-year-old force. "They let me see Sandy when she was in the hospital."

Auntie Esmae kept crying. I guess her branches on the family tree cry a lot, "They won't let us in now, but they will call later when he stabilizes."

Well, I couldn't argue with that. However, I did try and suggest that they should leave me alone here at *my* house. I did not need to go with them.

It was no use. They insisted that it's against the law for a nine-year-old to live alone. The cops would get involved. There would be trouble.

I packed three duffel bags with some of my important stuff.

We went to their house.

Sandy, sitting-on-my-shoulder, said, "Don't be a troublemaker. You are likely to lose this one, anyway. Go with the flow."

I knew it, this was that.

Before leaving I brought the blanket back out from the storage closet. I needed it now. Forget the *"you are a big boy now"* stuff they said when they took my security blanket away.

The blanket is comforting. That's what I need now.

Comforting.

Other People's Plans

Although they all say I have met my Gramps a *few* times, I don't really remember. Maybe I was too young. Auntie Esmae insists we definitely all got together before the first wave of the pandemic for various family functions a few times. I was younger back then, and who knows what was going on those days. We were a complete family back then. Nowadays, dad and me don't make a family. Besides that, dad is all messed up and, in some new hospital, somewhere. Something's wrong with dad, but if they know what it is, they're not telling me.

I was only six or seven years old when the first wave of the last big pandemic started. So, I don't remember much about Grampa Earl, other than he was really old. Mum showed me his picture and said Earl is *seventy* years old. Gramps is my dad's dad. My dad is forty-one.

Mum was thirty-nine when she got killed. Almost made it to forty, she was two months shy.

Mum's dad died way before I was even born. He had lung cancer. He died young at age fifty-seven. He smoked cigarettes and breathed in wood fibres from carpenter work. Sandy says that stuff screws up the body's warranty. If I asked, she'd explain what warranty meant, but I didn't care. Don't sweat small stuff, right? And, you know, it's all small stuff.

My mum's mum died when I was a baby from a heart problem failure cardiac crash. Now my mother and sister are *both* dead. I don't know what that says about the family tree, but the branches are falling all over the place.

Sandy always said, "Stop it, Cliffie, don't *obsess* about stuff that doesn't matter." Sure, that was fine, then, but now that Sandy's gone, I don't have anyone explaining anything thing to me. Dad didn't explain things before and now he's all messed up anyways. So, you know you can't count on him to do some explaining.

Sandy always said, "If I can't explain something to *you* then that means I don't understand it well enough."

I've been living with Katy, Uncle Jules and Auntie Esmae for the last few weeks. They are a nice little family, but they are not *my* family. I am a visitor, an interloper. Now that school is finishing for the summer, they've decided I should spend time with Grampa Earl at his place on Mayne Island. Of course, I told them that was not what I wanted, but when they asked what did I want? I explained I just wanted to go back to my real home.

Dad is in a different hospital now. They don't know when he can go back home, yet they assure me, "He's not going to die. It's *not* a life-threatening situation."

"Don't worry Cliff," Uncle Jules lamented, "your father will join you on Mayne Island as soon as the doctors clear him for travel."

"Okay," was what I said, but I was thinking, "whatever." I know my dad is messed up. And I know you are just talking jibber jabs. I kept my thoughts to myself. Sandy says, "Don't be a troublemaker."

I still don't really know what is wrong with dad, but this isn't a debatable discussion. They were making plans to kick me out of their place to go to some deserted island in the middle of the ocean in the middle of nowhere. They say I know Grampa Earl. I say I don't.

So, too bad, so sad, Clifford's getting evicted and that's that. I had some various thoughts about these things. However, that's how it goes, was mostly what I thought. I have no say anyway. Time to move out.

See you later alligator.

In a while crocodile.

I want to go back to my real home.
This island stuff is dumb.
Other people making plans.
Plans for perfect people.
Sucks to be a kid.
Nine-year-olds have no say in nothing.

Mayne Island

I am definitely no good at packing stuff. My mum knew how to pack bags. If there's some sort of trick to it, I don't know it. Today I'm just packing only the summer stuff and leaving the rest behind. Let auntie deal with it later, I guess. Whatever. Packing sucks. This whole thing sucks.

Upstairs I could hear Cousin Katy and Uncle Jules loudly bickering about which boat *we* should use to dump me off on Mayne Island. Katy wanted the sailboat. She likes the wind. Uncle Jules said, no way, sails take too long. The powerboat is the *best* way to cross the Salish Sea.

Sandy sitting on my shoulder says, "These are rich people problems. First world problems, *which* boat to take, OMG."

Cousin Katy shouts down the stairs, "Clifford, you need any help with packing?"

I did need help, but for some stupid reason I yelled back, "No, thanks, I'm good to go."

"Alright, let's get going." Katy screamed down the stairs.

Sandy always said, screaming was not a good thing. "Don't do it unless you have to."

Cousin Katy is eleven years old. She's two years older than me and two years younger than Sandy. I like Katy. Sandy said, "Katy is a bit hyper, immature and impulsive. Otherwise, she's okay. Most notably, Katy doesn't lie, cheat or steal stuff."

Cousin Katy said she was sad that I was moving out. She always wanted a little brother. "Now, we are both back to being *only* children." Katy said trying to console me as we loaded my stuff from the minivan, down the steep low tide ramp to the powerboat.

"Well, you still have two parents," I reminded her. "My mum and sister are dead. They are not coming back. And my dad, well, who knows what's what with him?"

"Yes, that's the truth," Katy said in agreement, "my mum, says your dad, who is her brother, is not dealing well with anything. He's got new meds and new doctors, but he's not getting any better *at all*. Mum went to see him." Katy shakes her head, "It wasn't good. She came home in tears."

"Well, at least she got to see him," I sighed. "They won't let me anywhere near him."

"That's because you are a nine-year-old kid. They always treat us like little kids."

"We are kids." I sort of scowled at her.

"Yeah, guess so," she held up her palms and shrugged her shoulders. "You want to go below and eat cheese nauchos while my dad does his safety shove off the dock and boat fuelling stuff. It is boring to watch him."

"Sure, nauchos are good." I smiled, giving the thumbs up sign.

*

By boat it takes about three hours to cross the Salish Sea from the lower Vancouver False Creek Marina. Today the ride was rough. A couple times we had waves pounding the boat making it wobbly. Katy screamed, "This is the best part!" She likes it when things get wild. Again, Katy has no fear. I think she is crazy that way.

Uncle Jules patiently explained that when the tide changes and the Fraser River is running high from up country runoff, the two forces come together, and big waves are produced. The delta does that. "Some ships have learned that lesson the hard way," according to our Captain Jules.

Uncle J let me drive the boat when we were in calmer waters. "C'mon over here Clifford," he gestured, "Take the wheel. Keep us heading west for a while."

"Okay, but west, north, east or whatever mean nothing to me. I haven't got turn left or right straight yet. I usually go the wrong way."

"That's not a problem Cliffie. You got this."

We were out in the open water, nothing was near to us on any side, so it was straight forward steering. Katy yelled at me to crank the speed up. Uncle J rolled his eyes, shook his head, and said, "You are doing just fine Clifford. Steady as she goes, we are cruising fast enough. There's no reason to go any faster."

Katy was up front doing poses and howling, *"I have the need for speed."*

Uncle Jules looked over my way, shrugged his shoulders, and said, "I don't know where Katy gets these things from, but the need for speed usually is not a good symptom. Her mother keeps saying Katy will grow out of it. Be patient and give her time."

I shrugged, "Ya, maybe it's a phase?"

He just sorta whistles, and said, "Last week she rode her bicycle down the steep Blanca Street stairs. Seven stitches, a chipped tooth, and Katy was ready to go again."

I remembered hearing about that, everyone was mad at Katy.

I didn't care. Uncle J's disclosures didn't matter to me. Sister Sandy called them *family dynamics*. We all have them, I guess. Today turned out okay, I was having a good enough time. We were out on the wide open sea, and nothing was bugging me! Katy was Katy, and that was just the way it works.

Sandy says individual differences are good. Otherwise, we would all wear the same clothes, think the same way, show up at the same restaurant at the same time and order the same food. That wouldn't be good. "Individual differences are important; we should value them. Personalities and culture are what we are about."

All of a sudden Katy starts jumping, waving her arms, gesturing with her pointer finger across her throat, "Whales, we got a pod of Orcas starboard!" She points with force, "See 'em? Slow down."

Starboard means nothing to me. Again, I'm nine years old and have not perfected yet the turn left or right thing. Turn north or west is meaningless. My maturity is not in question according to Sandy. She said there are mental maturity, social maturity and physical maturity. "Cliff is clear on all accounts. Look for another issue." Sandy was protective.

Katy motioned, "See 'em?" Then she did her whisper scream, "Look over there!"

"Nope, Katy," I gave her a thumbs down sign. "I don't see anything."

Uncle J came over to take the wheel, cut the engine speed to slow, he guided my vision by pointing with purpose, "Clifford, look this way, you can see them?"

"Whoa, oh, oh," I got wide-eyed, "Yes, I see them. That's cool!" I had never seen whales in the wild before. Oh, I *wish* Sandy were here. This is something she would really go crazy about. She used to show me videos of wild animals on the interweb all the time. Sandy didn't like zoos. She said they should just let animals live in their own space, not ours. Zoos just want money. "Capitalism has some down sides."

There were four *big* whales, adults I guess, and a baby whale in their pod. Orcas can weigh up the *nine* tonnes. Although Katy wanted to get closer to see them, Uncle J explained that keeping a safe distance was important because too many people harassed whales by getting too close for comfort. "We won't be doing that."

The pod of orcas was swimming towards Active Pass, which separates Galiano Island and Mayne Island. Of course, Katy wanted to follow the whales, at the correct distance, but Uncle J said, "No way, we aren't going that direction because it's the extra-long route to Gramps' place. We are going the regular route."

Uncle J explained that we would be going around the Mayne Island lighthouse, past the Oysters Cove and then through the narrow passage than opens up to Julsons Bay. "High tide is the best time for the boat to go through that passage."

Evidently, Gramps is considered the King of Julsons Bay. He's got a big house, boats, bikes, barn animals, and small farm stuff. Katy says she's been to the property a bunch of times. "Other than Gramps grumpiness, it's a cool place. He has an ancient Labrador retriever dog. Those dogs come from Labrador. They are natural swimmers with a tail shaped like a rudder. You'll see. Things are going to be okay you know. You're gonna be fine here, Cliff. You gotta give the place a fair chance, eh?"

I gave her a small lopsided grin, "Yes, I suppose you are right. This isn't my fight. Well, not one I might win. Anyway, I'm not a good fighter. I tend to turtle."

"Wish I could stay here longer," Katy glared at her father. "We are just here for the night. We leave tomorrow."

The wind was whistling so Uncle J couldn't hear anything Katy was saying. He just smiled, waved his hand, and accelerated the boat forward. "We'll get there soon. We are riding a strong current in our favour," Uncle J shouted to us.

Katy shouted back, "How many knots the current running?"

"Charts on the laptop say current is four, but I think it's higher."

I had to ask, "Hey sailor Katy, what's a current knot?"

She smiled and started a story about how she learned about currents the *hard way.*

"Everyone knows about high tide, when the water is close to shore. Low tide is when it has ebbed out and you have to walk a way to get to the water. Forget about that, it doesn't matter. Currents and knots that's what matters."

"Okay, if you say so."

"Yes, I say so!"

Katy is all too familiar with people getting angry with her over behavioural transgressions. Evidently, on a previous visit, she took one of the kevlar kayaks out for a paddle. She says the kevlar kayak is good because it's light, but you'll catch trouble for scratches. Kevlar scratches easy, but it is lighter to carry than plastic.

Lots of stuff Katy tells me makes no sense at all, yet I know she isn't lying or anything like that. Sandy would say that Katy is from Mars and I'm from Venus. We're just from different planets twirling in different orbits.

Apparently, Katy took a kayak out at high tide, started chasing some seals, and eventually wound up in deep sea trouble. Katy hadn't accounted for the changing current's speed and the tide turning. She got caught paddling on the wrong side of Curlew Island with the ocean's current pushing her towards the USA border.

Katy says, "Grampa Earl has little GPS devices installed on just about everything!"

I gave her my grimace, "GPS?"

"Yes," she said with a whistle, "even the bikes have Global Positioning System devices under the seats."

"Why?" I wondered out loud with tone.

"Modern tech, I guess," Katy shrugged, "and Gramps likes to know where his stuff is. For an old guy, he's quite tech competent."

Katy often topic hops. "What happened next?" I asked.

"Well," she took a breath, "Gramps was tracking me because my mother, his daughter, would go stark raving crazy if anything happened to me while I was at *his* place. From the GPS readings he could see I was being pushed the wrong way by the current."

She always strays to a tangent. Sometimes she comes back, or she meanders elsewhere. That's Katy's speaking style, I guess.

"So, you know Cliffie, an experienced kayaker can paddle three knots against the current without a problem. Anything higher is a problem. That day the current was running five knots or so through the tight channel. Consequently, it became a problem for me. I was in some bit of trouble, and it was getting worse."

"What happened?" Katy had my curiosity ramped up.

"Oh, well, Gramps got in the skiff, motored to where I was floundering, came alongside the kayak, barked at me, and hauled me into the skiff. We tied a rope to the kayak and towed it back to the dock and went home for dinner."

"Was he angry with you?"

Katy gave me her weird smirk, "Not really. Gramps says the only people who fail are those who don't try. It was a *teachable moment* for him. After dinner he taught me how to read the charts. I had to promise not to do dangerous stuff again. We were copacetic."

While we were talking about Katy's misadventures, Julsons Bay appeared twelve o'clock, dead ahead. "We're here," Uncle J bellowed.

I could see a long skinny dock thing that leads from the big old wooden house to the sea. "Big house, eh Katy?"

"Ya, I guess," she scrunched her eyes. "Hey, look, top of the dock, that's Elaine and Jaspar waving to us. I didn't know Elaine was going to be here. She's the coolest cousin we got!"

"I don't know who is who. One is a dog."

Katy grinned, "Jaspar is the dog. He's the Labrador retriever I was telling you about. Elaine is our cousin from Seattle." Katy started waving wildly and yelling, "Yo, yo, yo, Elaine, what's up!"

Katy doesn't need a microphone or an amplification machine; her voice puts a foghorn to shame.

Sandy sometimes suggested, "Use your indoor voice, even when you are outside. Shouting is unbecoming."

Katy makes a lot of loud noises.

"Yodelayheehoo!" Katy announced our arrival, loudly.

Elaine's from Seattle

Here's the part where I really miss Sandy's clear stated explanations. I miss her pencil drawings, mind mapping concept illustrations, and line diagrams. Sandy could break down complicated connections into understandable chunks. "Let me re-frame it for you."

Apparently, Elaine is our cousin because her mother is Gramp's daughter, and that makes Elaine our cousin. Or something like that. Sandy always said genograms are a good way to think about these anthropological algorithms. "Drawing the family tree from the top down with branches."

I am okay with most math calculations. But these family tree things are confusing. Especially, without Sandy's explanations. Oh, how I wish Sandy were here. She'd know what's what. Sandy could figure things out quickly. Given some time and steps, I can figure things out, just not as quickly as the way Sandy could reason. "Information processing speed is not the be all end all thing. Don't worry about it." Sandy would say.

"Elaine is from Seattle." She's sixteen. Elaine is in the middle of the teenage years. Sandy didn't get that far. She was only thirteen, at the beginning of the teenage years. I haven't even started. Nine is a single digit.

"You must be Cousin Clifford," Elaine said as she stuck out her hand towards me. "Nice to meet you."

Last year, dad had enrolled me in what Sandy called the para-military. I was with them only for a short while. I got to quit the paramilitary when I started soccer. Mum said I didn't have to do *both*. One was good enough. Perhaps if I had stayed longer with the Cub Scouts, I would have learned how to shake hands properly. Instinctively, I reached out my dominant left hand and grasped Elaine's extended right hand.

Katy let out a loud whoop, "Clifford, you are such a geek! That's *not* how you shake hands."

"Okay." I didn't know that. I'm not really much of a hand shaker, or a hug maker either. It's not that I'm averse to tactile touching, I'm just not very good at it. No practice effects.

I did, however, notice that Katy didn't shake hands with Elaine, rather they did big bear hugs and European cheek kisses. Obviously, they know each other. Katy tried to kiss me before, but it weirded me out. Maybe Katy is a kisser or something. I'm not really the kissing type. Seems sorta germy, and when COVID was rampant, kissing would have been banned for sure.

Katy gestured to my direction, "Cliffie is our cousin from Vantown." She grabbed Elaine's shoulders. "I'm so glad you are here. You got some work ahead of you teaching Cliffie the ropes here at Julsons Bay."

Elaine smiled, gave me a small shoulder slug, "That's why I'm here. ESP sent a plane down to Seattle yesterday to get me. He said when Katy leaves tomorrow, I'm supposed to take over and look after Clifford. You know, make sure he has some fun here. It's his time to shine."

Katy seemed happy to hear such, "That's terrific. Cliffie is okay. He's a bit awkward, gets confused sometimes, but you can teach him the ropes."

"For sure, that's the deal," Elaine grabbed two of my bags. "Let's go up to the house. ESP is around somewhere. He'll surface sometime."

The girls were what Sandy calls *high strung* and a bit overwhelming.

I whispered to Katy, "Who's ESP?"

Katy chortled, "ESP is Earl Sanford Porter. That's what Elaine calls Grampa Earl." Katy seemed pleased, "That's so cool Gramps sent a plane for her. You are going to love Elaine. She's the bomb."

"I like her dog," I said with a smile.

"Jaspar isn't *her* dog. He lives here. He's Gramps' dog. He comes with the place."

Jaspar and the girls took me up to the house. We plopped my stuff in the bedroom assigned to me, just down the hall from where Elaine and Katy were bunking.

This house seemed to have two eating areas. One was in the kitchen and the other, which looked more seriously fancy, was on the other side of the kitchen overlooking the ocean.

When I got down the stairs the girls were mixing some sort of drinks things in a twirly machine. Elaine smiled, waved me in, and pointed to a kitchen stool by the prep island, "Hi Cliff, pull up a seat. You want something to eat or drink?"

Katy chimes in, "Clifford *always* wants something to eat. Although when he stands sideways, he's so skinny you can't see him. Cliffie, the human swizzle stick can eat more food than anyone my mum has *ever* seen."

"That's terrific!" Elaine seems impressed. "Would you like sand-wiches, or eggs from *our* chickens, or whatever?"

"A sandwich would be nice. I like grilled cheese." I gave her the thumbs up signal.

Elaine started telling Katy what to do in the kitchen. Which I thought was quite cool because Katy doesn't usually take instructions from anyone ordinarily.

Elaine turned to me, and said, "Sorry to hear about your father's nervous breakdown, Cliff. That must be hard for you."

"No, not really." I replied. "My mum and sister dying has been way worse. I really miss them."

"Ya, I can't imagine," Elaine sighed. "ESP and I went to the funeral. It was tough stuff."

"I guess," I shrugged. "It's all a bit blurry. If I had it to do over again, I wouldn't do it again."

"What does that mean?" Katy asked.

"It wasn't worth it," I explained. "My sister, Sandy, always said, don't do things that aren't worth it."

Elaine says, "Ya, I agree! I didn't want to go either, but ESP said I had to accompany him. He *needed* me. So, what could I do? I had to go."

"Didn't see you," I said, shaking my head.

"Ya, we were in the back, didn't talk to you, only waved and nodded. ESP and your Pops seemed to need the space or something. I don't question ESP when he's like that. Just go with the flow, that's what I do in those instances. They still have father/son stuff going on."

I just bobbled my head in agreement, "Ya, that's the truth, everyone has something going on, I guess."

"Do you know how to kayak?" Elaine asked.

"When I was in the paramilitary we went kayaking," I replied.

"Single or double kayak?" Elaine asked.

Katy did a neck snap in my direction, "Wait, wait, what," she bellowed. "You were in the military?"

"Yes, the paramilitary," I explained. "My dad made me join the Dunbar Beach Cub Scouts troop, but my mum said I could quit when I joined the soccer team. Mum said I didn't have to do *both*."

Elaine did the Boy Scout three finger salute, "Cliff, your mum was so cool! I have all her albums downloaded on my devices."

"My mum has *albums*?" I asked, "What kinda albums?"

"You mean music genre?" Elaine asked.

"Dunno," I shrugged, "What does music genre mean?"

"How'd you get into the military?" Katy interrupted.

"My dad's a lawyer." I put a palm up.

"How are Cub Scouts military?" Katy was confounded.

"Sandy said it was the uniforms, ranks, salutes and chants. That's the paramilitary."

Elaine scoffed, "Whatever," she raised her index finger, "you two want to go to ESP's studio and listen to Clifford's mum's music? He's got her all her videos, too. ESP has excellent video display and music equipment."

"Yes!" I said enthusiastically. For sure I wanted to see my mum's videos. I didn't know she had videos. Wonder whether Sandy knew about the videos.

Elaine points to Katy, "Absolutely no food or drinks in the studio."

Katy tipped her head back, gulped what remained of what they called *smoothies,* "Sure, I'm cool," She assured us. "Let's go, I've *never* been allowed inside the studio before."

ESP's studio was at the top and front of the house overlooking the bay. Elaine said, "When I was little the studio was off limits and I was *not* allowed access. Then, when I was older, ESP hired me to catalogue and clean the studio. Ever since I can come and go as I please. But when he's working, we leave him alone. Don't go in then. Could be a *mood maker.*"

"Thanks, that's good to know."

Mood makers.

The Nancy Walker Band

I never knew my mum had a band. And I always knew her name as Nancy Porter. Evidently, she changed her last name from Walker when she married dad. Some women do that sort of name change thing. I've seen their wedding video a bunch of times, but never ever seen any of mum's music videos. Who knew Mum could play guitar, sing *and* dance. She was lead singer in the Nancy Walker Band!

We were watching the videos on the big screen with the sound booming loud. For some reason I started crying. It wasn't really sad tears. Don't know what the tears were about, but it made Katy and Elaine feel bad. Then all of a sudden, the studio door flies open, and Grampa ESP came thundering through into the middle of the room, "What's going on in here?" He asked with authority.

Elaine jumped up, "Hi Gramps," she started to explain, "We were just showing Clifford his mum's music videos. He's *never* seen them before. Sorry, didn't know if we should have asked you first. It's my responsibility. I didn't want to bother you while you were working in the barn."

"That's okay." He smiled, came over to me, picked me up and *twirled* me about. It was for real twirling spin about stuff. "Hello Clifford, I'm so happy to see you." He kissed me on the forehead, hugged me hard, wiped away my tears, and said, "And who's this little munchkin in the corner?"

I snivelled, and said, "That's Katy."

"Oh, so, Miss Katy Porter, you say."

Katy waved, "Hi Gramps, how's it hanging?"

He let out a big belly laugh, twirled me again, put me upside down on the big stuffed chair. Then he went over to Katy, "Things are hanging just fine Miss Katy. When did you miscreants arrive?"

"A couple hours ago," Katy replied, "We came on Pops motorboat. I wanted to sail over. He wanted to power over. He says we have to go home tomorrow."

"Nonsense," ESP scoffed. "Where is Julian?" he asked Elaine.

"Down on the dock, sitting in his boat, doing something with his computer system."

"Perhaps someone should go get Julian," Gramps said, sort of in Elaine's direction.

She said, "Yes, of course, I'll let him know it's time to surface. He knew you were working."

"That's fine." ESP walked over to the wall, took down one of the guitars that was hanging on a hook, "Do you play guitar, Clifford?"

"No, there are two guitars in our basement," I replied. "Guess they must have been my mum's. We got a lot of stuff in the basement."

"What? You don't play guitar," ESP shook his head. "How old are you?"

Katy answered for me, "He's only nine, and I'm eleven, going on twelve."

ESP nods, and says, "Well then, you both are certainly old enough to learn some of Nancy's songs. I'll teach you some tunes." He handed Katy the guitar.

"Thanks," she started strumming or something like string picking. Katy likes to thump stuff. She should be a drummer.

Gramps went over and got two more, one for me, and the other for him. Gramps has a lot of guitars on hanging on the walls.

Gramps handed me a guitar, "Clifford, my man, this is a small body Martin concert guitar. The scratch plate is special because there were only eleven made back in 1930. Blaine, Craig, and the boys at Rufus Guitar Shop designed this one when they were in Nazareth,

Pennsylvania at the factory. It's a dandy. Let's do some picking and strumming."

I carefully grasped the instrument and gave it some plunks.

"That's good," Gramps seemed to approve, "but you're no Jimi Hendrix. You got it upside down. Your mother was left-handed, too. She was a great guitar player. She had a fancy Gibson Bird, a Fender, and her favourite was an old Jèan Larrivée maple midsize."

"Cool," I smiled, not that I knew what he was talking about, other than it was about my mum, the lead singer in the Nancy Walker Band.

"You know she gave up singing when she married my boy, the ball player?"

I gave him some raised eyebrows, "Yes, Sandy said something like that. I wasn't really paying attention back then because I was busy learning how to ride a bike."

From across the room, Katy bellowed, "We got lots of bikes here, right Gramps."

He sort of seemed to nod some agreement, "Well, we have a few, but never too many. Maybe, we'll go for a trail ride after dinner."

Katy the bike rider enthusiastically said, "Sure, but I am not allowed to ride in the dark anymore."

"Why's that?" Gramps wondered.

I jumped in, "Because Katy's taken too many tumbles in the dark."

"Put a light on the handlebars," Gramps grimaced.

"Doesn't matter, my mum, your daughter, made me sign a piece of paper saying I promise not to ride at night anymore. And, you know, a promise is a promise. My mum, your daughter, says *contract law* is the most important law. Forget criminal law because if contracts aren't honoured, *nothing matters.*"

"Well, don't you worry, we're not going to ride at night. We're going after dinner. So, therefore, it's alright. Doesn't get dark until after eight or so."

Katy punched her clenched fist in the air, "Power to the people," she screamed.

Gramps gave her a wink, "I can deal with my daughter, Esmae. That's not a problem."

Katy gave him a big grin, "Sing us something, Gramps." Katy pleaded.

He started strumming the guitar, warming up, I guess, paused for a second, looked up, and said, "Here's a song Nancy wrote. She had a couple different titles for this one. Sometimes she called it her *John Lennon* song. I think it was called *Coming Home* on her second album. The chorus goes like this."

> All you need is Love,
> John Lennon said so.
> All I need is you,
> Watching our love grow.
> First Verse:
> I've been away so long,
> Oh, I was just chasing some dreams,
> But I'll be coming home soon,
> Just as fast as this bus can carry me.
> Carry me home, home,
> Oh, you know it's where I belong,
> I'm coming on home.
> Second Verse:
> When we were young,
> They said the sky is the limit,
> Yeah, but I know now,
> It doesn't mean a thing,
> If you are not in it.
> So, I'm coming on home,
> I'm coming on home.
> Third Verse:

The new book is doing really well,
All the critics seem to agree,
This one's really gonna sell,
Oh, you just wait and see,
And then I'm coming on home,
Home, home, I'm coming on home.
Chorus:
All you need is LOVE,
John Lennon said so.
All you need is LOVE,
And you should know,
Because I love you so.

Gramps ended the song, looked over to me, "I can't sing it like your mother could sing. It's a sweet song. I've always liked it."

Katy piped in, "I like that song, too. Gramps, you are a great guitar player and singer. Even though I don't understand the song."

He put his lips together in a strange way, sighed, and said, "Nancy wrote that song for my boy, the ball player, when they were having some differences."

"Okay, that's cool, everyone has their differences," Katy replied. "Sing us another, please. Pretty please, sing us another. I like the Stones."

Gramps laughed, started singing some more songs. He tried teaching us how to accompany him on the guitars we were holding. Katy mostly thumped hers and did some howling noises. I enjoyed plunking the strings, humming, and thinking about my mother.

My mother was the lead singer in the Nancy Walker Band.

News to me.

Earl Sanford Porter

My sister Sandy was a wiz on the computer and other techno type things. She also played piano and sang opera songs.

Probably because Sandy and mum did everything for me, I never learned as much as I should have. Now they are gone and I'm on my own. Everything is a lot harder. Last night Elaine gave me a tablet type phone thing to use. She showed me how to work it, but now I can't remember how to turn the thing on. Sandy would know. Sandy was smart.

Sandy said trolling people on the computer wasn't such a good thing to do. Similarly, she said eavesdropping on other people's conversations was bad manners. Don't do it. Nevertheless, there I was listening to Gramps and Uncle Julian *discussing* Katy's situation. Obviously, there must be a bunch of background stuff that got them to where they are now in their conversation, but what did I know? I'm just a nine-year-old interloper sitting on the top stair.

From what I could gather, while sitting quietly, stuck in between the bathroom and stairs down to the other level, the discussion was whether Katy should go home today with Uncle J or stay on longer here on the island. Seemed like an awkward conversation.

"I will have to call Esmae and ask her opinion," Uncle Jules *tried* to explain to Gramps.

"What," ESP scoffed, "you *have* to ask permission?"

"Yes, Earl, that's how cooperative parenting works."

"Perhaps I should call?" ESP asked, "I'm not afraid of my shadow."

I winced; this is what my sister Sandy called *baiting*.

"No, that's fine, thanks Earl." Uncle J replied with some tone. "Katy can stay here for the time being. When Esmae and I have things sorted out we will let you know."

I didn't know at the time I was eavesdropping, but found out soon enough, Auntie Esmae and Uncle Jules were getting a *divorce*. That's a complication likely to be difficult for Katy.

While I was sitting there on the top stair, Elaine quietly snuck up behind me, tapped me on the shoulder, and said, "Whatcha doing?"

Scared the crap out of me. "Geez Elaine," I moaned quietly, "where did you come from?"

"The back passage stairs. We've been buzzing you, but you didn't answer, so I figured I'd better come and get you."

"You've been *buzzing* me. How does that work? Buzzing?"

"There's an intercom in your bedroom, and I gave you a cellphone yesterday, remember."

"Yes, but I couldn't figure out how to work the little tablet thing and I didn't know about any bedroom intercom. Where is it? Anyhow, I was trying to go to down these stairs, but I could hear Gramps and Uncle Julian doing difficult discussions. In my family we were always told not to interrupt or inject yourself somewhere you shouldn't be involved. I've been waiting for them to finish. Where's the back stairs, anyway?"

Elaine smiled, gave me a hug, "Katy was correct, I've got some work to do teaching you the ropes here."

"Okay, but what does that even mean? Teaching ropes."

"Ha, it's sailor talk. It's simply teaching a new person how the sailing ropes work on the new ship. That's us Cliff. I'm going to teach you how things work here."

"Thanks."

"Don't mention it, that's why I'm here."

"Ya."

Elaine winked, "Yes, ESP sent for me when he made arrangements for you to come to the island. You're his *favourite* grandson."

"Katy says I'm ESP's *only* grandson."

"That's true."

*

Elaine is quite cool. She's got a good way about her. I'm glad she's here to help me with the new ropes thing. Otherwise, I'd be sunk. Elaine knows a lot about how to do things that need to be done. She says she's been coming up here to visit ESP all her life. She stays protracted periods. That's because when Grandma died, they didn't want ESP to be alone. Elaine looks after him, keeps him company.

Elaine was born in Seattle and that's where her parents live. She's been home schooled most of her life. Gramps has helped with her education. Elaine's mum is a computer nerd working with a large Seattle computer artificial intelligence conglomerate. Her dad builds special powered airplanes for Boeing."

"My parents met when they were students at Stanford University," Elaine said with a nodding head.

I replied, "Sandy said our parents met when they were students at UBC. Then my dad was MLB drafted and became an all-star baseball player."

"That's a big deal! What position did he play? Whom did he play for?"

"Sandy had dad's rookie card when he played second base for the Montreal Expos. Then he got traded to the Giants. I've seen lots of dad's baseball pics and videos, but I never knew about my mum's singing stuff. I wonder if Sandy knew."

"Dunno, I can't remember if I ever met Sandy. Wish we had gotten together before the accident, but you know how family stuff goes, right?"

"No, not really," I sighed. "I don't really know much about these things. No one ever told me."

"Ya, well, your dad and ESP had father/son issues from some time ago. I don't think they've ever mended their fences. And that's why we haven't ever got together before."

"What was their problem"?

"Dunno, ESP won't talk about it. I've asked."

"How come?" I asked.

"Historical."

I didn't know about dad and his dad having fences with holes or something.

Farmers mend fences?

Relationships and family foibles.

Belle Chain Islets

We stayed up quite late last night watching scary movies on the big, curved screen machine. Previously, my mum did not approve of gory gutsy movies when I was little. "That will give you nightmares."

I don't have as much experience with scary stuff as Katy and Elaine. They were nonplussed with the blood and mayhem. I, on the other hand, winced with the murder scenes. Ouches everywhere. That's gotta hurt, eh?

Elaine explained that our family's ancestors were Vikings. I didn't know that. Wonder whether Sandy knew about the Vikings in our past. I really miss Sandy – all the time!

"Yay, we're not Anglo Saxons," Elaine proclaimed. "Our ancestors were Norsemen!"

Katy punched the air with a raised fist, "And women. Don't forget the women Vikings who were fierce warriors."

"No shit," Elaine agreed, "Viking women ruled."

This was all news to me. Mind you I didn't know about having a cousin called Elaine either until two days ago. Ancestors are even farther back branches on our family tree. "Those that died before us."

*

I *can* get out of bed early, but if I don't have to then I don't. Especially when we were up late the night before.

So, anyway, there I am in the middle of a Viking dream where Elaine, Katy, and I are defending our fleet against the marauders. We're swinging swords, shields smashing the heads of the enemy, and blood was spurting out everywhere. When all of a sudden, I feel something poking me.

"Hey Cliffie."

It's Katy.

"Cliffie, wake up," she poked me *again*, "You're supposed to be awake, dressed, and downstairs by now."

"Why?"

"We're going kayaking with Gramps today. Remember?"

"No, I remember absolutely nothing," I shook some cobwebs from my mind. "What are we doing?"

"Kayaking."

"Okay, okay, you don't have to shout at me."

"Pitter, patter, let's get at 'er." Katy pulled the covers off me, started to tickle, and roughhouse. Katy *loves* to rough house.

I rolled out of bed, "My ancestors were Vikings!" I shouted and started wrestling with her.

We were flopping around the floor wrestling. A lamp accidentally got knocked over when Elaine came bursting in through the door saying, "Knock it off you two goofballs." She pulled Katy off me. "It's too early to be making so much noise."

In unison we said, "Sorry."

*

I quickly got dressed and dashed down the stairs. Although I was not sure what kind of costume kayaking required, I went with shorts and polo shirt. Whatever. I knew they'd tell me what was acceptable.

Gramps was sitting at the head of the table, eating and reading a physical hard copy newspaper. My mum would do that stuff too.

Katy was net surfing with her small tablet thing. Elaine was cooking and serving food from the kitchen to the dining table.

Gramps lowered his newspaper, "Good morning, Clifford, how'd you sleep?"

"Fine thanks."

"C'mon, grab a seat, you hungry?"

"Cliffie's *always* hungry," Katy replied on my behalf. "Even though he's a human swizzle stick, he can eat a tonne of food."

"Oh, is that so," Gramps scowled at Katy. "Don't think I was asking you, Miss Katy. Remember, your manners, please."

"Sorry Gramps, but it's *true*, Cliffie is always hungry."

"That's because he's a growing young man. He needs to eat to be strong."

I saluted, "Yes, that's right, my ancestors were Vikings."

Gramps gave out a big belly laugh, "Vikings you say."

"Well, that's what Elaine said."

He nodded, "Elaine knows the family history for certain."

Elaine came walking in from the kitchen, "Yes, and ESP's father said his grandfather was around when we switched from sails to steam."

Katy looked puzzled, "When did we switch from sails to steam?"

"More than hundred and fifty years ago," Elaine replied putting a pile of pancakes in the middle of the table.

"Well, I love sailing more than powerboating." Katy said nodding her head. "I like the wind. I like it when the sailboat feels like it's going to flip and tip into the water. It never does because the keel is so deep, and my father would see it as a failure. My mother *never* comes sailing with us."

"How do you feel about kayaking?" Gramps asked. "Didn't we discuss that last night?"

"Yes, I love kayaking," Katy replied, as she stabbed some more pancakes. "My father says that he is a boat enthusiast. Truth is he's not much interested when it comes to kayaking or canoeing. Father likes big boats. I like canoes, except they are heavy, and you really need two people to carry and paddle. Kayaks travel faster. Elaine said she'd teach me the Inuit roll this summer." Katy turned her head to the kitchen and yelled, "Didn't you Elaine?"

Katy's loudness brought Elaine from the kitchen, "Katy, indoor voice please." Elaine put her index finger over her mouth for the shushing signal. "Didn't I what?" She asked.

"You said you'd teach me how to Inuit roll the kayak."

"Yes, sure, we can do that. What do you say Grampa ESP?"

He made a snortling sound, and replied, "I say we better get going. Let's meet down at the dock in a half hour."

"Yahoo," Katy yelped, too loudly, and then bowed her head, "Sorry."

When I got down to the dock Elaine had everything lined up. Katy was her assistant. "Hey Cliff, you need a hat," Elaine said as I walked down the dock. "You can borrow one of mine?"

"Why do I need a hat for kayaking?"

"Sunstroke." Elaine pointed at my head, "You have red hair. The sun reflects off the ocean and hits red heads hard."

She opened up one of the hatches on the red kayak, "Here, try this one."

"Thanks," I put it on. "Where's Gramps?"

"On some conference call with his people," Elaine motioned to the house. "He'll be down soon. Let's get you fitted for a life jacket. What colour do you like?"

"Blue."

Katy was already paddling around in a green kayak. "Ahoy Cliffie, she shouted as she came along side us. Nice hat."

"It's Elaine's."

Gramps, Jaspar the Labrador retriever, and I were all going in a yellow double seater kayak and the girls were in separate singles. Gramps sat at the back where the rudder and steering controls were located. Jaspar sat in the middle, and I was up in the front.

I remembered back when I was in the paramilitary. Dad and I went kayaking in a double seater. My dad was in the back seat. We only did it twice and then I quit the Cub Scouts troop. Dad didn't object too much. I think he preferred soccer.

It was a sweet sunny day when we pushed off. Goldilocks weather, not too hot, not too cool, just perfect. Gramps taught Katy how to use the computer to check the tide and current conditions for our söjourn to the Belle Chain Islets. We wanted not to get caught going the wrong direction when the tides turned. Katy learned that lesson the hard way a while back. Gramps called it a "teachable moment."

Earlier, Katy showed me the map and explained our paddling plans. I had never heard of islets before. Evidently, they are small uninhabitable little islands. The Belle Chain Islets are part of the Southern Gulf Islands National Park Reserve. They were named after Mr. Belle, who was a crew member on the Wilkes Expedition of 1841.

"When the tide is high some of the smaller Belle Islets chain are submerged," Katy explained. "Some sailors have learned that fact the hard way and ran their ship onto the rocks."

We were paddling far from shore, couldn't see the dock anymore when I looked backwards. I was having fun. Jaspar was sleeping. Gramps was humming. He likes to hum. Lots of seals would poke their head up out of the water to check us out.

Katy is a good paddler. She can make her kayak move fast, do doughnuts, and buzz about. "Yo, Gramps," Katy hollered as she spun her kayak alongside us, "you two wanna race to the other side of the big Belle?"

Gramps gave out a harrumphed sound, "No, that's fine Miss Katy, you go on ahead and let us catch up to you on the other side."

"How about you, Elaine?" Katy asked.

"Let's go," Elaine replied, as she dipped her paddle into the water and took off churning the sea into froth.

"What a wake she makes, eh?" I said to Gramps as we watched Elaine paddle furiously towards the biggest of the Belle Islets.

Gramps made another harrumphing noise from the back of the kayak. "Yes, Elaine is a strong paddler."

Jaspar sleeps a lot. He's an old dog. Elaine says Jaspar is eleven *calendar* years old, but in *dog years* he's like eighty years old. That's because one calendar year is the equivalent of six dog years. Or something like that calculation. All l know: Jaspar is *old.*

So, there we were, watching Katy and Elaine racing. Jaspar *was* sleeping in his spot on the kayak when suddenly he started acting weird. He was now quite alert making strange noises. Gramps whispered, "Jaspar can sense something."

"Like what?" I whispered back.

Meanwhile Katy and Elaine were paddling like crazy. Elaine suddenly stopped paddling. She was in front of Katy. Elaine raised her paddle in the air, trying to get Katy's attention. It was no use. Katy started paddling faster.

It was at that point we could see what Jaspar had sensed with his dog senses. A large pod of Orca whales was on the other side of the islet. They were now swimming *towards* Katy. Their dorsal fins were large, sticking out of the water, looking magnificent. One whale surfaced next to Katy's kayak. He, or she, was a huge whale.

Katy was undaunted. She has *no fear.* The gigantic whale made a loud blowhole noise or something. Katy started singing, Jaspar started barking, and I suggested to Gramps, "Maybe we should get out of here!"

"Just hold your horses," Gramps cautioned, "we're far enough away to not be worried. Miss Katy, on the other hand, is in the thick of it now. If she overturns, we will need to help her."

"Okay." What else could I say? Seemed like I was the *only* person nervous about this situation.

Katy did not phase the whales. They just swam by her kayak without thinking twice. They created waves as they cruised by, but of course, Katy loved the waves rocking her boat.

"Did you see that?" Katy screamed at us. "Wowzers, that was something I will *never* forget. All those whales *breached* beside me!"

"Me neither, Katy," I said softly. "I've never seen anything like that before in *real time*."

Gramps paddled us up alongside Katy, "You're a lucky young lady, Miss Katy," Gramps smacked his lips. "Those were magnificent mammals. We were fortunate to cross their path. You were fortunate not to tip over."

Elaine smiled, "Ya, I'm teaching Katy the Inuit roll today when we get back to shore. You could have been easily overturned by a flick of the tail."

"No fooling, I was in the middle of them!" Katy was beaming. "This has been the *best* day of my life!"

I was glad to see Katy so happy. She was having fun. I was feeling the same way. Except I wished Sandy was here. Sandy would have loved to see whales in the wild. She would be better than me answering Grampa ESP's questions. I never know what to say. Sandy knew lots of science stuff. She was a good talker. Questions were fine for her. She and Socrates were fine with interrogatives.

"Clifford, you in the middle of a daydream up front there?" Gramps said with a soft sort of tone. "What did you think of those whales?"

I turned around in the front kayak's cockpit, "I thought the whales were awesome. I'm sure glad Katy didn't get bumped or dumped out of her kayak."

"Me too." He chuckled. "Let's paddle onward, eh?"

"Yes," I smacked my paddle down, "I'm ready, let's go."

We kept paddling until we cleared the last of the Belle Chain Islets. Then we cruised over to the beach at Grainger Point on Samuel Island so Gramps could get out, stretch his legs and have a pee in the woods. Jaspar followed behind him.

"Old men pee all the time," Katy explained, as Elaine pulled out the cooler with some sandwiches and drinks for our beach picnic.

Elaine passed us the sandwiches, "Ya, ESP says if he isn't peeing, then he's thinking about it. He's old, but healthy otherwise. ESP says the warranty wears out after fifty."

"My dad's forty-one," I added to the convo. "Gramps is his dad."

Katy whistled, "Cliffie, we knew that. We are *all* related. ESP is grandfather to each of us."

"So how come you've never known much about Gramps?" Elaine asked. "How come I've never met you before this summer?"

"Gramps and my dad have unresolved issues and misunderstandings is all I know. If my mum were still alive, she'd be able to explain. My dad is different that way, but you know, he's the only dad I got."

Jaspar and Gramps came out from the woods and started shuffling towards us, "My ears are burning."

"What happened," Katy asked. "Burning ears?"

Elaine smiled, "When someone says their ears are burning that means they *know* you were talking about them."

"Oh, yes, that's true," Katy did some sort of finger crossing thing in front of her chest. "Cliffie said you were a slack paddler and he had to do all the work."

"Katy," I was surprised, "Don't be a liar."

She gasped, "Clifford Porter, who are you calling a *liar?*"

And then she dove on top of me, started wrestling, and trying to tickle me.

Jaspar started barking, dancing around us, and causing a commotion. Gramps grabbed Katy and pulled her off me. He was laughing, tickling her, and Jaspar kept barking.

I sat there on the beach log, smiling, and enjoyed the moment. Katy was getting a taste of her own medicine. I was having a happy day. Summer is the best. It's nice to be here. I hadn't known what to expect. Sorta thought this place might suck. I was wrong. So far so good. Except my mum and Sandy are dead.

We finished eating, cleaned up the zone, "You must leave it *better* than you found it," Elaine announced.

Katy and I both saluted, put our life jackets back on, and prepared to shove off. "Which way we going now?" I asked softly, just in case it was an uncool question.

Katy softly poked me in the ribs, "We follow the curve of Curlew Island until we reach Horton Bay, and then the current will slingshot us back home. Remember, I showed you the map."

"Naw, I remember nothing. I'm the epitome of *learned helplessness.* Until now, my mum and sister took care of everything!"

Elaine put her hand on my shoulder, "You are going to be okay, Clifford. We gotcha. You're with us now. It's cool."

For some reason I started crying, "Thanks, oh I wish Sandy was here."

Katy had moved on already and had started organizing her paddle, snacks, and kayak equipment. She dropped everything and charged towards us, "Group hug!"

Jaspar joined in by barking. Gramps shook his head, smiled, "Come on, we got some paddling to do. We'll catch-up on the lovey-dovey hugs when we are back home."

I pulled myself together, climbed into the front of the kayak, and we pushed off paddling down the channel.

"How you doing, Clifford?" Gramps said softly from the back of the kayak.

I turned around and said, "I'm okay."

"That's good," he winked at me. "Did you ever hear about the time Miss Katy took a kayak out by herself and got stuck in the middle of the channel with a changing tide?"

"Yes, I heard she got into water troubles, and you had to save her."

"That's true, her mother would have been quite angry with me if things had gone south."

"Have I met Elaine's mother?"

"Yes, some time ago when you were a little munchkin, we all got together in Seattle when Emily received her science award from Michelle Obama."

"I don't remember."

"You were a baby."

"Katy says I'm still a baby."

"Nonsense," he scoffed, "Katy is mistaken, and you are almost ten years old. Double digits my man."

"Thanks," I smiled back at him, "hadn't thought about double digits before."

We paddled along down the channel. Katy was in the middle kayak slot, singing something. Jaspar was snoring. Elaine was the lead kayak. I was feeling fairly fine. Don't know why I get teary eyes for no real reason, but Gramps said to just roll with the feelings. It's nothing to fret about.

"Everything is going to be okay, trust me." Gramps said softly from the back of the boat.

I trust him. Right now, Gramps, Elaine, and Katy are all I got. Jaspar made a grunting noise. "Thanks, Jassy," I've never had a dog before. My dad said he had allergies or something and we should *not* get a dog.

We made it through to the end of the narrow channel that separates Curlew and Samuel Islands. We entered Horton Bay where, just as Katy predicted, the current was in our favour and was *pushing* us back home. Sorta like having the wind on your back when biking, but different. We didn't even have to hardly paddle now, yet we didn't want to lag behind.

Julsons Bay was quickly coming into sight. Jaspar had been sound asleep and snoring. He woke up and started making happy dog noises. Gramps explained that's because Jaspar knows dinner is on the near horizon.

As we got closer the dock came into view. We could see that there were two men standing at the end of the dock waving to us.

Katy turned and yelled at me, "Clifford, is that your dad on the dock?"

I looked closely. Sure enough, that *was* my dad on the dock waving wildly to us!

Katy's dad, my Uncle Julian, was standing beside him. I could see that they'd come over on the powerboat.

Gramps gave out a snort, "Looks like we got some company for dinner."

I could see that dad was awfully skinny now. He used to be so big and strong. He must be okay because Uncle Jules brought him here. Jules is competent.

"Clifford," Gramps sort of whispered, "Raise your paddle and wave to your Pops, eh?"

I did as he suggested. Katy was in front of us, and she bellowed, "Ahoy matey." She knows pirates' languages. Katy watches too much television.

Uncle Jules yelled something back, but I didn't understand anyway. I can't remember when I last saw dad. It was before the hospital stuff.

He seemed to be smiling. He *must* be okay. Sure is skinny.

He's out of the hospital and waving at us. Jaspar started barking.

"Don't rock the boat." I said with a nervous tone.

Gramps laughed because this was funny for him.

Not *My* Prerogative

Prerogative - Elaine taught me a new word today.

So, you see, *everyone*, except Katy, now knows that her parents are separating and getting a divorce. However, Elaine says, "It's not our *prerogative* to tell Katy about it."

I tried to explain to Elaine, "My mum always said secrets from friends about them are bad. Katy's my friend?"

"This isn't like that," Elaine shrugged, "it's different."

"Okay, if you say so."

"Yes, I say so. Not our prerogative. Walk away."

Last night Elaine and Gramps put on a big dinner together. Everyone seemed to have a good time. Certainly, lots of drinks and food fit for an army.

My dad explained that he's on a *pass* from the hospital. Auntie E signed him out so dad could come to Mayne Island with Uncle Jules. He's going back to the hospital in a day or two.

Quietly, Elaine explained to me and Katy, that Uncle J and Esmae have taken *legal* responsibility for dad while he's on the pass. They are the supervisors, legally speaking. "Gramps seemed pleased."

Gramps leaned back in his chair, "So Julian, tell me, is my daughter Esmae still working for that big bucks law firm?" Gramps asked quite politely.

"No," Uncle J shook his head, "she's had her own firm for five years or so."

Gramps made a weird face, "Well, whatever, please tell her I appreciate you two busting Erik out of the hospital so he could come over here for a visit. It's nice to see you, Erik. It's been too long."

Dad almost seemed caught off guard, he nodded his head and said, "Yes, my sister can be a tough lawyer to try and deal with when you don't know her ploy."

"Ploy?" I wondered out loud. "That rhymes with toy."

Elaine gave me a side-eye look with a slight headshake. I knew that meant for me to let it go, just be quiet. This was where we were to be seen not heard. No need to say any more. This was that social skill situation where cooperation is important.

Gramps sort of made a croaking sound, "Well, whatever. It is indeed a pleasure to see you, son."

My dad seemed surprised, and he said softly, "Thanks dad, it's very nice to see you and Clifford, too. Jules has been looking after things for me while I've been in the hospital. I'm *trying* to get better. I'll be back on my feet in no time." Then suddenly dad got up from the table, stumbled, "Excuse me," and took off for a breath of air outside on the balcony.

Jules looked over towards ESP, who shook his head, and said, "Let's just leave him be. These things take some time."

No one tells Katy what to do, she was already out of her chair and strolling outside over to the balcony, "Uncle Erik, would you like some water?"

"No, thanks Katy, I'm fine."

"All right," she patted dad's back as they leaned on the balcony's railing, "If you need anything, just call my name and I'll be there in a hurry."

"Okay, thanks Katy. You're a pal."

"Also," Katy emphasized, "I wanted to tell you that you've done a very good job raising Clifford. He has the *best* manners I've ever seen. Clifford is one of the nicest boys I have met. And normally I don't like boys. I'm eleven years old."

Dad tapped Katy's shoulder fondly, "Thanks Katy, but truth is Nancy, Cliffie's mother, and sister, Sandy, did most of the work teaching him manners."

"Well, yes, of course, likely that's true," Katy raised her index finger to make a point, "Cliffie talks about them *all* the time. He misses them massively, but you should know Cliffie misses you too, a lot. He says you taught him soccer skills. You know he needs you."

"I need him, too."

"Hey, after dessert do you want to go up to the studio and watch Cliffie's mum's singing videos? Gramps got a good sound system and big screen monitor."

"Yes, that sounds like a great idea. Thanks Katy."

"Alright, I'll set it up the way we like it. And you know we like it *loud*."

"That's the best way to do it."

"You know it." Katy smiled ear to ear. "Except lullabies, they are softer. You wanna hear one?"

"Sure," dad said with a small smile.

"Okay, this is from the Nancy Walker lullaby album. Cliffie says he now remembers his mother singing it to him when he was little. Gramps said she wrote this song for *you*. It's called Between the Clouds."

Katy cleared her throat and softly sang.

"Between the clouds, the sun's going to shine,

Between your dreams, you're going to find,

I'm still standing here, straight and tall,

You know I'll come running whenever you call."

She looked up at dad, gave him a slight slug, "That's the chorus, I gotta work on remembering the verses."

Dad pursed his lips together, gave Katy a return shoulder slug, "That's a beautiful lullaby, Katy. You've got the gift."

"Thanks, I'm working on it."

PART TWO

Dr. Randal Reilly, Psychotherapist

"Clinical Psychology helps people feel better."

When you go one step at a time, it'll add up, and sooner or later, you'll get there.

~Douglas J. McNicol (1955 – 2016)

Sometimes you just need to be patient, as a first step.

~Jenny Birtwell, ODNW, (1948 – 2023)

Randal – Do Me a Favour?

My sister, Annette, always leaves me lengthy long, long voicemails. She's a proficient professional talker. I think she dictates rather than typing text messages. Usually, she calls quite early in the morning. She's an early bird. The time stamp on today's call was 8:03. That's not *too* unreasonable.

"Hi Randal, it's your favourite sister leaving you voicemail. I need you to *do me a favour*. Okay, thanks, call me back and I'll give you the details. Ciao for now."

From an empirical perspective, whenever Annie asks me for a *favour*, I know it will be complicated, and I will wish I hadn't responded to the favour. Oh well, at least these days she's getting better with voicemail. Previously, she would always leave long, long lengthy, convoluted complicated voicemail with too many details. Even though I now have voice-to-text message display there's still a lot of words to wade through. And, thankfully, I'm a good reader.

I'm not together enough for calling her back straight away. First, I'll have a second cup of coffee. If she said it was an *emergency*, I'd respond quicker. Otherwise, I know she'll send a follow up email shortly. She always sends a follow up email. We'll take it from there.

I just poured a second cup and the phone started ringing, again. Call display showed it's my sister. Might as well take the call and find out about the *favour*. "Hi Annie, what's up so early?" I asked.

"What," she grunted, "this isn't *early*. Besides, it's a weekday and well after eight already."

These discussions go nowhere, "Okay, fine," I placated, "what's the favour you need?"

"You remember Esmae Porter?"

"No, who's Esmae Porter?"

"Esmae and I worked together when we were junior lawyers at the old firm. She's one of my best friends *ever.* You have met her before a number of times at my summerfest parties. She never misses."

"Okay," I didn't really know what she was on about, but that happens with my sister, "what's the favour you need, Annette?"

"Oh, I don't need *anything,* but Esmae needs a British Columbia licensed psychologist to evaluate her daughter and fill out government parent capacity assessment forms for her daughter's grandfather."

I exhaled loudly, "Sorry, no can do. I'm not taking on *any* new patients these days."

"Yes, you can, and you must do so because I said you would."

"Why did you do that?"

"Because Esmae is a dear, dear friend. She doesn't know who to turn to and she needs *our* help."

"Our help?"

"Yes, I said we'd help her."

"*We?*"

"Yes, Esmae and Julian are getting divorced. I am representing Esmae."

"Really," I exhaled loudly, "thought you *hated* family law."

"Well, I do not relish the practice of family law, but Esmae needs me. So, I'm on board and we need your favour."

I sighed, "Annie, let's see if I can find you someone to take this file. I don't want it, don't need it, and you should have a better batter up than me at home plate."

"No, no, no," she was winding up, "we want you."

Some beeping noises start to interrupt her speech.

"Annie, you still there?" I asked.

More beeps, "Sorry Randy," she moans, "I've got a conference call coming in on the other line that needs my attention. We've got a big merger mess with the federal government's lawyers. I will get back to you shorty."

Then I heard a *click* followed by the dial tone. She's gone on to something else.

Although she certainly knows, but has her own agenda, I'm a licensed psychotherapist. That's what I'm good at. My preferred area of practice is applied cognitive psychotherapy. People with PTSD, depression, anxiety, phobias, and emotional problems are people I can help.

Over the years I *have* done a number of family law custody and access assessments, parent capacity and court ordered evaluations. I am more than qualified to work in that area. I have the training, credentials and experience; however, I just don't like it much. Psychology's pathology-centric mandate is met with custody assessments. "What's wrong with Johnny's mother?"

The court needs to know: who should get the kids – mother or father?

Opinions from shrinks can make or sink someone's case. It's negative work. I'm not saying it is not important work because it is, but it's negative. Winners and losers, anger, and money. It's the judge's decision, yet the shrink's opinion shapes the scene.

I like doing adoptions. That's when the government agency retains me to let them know whether someone is, in my professional psychological opinion, likely to be a good candidate to adopt a child. Generally, this is positive work. I meet with the prospective parents, do some collateral interviews, and ask: Why do you want to be a parent?

Having said all that, the truth is I'm old now, tired, and thinking about approaching retirement. I've been working for quite a while. At age sixty-seven taking on new cases is not attractive. Of course, it is unethical to *abandon* previous patients. Sometimes they need my help, a booster session or two. I keep their files open and see them as needed. I'm managing current patients judiciously. I can only do so much.

The late, great, Jerry Jeff Walker, sang in his 1998 Guy Clark song, *Boats to Build,* "Days, precious days, they roll in and out just like waves."

That's my feeling exactly. I don't know how many precious days I have left. I'm sixty-seven years old!

*

After the 2020 first deadly wave of COVID-19, we all were forced to practice psychotherapy remotely using virtual technology. It was a government order. No more meeting patients in small windowless offices. Some customers and counsellors really liked the new cyber methods. I've always been kind of old school. Face-to-face was what I was trained with, but a caveat of changes is not necessarily something to avoid. Nowadays I maintain a *mixed practice.* Some patients I meet in-person and with others we do therapy virtually over the Internet.

I'm not exactly sure which wave of the virus we are in now because of the variants and mutations. It's been bad, but we are hoping for the best.

I've had *five* vaccine shots, and three variant *boosters.* Not to mention flu and RSV shots.

Due to the 2020 pandemic, the psychology business is booming. Things were busy before, but these days lots of people have problems.

I seriously must get my sister to understand that I'm *not* taking new files. No new patients – period.

Katy Shot her Father

Nowadays *no contact delivery* is the new normal. That means the courier knocks on my door, drops the package to the ground, and darts back to her truck. We don't talk or anything. No pleasantries. No signature needed these days. Someone, sometimes me, paid in advance over the Internet.

Although I thought I had insisted, *no new files,* my sister doubled down demanding I at least read the material she sent over. Would I "please do her a *favour?*"

My wife, Harjit, works as a British Columbia Court of Appeals judge. I often ask her opinion on these things. No one holds my best interests more than Harjit. Of course, she most often says, "Randal, you should do what you think is best. I cannot decide for you."

Okay, so from that I interpret that if I were thinking of doing the *wrong* thing, she'd let me know. Otherwise, it is likely not illegal or unethical. My wife prefers I steer clear of both of those endeavours. Harjit doesn't *give* legal advice, lawyers do that. People always ask her advice; she seldom delivers such sentiments. She's the judge.

My sister, and lots of legal community people, prefer *hard* copy materials. Not me, I'm fine with electronic copies. Easier to store, search for key words, and no paper involved. That's the part my sister can't cope with - she's a paper person.

I opened the thick hard copy multiple pages file with the label on the front:

Katherine Angelita Porter – age: eleven.

I thought to myself, oh boy, here we go, because right off the bat, *eleven*-year-olds are in that grey zone of cognitive and moral development. Psychologists disagree on many things. Psychology is a *soft* science. Unlike our friends in the hard sciences, psychology does not have a formal language to deliver and explain concepts. French chemists, Russian or Spanish all have a uniform agreement language to discuss chemistry. Same thing with physics, mathematics, engineering and technology. The hard sciences build on accepted theories and principles.

Psychology is a social science. It's not the same system as the hard sciences. Having said that, however, one of the intercultural agreements we see around the world is Jean Piaget's genetic epistemology. Piaget's theory of cognitive development stages occurs throughout the world in developing countries and western societies. All psychologists agree that children are not, as Piaget explained, little adults who simply know less. It's not just language development that makes children different, they *think* differently. Adolescents use deductive reasoning; younger children use inductive reasoning to solve a problem. Younger children are *concrete* thinkers. The ability to think *abstractly* is beyond the cognitive ability of younger children. They have not developed that far.

Little kids learn *how* to read. Adolescents read to learn. Big difference between them. Cognitive development in stages is the explanation.

Eleven-year-old Katy is in a grey zone. She isn't a little kid, and not an adolescent either. Katy is in between, on the cusp, creeping along the age developing continuum. But, on the other hand, it's all relative.

Generally speaking, cross culturally, the ability to think abstractly is a cognitive stage that happens with most children *around* age twelve. The concrete thinking child is shown two piles of coins. One pile has five nickels, the other has two dimes and one nickel. Which pile has more money? The concrete thinking child picks the five nickels.

If we pour fifty millilitres of water into a short squat clear container and fifty millilitres into a tall clear container and ask which has the more water, the concrete thinking child picks the tall container.

Lawrence Kohlberg extended Piaget's work with his explanations of moral development in childhood. Ethical decisions and moral dilemmas are different for young children. The *brotherhood of man* is an advanced level of ethical thinking and moral development.

My attention was interrupted with the phone's vibration. The ringer was turned off. As I suspected, my sister was calling. I let it go to voicemail. I couldn't talk, then.

*

The title page: Katy shot her father.

Lawyers like large paper trails, my sister is no exception. A raft of documents, drawings, briefs, pictures, and memos confronted me as I pawed through the pile. Fortunately, one of Annie's junior lawyers, as well as a legal secretary, and two articling law students had put this package of material together. The first few pages summarized what the case is about.

As my sister well knows, I've been doing this type of work for quite a while now. One thing that's consistent with these cases is that the children involved invariably feel awful about the thought of their parent's divorce, custody, access, and the notion of "Where will we all live afterwards?" prevails. Katy Porter was no exception.

Apparently, eleven-year-old Katy had spent the summer on Mayne Island with her grandfather and two cousins. When September arrived, it was time for Katy to go back to school. Upon returning to the family home in Vancouver her parents disclosed that while Katy was away their marriage recently detonated with the discovery of her mother's extramarital affair. This was something Katy did not really understand. Why would her mother do that? However, her father's explanation that he no longer could live with Katy's mother made Katy unravel.

"It's not your fault Katy."

The mother, Esmae Porter, was having an extramarital affair with one of the lawyers from her firm. The father, Julian Kroberts discovered a love letter Esmae was writing to Bryan Petersen. Thus, the letter detonated their marriage.

Evidently, the various documents and notations indicate that Katy has a well-documented behavioural history of impulsivity. A partial list of impulsive behaviours was on a separate page.

Apparently, after the family discussion about the dissolution of her parent's marriage, Katy briefly went to her bedroom. Her father then went to the master bedroom to continue packing clothes. He was emptying his nightstand and dresser drawers into cardboard moving boxes. Katy entered the room, walked over to the nightstand where her father kept a firearm. She picked up the pistol, pointed it at her father, and shot him.

I set the file down. Took a look at Katy's picture. Got up walked to the window and wondered why this happened to Katy and her family. Gazed out the window for a while returned to my desk and kept pawing through the materials.

Fortunately, the thirty-eight-calibre bullet passed cleanly through Julian's shoulder. His clavicle was shattered, and he was certainly injured. However, he did not have life-threatening injuries. The ambulance arrived quickly taking him to Vancouver General Hospital for surgical treatments. He would survive.

The police came, took Katy and her mother into custody for investigative purposes. Katy's mother is a lawyer. Normally, that would be helpful. Esmae, however, was certainly in shock. Her daughter just shot her husband. Everyone here needs help.

Of course, the 2003 Youth Criminal Justice Act clearly stipulates an eleven-year-old like Katy cannot be charged with a *criminal offence*. She is too young to commit a crime in Canada. Nevertheless, the fact remains, Katy shot her father.

I suppose some lawyers would say it was an *accident*. The question will be asked: did Katy intend on shooting her father? In terms of cognitive capacity, did Katy *know* what she was doing?

Guns are bad. I shook my head and sighed.

I took another look at some of the photos, one after another, and then I started putting the file back together. Unconsciously, I had scattered stuff all over my desk.

I didn't want to talk directly to my sister, don't want to get into the legal details and logistics. So, I simply sent her a text saying: Yes, I will take this file. Please make arrangements for Katy to meet me at my office on Monday morning at ten.

Annette immediately texted back asking: How about tomorrow at ten?

Not wanting to volley back and forth I responded: No, tomorrow is Friday. I never work on a Friday. Monday is soon enough.

She replied: Yes, you got it.

For the longest time, I have known that the days of the week mean *nothing* to my sister. Every day is the same for her. By that I mean to say she works every day. She's always been that way.

Not me, I need tools down time. Unwind, chill out, or whatever you wish to say, I can't work every day.

I like to stare out the window and watch the world go by. In the summer my favourite pastime is sitting on the deck watching waves rolling in and out. Figuring out whether the tide is coming in or going out can take some time.

Katy's mother put a love letter in a book.

Katy's dad discovered the book.

Katy shot her father.

*

Monday will come soon enough. I'll meet with Katy Porter.

Looks like I'm opening a new file – paper and electronic.

Part Three

Clifford Martin Porter

"Summer is almost over – Fading Like a Tan."

Summer is Almost Over

Summer is almost over, fading like a tan.
Labour Day is coming, the hourglass running out of sand.
Soon the leaves are falling, and summer goes in the can.
Summer is almost over, fading like a tan.

To my extreme surprise, summer on Mayne Island has been a lot *more* fun than I thought it would be. My expectations were low. This summer we were often doing something as a trio. The girls are great. They know how to have a good time. Katy has no fear of nothing. Elaine is much more mature. She seldom does stupid stuff. She's sixteen going on seventeen. Elaine drives cars and trucks.

If Gramps isn't wrestling with a deadline, he sometimes joins in with our adventures to make us a quartet, but he often has stuff to do. Really early in the morning, Gramps does some sort of Montreal market exchange, Toronto numbers work, but I don't *really* know what he does all day other than chores and chopping wood for winter. He does that almost daily. We've got a lot of firewood. I suspect that I'll be long gone before winter comes on. On the other hand, who knows which way the wind blows? I'm starting to like it here.

Elaine says Gramps is a country gentleman. And that's on the other end of city- slicker stuff spectrum. I am what the local islanders call a city slicker. Elaine says, "You'll adjust."

Katy had to go back to Vancouver yesterday. She's still about the only one I know that doesn't know about her parents' pending divorce.

Today, while we were waiting for the pontoon plane to pick us up at our dock, Elaine was describing the beauty and high points of the four equinox seasons. I listened closely. She knows stuff. I can learn a lot by listening.

"Cliffie, you have to enjoy *each* season. They all have something special," Elaine tried to explain. "The same with colours. Quit saying *blue* is your favourite colour. All the colours are spectacular. You gotta *like* all the colours."

"Okay, yes, you make sense." I couldn't argue.

If Katy were still here, she'd likely argue about the seasons and colours. Katy likes to argue about everything. When Katy grows up, I suspect she'll be a lawyer. She's good at it. She'll be a professional arguer. Elaine says Katy is a contrarian.

Elaine knows whats going on in the world. She's sixteen going on seventeen. Me, I'm confused about a lot of things. I often don't know what's going on.

A couple nights ago, while we were sitting on the dock, under the stars, Katy and me had decided that summer was the *best* season. Katy likes summer because, "No school and their stupid school rules."

I like summer because when my mum was alive her rule was "home before dark." In the winter the sun sets so early. You gotta get home much sooner than later. No dallying along the way.

"Summer is the best because all the sunlight's up 'til late at night."

Elaine agreed, "Yes, that's the truth, the Pacific Northwest is the most excellent place ever! We've got Goldilocks weather – not too hot and not too cold. When my parents lived in California, it got hot. And there are these crazy wildfires burning down whole towns. Climate change is real!"

*

While we were waiting for the airplane with pontoons to land at our dock I thought about my family. Previously, we had flown on the giant airplane that goes nonstop direct from Vancouver to Montreal. The year before last, our family flew altogether because my dad had some business thing to attend. Afterwards we went and stayed at his friend's cottage on the St. Lawrence River. We watched Beluga whales. It was a great trip. My first airplane trip. Our last family trip.

Back then, I was somewhat nervous about flying, but I sat beside Sandy on the giant airplane. She reminded me about when we were riding the roller coaster at Playland. Same thing as the plane. I was squeamish the first time and screaming the sixth time with joy. Fear fades sometimes.

Sandy said, "The amazing thing about flying is you sit in a chair, and you fly. Get it. Flying."

Sandy still sits on my shoulder these days. She tries to help me figure things out. Sandy convinced me when it was time to let go of Arthur, my invisible friend. I didn't want to do it, but she said I'd be okay. Artie was the best invisible friend, *ever.*

These days I'm certainly sure that I am not letting go of Sandy. She still sits on my shoulder making suggestions. Maybe someday, she will go, when if it seems okay or something like that. I'm in no hurry. I need her.

I've never been on a pontoon plane before. Gramps had to leave the island to go do something somewhere. He suggested that we should visit Elaine's parents in Seattle while he was gone. I've never been to Seattle, so sure, let's go. I thought it was an excellent plan. Elaine's parents' place is in South Seattle on Lake Washington. It's near the Boeing beach community. Lots of Boeing people bought property on the lakefront. They carpool to work.

Jaspar was giving out growly soft barks and woofs. He is a surprisingly smart dog with supersonic hyper hearing. Our backpacks and luggage bags on the dock gave away the fact that we were leaving.

Jaspar knew what luggage represents. Gramps was long gone, at the crack of dawn.

Jaspar knew that and he wanted to come with us. "Sorry Jassie," Elaine said, rubbing his ears, "we can't take you across the border. It's too much hassle and too many forms for filling out."

Jaspar barked again. I'm guessing he didn't believe her. Jaspar wanted to go with us. Whether we were on the water, riding bikes, or whatever, Jaspar loved to be with us. He's a sweet dog. He understands our language. And Jaspar is an excellent swimmer. Katy pointed out how Labrador retrievers have a tail that serves as a rudder for swimming. Steering made easy.

My dad, Erik, says he has some sort of dog hair allergies. So, we were never allowed to get a dog, or a cat. I did have a turtle for a while, but something happened to the turtle. Timmy Turtle went missing. My mum said the turtle probably escaped.

Sandy said the turtle was likely dead and I should leave the issue alone and not make mum upset. "Just do it. We are *not* getting a dog." Sandy pointed her finger of doom at me.

Jaspar has dog-ears and can hear sounds we can't. He heard the airplane coming way before we could. He barked and jumped about to announce the arrival.

Pontoon propeller planes are *loud.* This one was painted red and white. Canadian colours, I guess. I thought it would be bigger.

Keven Parker is our Mayne Island handyman, caretaker, and all-round fixer. Keven seems to like working for Gramps. He lives on the other side of the island, but he comes here almost every day to do stuff for Gramps. Keven is usually late because he's on *island-time,* but today he was spot on schedule. He helped tie the pontoon plane's ropes secure to the dock.

The pilot came out to greet us. Keven threw our luggage into the back of the plane, and we got on board. This was my second airplane ride. I wished Sandy was here with me. Elaine is wonderful, but she's not Sandy. This is a small plane compared to the giant one I went on with my family. Elaine says they can't put pontoons on the big airplanes.

"I suppose, theoretically, hydraulic pontoons on a jet *could* be possible, but the logistics and engineering are likely problematic. Let's ask my Pops. He'll know." Elaine seemed confident.

We buckled up, and the plane roared off heading south for Seattle. From my window seat I waved to Keven and Jaspar who were left standing on the end of the dock. Jaspar barked and Keven waved back at us. We were on our way.

"Whew-eee," I wailed, but not too loud, as the airplane started gaining height soaring up high in the sky. The horizon was clear, I could see for miles and miles. Within a couple minutes we were flying high above the San Juan Islands, and then the Olympic Peninsula appeared. We kept going south into some cloud cover. That wasn't as exciting. I didn't like the clouds so much. Maybe I looked like I was getting nervous. Elaine reached across the aisle and gave me a slight shoulder slug.

Katy was forever punching me on my arm, shoulder, and tummy, saying, "That's for nothing. Just wait until you do something." She always thought that was funny, I didn't.

Now that Katy had gone back to Vancouver, I almost miss her antics. Although, statistically, we know Katy is for sure certainly quite crazy, she does make me laugh. Whenever she delivered a playful punch, I started play punching her back saying, "Play with the bull, you get the horn." That's what Elaine told me to say to Katy as retaliation.

Every now and then the clouds parted, I could see the ground. Mostly forest, trees and stuff. I told Elaine, "Washington State looks just like British Columbia from up here."

She scrunched her face, like she does, and said, "What were you expecting?"

"Dunno," I shrugged, "different country, three coloured flag and all, I thought it would look different."

She just smiled. "You can lean the seat back by pushing this button." She showed me where to push. "Just lean back and relax. We still have some distance yet to travel."

"Okay, that's a good idea." I leaned back, thought I'd close my eyes only for a minute or so. I remembered last week when Katy and I took a couple bikes to go trail riding. Elaine couldn't come because she had some home school university project that needed completing. She's a serious student.

Katy led the way, "We're taking fat knobby tire bikes with disc brakes today," she said as we entered the part of the barn where the bikes are kept. "We have road bikes with skinny tires," Katy pointed out with a sweeping gesture, "that's what we need for speed when biking to the Mayne village on pavement."

"Okay," I replied with a nodding head. Of course, I am able to ride a bicycle but didn't know one style from another. Katy does. And I never argue with Katy. There is no point to that. That's what sister Sandy called a *blind alley*.

Katy is good with wrenches, tools and stuff. She pulled out a nice-looking red bike, "This is a good one for you, Cliffie. First, we check tire pressure, then we will adjust the seat's height here." She makes groaning noises sometimes.

I learned that bicycle seat height is important for pedaling power going up trails. Down trails it's a different deal. Katy had me sit so my one leg was almost straight down and the other bent slightly, but not too much.

"How does that feel?"

I nodded, "Ya, it's good to go. I'm ready."

"Alrighty," she smiled as we pushed off down the path, "Pitter patter let's get at 'er," Katy shouted.

"Bingo bango, let's do the tango," I screamed in response.

I followed as best I could, trying to keep up with Katy's pace. She often does stunts while riding. I don't do that stuff, but it was fun watching her. We were cruising. We took the twisty trails that run alongside the bay and then turned inward and started heading up the road toward Mount Parke.

"It's the highest point on Mayne Island, wait until you see the view from the top," Katy was excited. "When the sky is clear you can see for miles and miles. It is beautiful!"

I was huffing and puffing, shifting gears downwards just like Katy had shown me. "Don't stop on a hill unless you *have* to because it is harder to get going again," Katy emphasized. "The science of biking up hills."

Elaine explained it was basic principles of physics. Sandy always said if she couldn't explain something, so I understood then she didn't understand it adequately. Elaine was the same.

Eventually we got to the top of the peak. Katy was correct. The view was magnificent. We could see Pender Island, Vancouver Island, and Friday Harbour on the American San Juan Islands. We sat for a while slurping our water bottles, taking in the view, and catching our breaths.

"Cliffie, you did a good job on those trails," Katy slugged my shoulder, "you're becoming a good biker."

"Thanks Katy."

"You ready to go down?"

"Sure, pitter patter let's get at 'er," I replied.

"First, I gotta lower your seat. I'll show you how to do it so as you'll know for next time."

"Okay, why are we lowering the seat?" I wondered.

"Well," Katy started to explain, "Now we're going downhill on some *steep* trails. Although these bikes have disc brakes, they can stop on a dime, you want the seat lowered a bit in case you need to stop and plant your feet firmly."

I climbed back on the seat, but she wasn't happy with the height, did some more tinkering.

"That's got it," Katy slapped the seat, "let's get going. I'll lead, you follow, but not *too* close. Okay?"

"Ya, let's roll!" I said pointing up to the sky.

So, you know, all summer I've been riding around the island with Katy many times to this point. Elaine's usually rides with us, and she keeps Katy in check. Now, today, with no theoretical cautionary guardrails or sober suggestions, I sorta knew Katy was going to blast down the trail at full tilt. Katy thinks brakes are just decorations on her handlebars.

I needed to keep her in sight because otherwise I might get lost on the twisty mountain trails. If Katy turned one way down a trail and I missed the turn it could be a problem. Getting lost sucks. I *hate* getting lost.

*

Elaine writes essays for her university computer school. They are really just stories, but the official academic school word is essay. Just like my sister, Sandy, Elaine always explains things so I can understand. Sometimes it takes a while, and she has to try different tacks (like in sailing with Katy's Pop). Last week, Elaine patiently explained the genetic human XX and XXY chromosomes. And that Katy's need for speed is likely a neurological thing.

"Sensory thrills," Elaine elaborated how, "Katy's need for speed is a neurological event. I've been reading and watching a variety of video series about whether it is the hypothalamus activation or amygdala. Personally, I'm suspecting sensations shared between the two."

Smiling and head nodding, I said, "Ya, that's our Katy. She has the need for speed."

Elaine pointed her finger at me, "Next week I'm sending in my paper on personality and genetics. I've been analyzing the relationship between genotype and phenotype."

"That's cool!" I did an imitation of a Katy fist punch to the sky. "I can't wait to hear about it, but right now gotta go pee. See you later alligator."

Elaine snorted, "In a while crocodile."

I started to scoot off down the hall to pee, and Elaine did her whisper shout thing, "Cliffie, aim straight will you? No more messes *please.*"

*

Now we were both going quite fast down the mountain, Katy let out with some whoop whoop shrieks. I just concentrated on keeping her in sight, but at the same time, *not* crashing my bike. Unlike Katy, I don't *lean* into turns and corners scraping the pedal, I like to keep the bike upright. Actually, I get sorta scared when the rear wheel slips in the loose dirt. Katy doesn't get scared, she likes it.

Katy swerved to take a narrow fork in the trail. I followed. She kept going straight down the trail and started to slow her speed, pulling off the side. I saw this as my opportunity to pass and have her follow me for a while. Wrong decision.

Whizzing by Katy I shouted, "So long sucker! You try and keep up with me now."

"NO, no, no, Cliffie," Katy shouted back, "there's a jump coming up. You are going too fast."

So now I know why Katy had pulled over to the side of the trail. She thought I would have stopped alongside her to converse about the situation. That *would* have been a good idea. However, it was now too late for discussions I hit the jump going full tilt speed. Uh oh, I thought as the bike launched up high into the air. I was *flying.*

Cousin Elaine has been assigned to teach me and Katy science lessons. Gramps' idea, he says we shouldn't goof about all day every day. I'm trying to remember was it Plato, Newton, or Socrates who said, "What goes up, must come down."

Doesn't matter now which theorist said it because I was coming down hard and fast, head over heels, releasing my grip on the handlebars. I landed in the bushes with a thud. I was hurt, but nothing serious. However, as Katy came down the hill towards me shrieking, "Clifford, are you okay?" I malingered a smidge.

"Oh no I can't breathe." I moaned and groaned. "Katy, I can't move my legs."

Katy was freaking out, "Okay, okay," she whispered in my face, "Just stay calm. I will get help. Gramps and Elaine will know what to do."

At that point I burst out with a raspberry laugh, "Oh no, don't bother Gramps and Elaine, they're busy! I'm fine, tougher than a two-dollar steak." I started to get up, shaking the dirt and debris off my sleeves. "Did you see me flying?"

"Ya, you had some height." Shaking her head, she said, "Did you think about doing a flip or a 360 spin-about once you were up so high?"

"Next time."

Katy checked my bike out for damage. It was dirty, but basically fine, and only needed some slight adjustments. "This is a sturdy bike," Katy said approvingly. "Carbonfibre frame makes it quite light."

We decided to go the rest of the way downhill a little slower. Part way down we turned left for an easier trail, one without jumps or obstacles. Katy suggested we take a shortcut through the Deconvale Farm to take a swim in their freshwater pond.

"The farm's owners don't care about trespassers, just as long as you are respectful, stay on the path, and don't bother any animals."

I could have asked about what kind of animals because some scare me, but *nothing* scares Katy. My sister would say, "Just roll with it. Blind faith."

We finally got to flat land, where pedaling was easy, and arrived at the Deconvale farm's pond lickedly splitly. The water was clear and inviting. There was a rope swing thing tied to a large tree branch.

Katy quickly peeled off her clothes, gave me some swinging instructions that I didn't really understand because she spoke so quickly. She grabbed the rope, pulled back a bit, put her feet on the bottom knot and swung way out into the pond leaping and shrieking. Splashing down with some flair, Katy yelled up at me, "C'mon Cliffie, the water is wonderful!"

I took a firm grip on the rope, counted to three, and swung out over the water. Just as I was getting ready to let go of the rope, Elaine gave me a shoulder shake, and softly said, "Wake up Clifford, we're going to splashdown shortly. We made it, this is my hometown, Seattle. We're here for a week. You're going to love it here!"

"Okay." I shared some cobwebs.

I was only dreaming.

"This is Seattle?" I asked looking down from the window.

"Lake Washington." Elaine smiled.

Flying on a Floatplane

3:00 in the afternoon is usually snack time. Gramps calls it teatime.

*

Elaine explained that the pontoon plane was going to splash down in a *controlled* dive. She held my hand reassuringly. Just stay calm, everything is cool. Of course, I believed her. Still, I clutched the side of my seat tightly as the water's surface approached. This is the sort of thing cousin Katy would *love*. Me, not so much.

"It's not a landing because it's water," I small talked to Elaine. "Water not land, get it."

She smiled as we hit the water with a thud, no bounce. Then we floated for a bit and powered over to the dock to disembark from the plane. We landed safely.

From the window I could see Elaine's mother, (my auntie, who I am certain that I do *not* know), she was waving to us, and saying something I couldn't understand. I waved back.

"Geez Elaine," I weak whistled, "your mother looks like your identical twin, except older. You two certainly look alike."

"Basic genetics." Elaine smiled, "But I got my daddy's hair."

I asked where her father was, and she said no way would they *both* take time off from projects or work to meet us. Pickups are a one-person job. Looks like Ma drew the short straw.

"No way, I think your mum's the *winner!* She gets the pleasure of picking us up." I gave Elaine a shoulder slug. "My sister said never sell yourself short."

Elaine smiled, shook her head, "I'm with the socialists."

"Me too!"

Elaine skipped towards her Ma. They had some hugs and kisses, then turned to me.

"Hello Clifford, how sweet to see you again," Elaine's mother hugged me hard. *She* certainly seemed sure that we had met before.

Okay, in my mind I figured whatever you say is fine with me. I guess she must be probably correct. I wish my sister were here because Sandy's memory was the best. I struggle sometimes with some memory stuff when I get confused. Sandy says don't sweat small stuff. Anything worthwhile you will remember. Everything else is small stuff.

Elaine's Ma is slight build, but a strong lady. She and Elaine started wrestling and arguing about who would carry which bag. Ma was set to carry *everything*. Elaine insisted, "Ma, I can carry my *own* bags."

I carried my own backpack with the gadgets and electronics. The clothing bags didn't matter to me. Whoever wants to carry clothes is not my concern. Clearly, mother/daughter history issues happening here. Dunno, but we were safe and sound on the Lake Washington dock. I had no fear of flying (now that we'd arrived).

I remember my dad said I was on some sorta spectrum and *one* of the number of things I suffered from is *learned helplessness.* That's because mum and Sandy did *everything* for me.

Mum sharply said to dad, "Leave Cliffie alone! He's nine years old. He's *not* Sandra. He is fine the way he is."

Sandy always said when mum raises her voice, don't poke the mother bear.

Dad knew that to be true. My mum was the best mum ever. I miss her so much.

*

In addition to designing and engineering airplanes, rockets, and jet propulsion things, Elaine's father builds cars for fun. His latest prototype was waiting for us in the parking spot. "I'll drive," Elaine exclaimed as she climbed behind the wheel of the shiny silver car with the *hydrogen hybrid* engine with macro/micro self-driving capabilities. Elaine is sixteen so she's legal to drive on public roads. She passed the government's test. Gramps taught her how to drive the pickup truck on private roads around Julsons Bay when she was fourteen. You don't need a license for that stuff on the island. The big city has rules of the road.

I sometimes wonder whether my mum and sister would have survived the crash if they had been in a bigger and better car. Something sturdier than the Toyota might have saved them.

Elaine turned around to me in the back seat, "Seatbelt Cliffie," she wrinkled her forehead, and asked, "you okay?"

"Ya, ya, I'm fine, just my mind is spacing out like what Katy talks about. I was thinking my mum and Sandy should have been in a car like this one. This car seems sturdy, secure and safe."

Elaine's Ma did a head tilt-thing like we were code talking. Elaine explained, "Ma, Cliffie has a few phobias. We are working on them concurrently. One phobia is car crashes. We are practically over this one, right Cliffie?" Elaine turned to me with a head nod and a right-eye wink.

"Katy's the best eye winker we know, eh Elaine?" I replied.

"Katy's the best." Elaine smiled and started driving down the road.

"Ya, she's ambidextrous." I double checked the seatbelt.

Elaine's Ma turned around in her seat, put a grim look on her face, and said, "I can relate Clifford. I have a few phobias, too."

Elaine scowled, poked Ma's arm, "Ma, don't joke around, okay. You aren't funny."

"I'm not joking! This summer I've had a *bad* case of arachnophobia! Your father has been much, much less than helpful! You know how he tries to logically *discuss* the situation." She threw both arms up in the air, "There's *nothing* to discuss."

"What's arachnophobia?" I asked.

"Ma is *paralyzed* if she sees a spider." Elaine snickered.

"Katy says spiders eat mosquitoes and that's good because *nobody* likes mosquitoes," I suggested.

"I *hate* spiders!" Ma pointed her finger at Elaine. "When I see a spider, I think the spider should *die*. That way that spider is *dead* and will *not* have descendants. Your father, on the other hand, always wants to *capture* and *release* the spider back into the wild outdoors. It's his Punjabi background."

Elaine scoffed, "Ma, basic spider reproduction is a little more complicated than that. You know, eggs, hundreds hatching all at the same time."

"I don't care," Ma was adamant, "I *hate* spiders."

Thinking I could help, I asked, "Ma, do know our cousin Katy?"

"Oh yes, of course," she nods her head, "Katy is Esmae's daughter."

"Ya, Katy's not afraid of nothing," I explained, "certainly not spiders."

"*Anything*" Elaine chirps in on behalf of all the grammarians. "Katy is not afraid of anything."

"Ya, whatever you say," I saluted.

Elaine's Ma looked quizzically at me.

"Gramps thought Katy and me should not just goof around all day doing nothing all summer long. He and Elaine both do work and school project things. So, we were given books to read and then report back to him what we thought. Oral and written book reports."

"Oh, that sounds educational," Ma affirmed.

"Ya, so we were assigned the book *Charlotte's Web*. It was written hundreds of years ago."

Elaine made a nose noise, "Not *hundreds* of years, Cliffie. *Charlotte's Web* was written seventy-two years ago, 1952."

"Ya, whatever," I made the namaste hand sign, "it's a good book Ma. You should read it."

Without being too patronizing, because Elaine's Ma has a Stanford PhD in applied mathematics and theoretical physics, she asked politely, "What's the book about?"

"Well," I cleared my throat, "I'm getting better at book reviewing. I've learned that you aren't supposed to give the whole book away with the ending and everything. With a *good* review you're supposed to get the other person interested enough to read the whole book for themselves so that person can experience the pleasure of reading the whole book. If I give away the ending then that's a bad book review, right?"

Elaine nodded her head in the driver's seat, "That's right Cliffie. Just tell Ma what the book is about *without* giving away the ending."

"Ya, okay, so *Charlotte's Web* is an *old* book about a little girl and her two friends, a farm pig and a barn spider. The farmer plans to kill the pig to make bacon and stuff, but the spider spins webs with words. The pig becomes famous. The farmer doesn't kill the pig. And it's a good book. If you want to know how it ends, you'll have to read it yourself. I think you will like spiders more after you read the book."

Ma pursed her lips together, bobbled her head, and said, "Thanks Clifford, although I doubt there's much that could get me to *like* spiders, you have piqued my interest. I had better read the book."

"Ya, don't forget about the mosquitoes?" I reminded.

"Mosquitoes?"

"Ya, spiders eat mosquitoes. *Nobody* likes mosquitoes."

"That's true."

Seattle has a Space Needle

1962 ~ The Seattle Space Needle was built for the World's Fair.

This is my first trip to Seattle. I have never been here before. Actually, I'd never been to the United States of America before. My mum harboured some anti-American sentiments because of their wars, racism, and discriminating health care.

I asked Sandy to explain the deal, but she said just let it go because it involved complex capitalism, politics, and religious zealots. And those were things *she* couldn't understand. So, for sure, if Sandy says she didn't understand America, then there was no hope for *me*. Let it go.

My sister, Sandy, she's the smartest person I've ever known.

Nevertheless, if Sandy were still here, I'd tell her all about the fun I was having in Seattle. "It's a cool town." Of course, it's all because of Elaine. She knows how to have fun! This is her hometown. Elaine was born here. Auburn actually, but that's still considered Seattle.

Elaine can drive cars, trucks, and motorcycles. Her parents didn't really like us riding the freeway on her dad's motorcycles. I thought it was great. Elaine taught me *lane splitting*. She tells me ahead of time when to close my eyes and hold her tight before the scary parts happen. Katy would love lane splitting. Elaine says Canada does not allow lane splitting.

"Big fines *and* demerit points on your ICBC driver's license." She points the finger of doom at me. "Remember that when you start driving."

"Ya, I got it."

Elaine has lots of fun and works hard, too. Still, she says the work she's doing is sorta challenging but fun, too. Her current big project has something to do with tracking the earth's axis slippage and climate change in the Pacific Northwest. She's measuring temperature changes in ocean currents and the jet stream fluctuations through computer modelling using public domain indices.

On Tuesday we are scheduled to go to the University of Washington. Elaine calls it the U Dub. We are going there to pick up some old-fashioned *hard copy* books from some professors she's collaborating with. I'm her assistant. Most of Elaine's books and monographs are online. Actually, almost everything's online.

"After we finish with the academic stuff we will go to the Seattle Space Needle for lunch," Elaine said with enthusiasm.

Elaine's parents are vegetarians. Elaine and me, we are omnivores. We eat *both* plants and cheeseburgers. They have double patty cheeseburgers at the Space Needle restaurant. The one I had was great. Fries with gravy is a Canadian thing. Americans think it strange to put *gravy* on fries. Elaine says chips are English derivation and gravy is likely from French poutine influence. When Americans say chips, they mean the dried thin salty ones in tin foil type bags. English call them crisps.

Elaine's father is from the Punjab. He cooked us up a big bunch of curried vegetable somethings with pakoras. It was really, really good. Rice is nice.

✳

Tuesday night before bedtime Elaine told me to get a good night's sleep because on Wednesday, we are e-bike riding along the Lake Washington Burke-Gilman Trail. "You'll like it, but you need to rest up."

"Okay, no problem, call the sandman," I'm a good sleeper. Not like Katy, she can stay awake all night just piddling around with screen stuff. Katy is high-strung and hyper. That's the double whammy behaviourally speaking.

In the morning, both of Elaine's parents were long gone to work by the time I rolled out of bed. They leave quite early in separate vehicles. They got lots of vehicles. Engineers are like that. Elaine was busy doing some sort of computer video-tele call thing and gave me the *five* minutes signal. It's never really *five* minutes, but I don't care. Time doesn't mean much to me.

I wrestled up some breakfast and started watching American cartoons on their big screen curved dual monitor. On top of the house's roof, they got these radar satellite dish deals where you rotate them to get more channels from all over the world. American television is different than ours. I liked it. They got Española channels, but no French at all! We got lots of French back home. Katy went to French submersion school for a while, until something went wrong. We don't talk about that.

Around ten o'clock Elaine came trotting into the media room and turned off the television. "Alright, let's get a wiggle on it. Time to spin. Go get dressed."

Back home, my mum or Sandy, selected clothes for me. They would lay them out on the bed. I'm on my own now, clothes-wise. Katy will tell me if I selected something stupid. Elaine is different. She doesn't select which clothes I should wear, but she'll let me know when something is *inappropriate* for the adventure. Then she makes suggestions. When we were coming here, I packed my own clothes bags, and then Elaine re-packed them so we would be copacetic.

I'm quite confident bike riding these days. Elaine says one must have confidence *and* competence. I got both. I spent the whole summer riding around Mayne Island with Katy. There are some big hills on Mayne. Consequently, I knew the Burke-Gilman Trail wouldn't be a problem. It is flat. This trail used to be a railway, but the railroad went bust. So, they pulled up the train tracks and paved it over with blacktop. We like blacktop better than concrete. It's a smoother ride. Gravel is no good.

Elaine says today we will employ the tortoise and hare principle. We don't have the need for speed on the bike trail. Slow and steady as we go so pedestrian people don't get mad at us zooming. We stopped for a picnic lunch at Marymoor Park. Elaine had packed sourdough sandwiches, caffeinated iced tea and cookies.

"Best lunch ever," I said with a soft shoulder slug. I had worked up an appetite. Bike riding the trail was terrific. No scary stuff or vigilant attention required, just basic riding for fun.

We got back home in time for three o'clock snacks. After which Elaine wanted to do some project edits or something. So, I watched videos. Dinner is always at seven in Seattle. "Mathematicians and engineering nerds are precise," according to Elaine. "We are more relaxed on the island."

"Ya, Katy calls that island time."

In Seattle dinnertime is a quasi-formal time. No phones or gadgets allowed at the dinner table. My mum would like that sort of thing. At the dinner table we sit around and talk about how our day went.

On the island I eat some meals leaning over the kitchen sink. In Seattle we all sit down at the table. Dinner is a smooth slow go with *courses*. We start with some kind of hors d'oeuvres on platters. That's the *first* course. Then some soup someone has made fresh or frozen. After that there's a salad. Followed with what's called a vegetarian entrée. That's the main course. The other dishes are starter type things.

Our dinner is finished off with desserts and American coffee. My mum was a tea person. I don't know about dad. I've tried both beverages but neither do too much for me. Elaine loads mine with lots of milk, not too much sugar because that's why we have desserts as the sweet course.

After dinner Elaine and Ma always bicker about who's going to do the cleanup. Seems like they *both* want to do it. Eventually Ma capitulates. Elaine tells Ma, "We'll be back on the island in a few days and you'll be doing *all* the cleanup then!"

Elaine and I do the cleanup together. Elaine says it's bad manners to eat leftovers off other people's plates. I didn't know that. Cleanup procedures are complex. Not everything goes in the dishwasher machine. Elaine does most of the work. She's competent. I just seem to get in the way. She smiles, pivots and gives me a hair tussle. Sometimes she kisses me on my head.

"Whatcha wanna do tomorrow?" I asked.

"I was thinking the Seattle Museum, or the art gallery."

"Great, I like museums. Sandy took me to the Museum de Montreal when we were in Quebec. It was fab. She loved that stuff."

"That's cool!" Elaine put palms up, "I've never been to Montreal, but I'd love to go."

"You speak French?" I asked.

"Yes, I have lots to learn."

I nodded my approval. "Real good food in Montreal!"

"French stomachs require good food."

"What time we leaving tomorrow?"

Elaine wobbled her head and said, "We'll leave after the traffic dies down. We don't want any rush hour snags."

Traffic in Seattle is a *big* deal. You don't want to get stuck in traffic if you can help it. Sometimes you can't help it and that's the way it goes. Elaine showed me how to use the computer to monitor traffic flow. If it's heavy we wait. When the coast is clear we shove off. Seattle is a *big* city.

When I eventually went to bed, I'm sure I fell asleep as soon as my head hit the pillow. I was tired. All the bike riding, excessive eating, and excitement made me exhausted. It had been a happy day.

I was stage seven dreaming or deep beta wave sleeping when Elaine burst into my bedroom.

"Wake up Cliffie," she said somewhat loudly while softly shaking my shoulder.

"What's up?" I asked. "What time is it?"

"It is just past 6 o'clock. Can you get up and get dressed quickly, please?"

"Sure, no problem. What are we doing?"

"We are going to Vancouver to meet up with Gramps."

"How come?" I started getting up, "thought we were here for a week."

"Katy shot her father. We have to go to Vancouver to be there."

"Okay."

Elaine started to leave, turned and said, "I'll be back in twenty minutes. You be ready, okay."

"Yes, no problem." I gave the thumbs up signal. "I *will* be ready."

Muttering to myself, "Katy shot her father?"

Elaine poked her head back in my room, "Put on travel clothes, okay."

"Yes," I gave the thumbs up signal.

All I could think was this is not good.

Two Wheels to Vancouver

While I was semi-methodically packing my backpack and duffel bag with essential electronics, I could overhear Elaine explain to Ma that we don't want to take a fancy car to Vancouver. Elaine wants a straightforward plain vehicle. "I don't need to attract unwanted attention with an expensive flashy hydrogen hybrid car. I'm crossing the border with Clifford."

"You could go *solo*, and leave Clifford here," Ma suggested. "I can look after him."

Elaine snorted, "I'm not leaving him here. You can't look after him. You've got work to do, numbers to crunch. Besides, Cliffie has special needs well beyond your pay grade."

"Okay, fine, fine, I was just trying to be helpful," Ma backpedalled, "Do you want to take the old pickup truck? It's an ordinary under the radar vehicle."

"Yes, good idea," Elaine said. "I'll go and check on his packing."

I could hear Elaine scurrying up the stairs, "Cliffie, how's the packing coming? We should get going soon."

"I'm ready,"

She came in, smiled, and patted me on the head, "Looks like you have the backpack ready." Then she grabbed the other duffel bag, "You are going to need some clothes, too."

"Why aren't we flying back?" I assured her, "I'm not scared or anything. Isn't flying faster?"

"No, we'd have to book a plane, get a pilot over here and then fly to Vancouver. Driving is actually faster." Elaine finished packing, looked around, and nodded, "We are good to go."

I held my index finger up in the air, "I think we should take the red motorcycle with the big boxer engine. We'd get there quickly on that bike. You know, flying on the ground, right?"

Elaine went wide eyed, nodding her head, "Yes, that's an excellent idea! Are you going to be okay sitting on the back of the bike for three hours or so?"

"Ya, I love the motorcycle."

Elaine smiled, "Yes, I agree, move to Plan B. I'll get the panniers and the bike gear ready to go. Ma will not like it but too bad. Pops is at work and he wouldn't care anyways. He likes the bike to get a good run. It's good for the engine."

I already knew that panniers and saddlebags were the same thing. Synonyms. Panniers are French and saddlebags are an American word from horses. Whatever, some re-packing will be required, but doesn't matter much to me. Elaine is in charge. My backpack is ready to go. I like riding on the motorbike.

Elaine predicted correctly, Ma preferred we take one of their cars or the old truck, however, Ma knows the bike gets through heavy traffic easily. We had some hugs, said some more goodbyes, Ma started crying. Elaine got huffy about the crying and told her not to be dramatic. Then we blasted off to Vancouver – full throttle.

It was a beautiful day for a motorbike ride. Halfway we stopped in Mount Vernon to pee and have some snacks. Elaine is always good with the snacks. While we were sitting at the rest stop picnic table Elaine said, "Cliffie, we should start rehearsing what *you* are going to say to the authorities about Katy when we get there."

"Okay, what should I say?"

Elaine put on her grim facial expression and started a serious speech, "The truth, we *always* tell the truth. I don't know the full complete story about what happened with Katy."

"Katy shot her father." I interrupted.

"Yes," Elaine wrinkled her forehead, "that's true, but we *know* Katy, right?"

"Ya, we love her!"

"Yes, we do. And that's why we are meeting Gramps in Vancouver. Katy needs our support now."

"Yes, yes, yes, she's got it," I saluted. "So, what should I be practicing?" I asked.

"Well, we are going to be character witnesses for Katy. If the cops, the juvenile judge, or the court appointed shrinks asks me questions about Katy's character, I'm going to say that Katy might be a bit impulsive at times, but she doesn't have a mean bone in her body! We are positive it was some sort of accident. Katy is a *good* person."

"That's true," I agreed. "Katy *is* a good person."

"And if someone asks us about Katy, we list all the sweet stuff she does. We don't talk about crazy stuff, right? We talk in a nice *normal* voice not your robot voice. This isn't a spectrum thing, Cliffie."

"Yes, no problem, I'm good to go. I won't mention about the time she rode her bike down the Blanca Street stairs, or the fire setting stuff, or the scissors thing, or the time she climbed up a tree to get a cat down and the fire fighters had to come and get them *both* down."

"When was the cat thing?"

"Just before school got out for the summer."

"The fire stuff was just a misunderstanding." Elaine pulled out her small gadget phone, "Gramps just sent me a message. Okay, he's in Vancouver now. Katy will be evaluated by a psychologist Monday morning. She's out of juvenile detention and back at home now."

"That's good news, right?" I asked.

"Yes, it is," Elaine put the device back in her secure pocket. "We are supposed to call Gramps when we reach Vancouver. You ready to get back on the road?"

"Ya, ya, let's go." I gave her the Cub Scouts salute, "I'm anxious to see Katy."

Elaine squinted, pushed out her bottom lip, "Me too."

Part Four

Dr Randal Reilly
"Katy is Eleven Years Old"

The Criminal Code of Canada

Section 13 of the Criminal Code of Canada states: "No person shall be convicted of an offence in respect of an act or omission on their part while that person was under the age of twelve years."

Youth Criminal Justice Act of 2003 replaced the Young Offenders Act of 1984, which replaced the 1908 Juvenile Delinquents Act.

Prior to 1908 all Canadian criminals were treated the same regardless of age.

Katy has an Entourage

"My truck sucks in the city!" Stuck in too much traffic, not much forward progress happening, thinking to myself, "Randal, tomorrow, take the bike."

Bicycle thieves in Vancouver have always been bad, but recently bike bandits have become brazen. Last year, I had my favourite red carbonfibre Brodie road bicycle stolen from the rack right outside my office. The bike was locked up tight with a kryptonite lock and cable. The robbers used some sort of jacking device to defeat the lock and bike stand. That day I had to walk home.

My wife, Harjit, couldn't stand my bike theft dejection. She bought me a special-order Brompton six speed folding bike with twelve-inch wheels. No more stolen bikes. It came as bike in a bag. The bike folds up easily and you put it under your table in a restaurant. I simply fold it up and bring the bike inside the office. I've taken it on the bus and train to get somewhere quickly and then pedal back leisurely. It's a decent commuter bike. We use bikes with shock absorbers on the front and back when we go on the trails at Whistler. City riding is so much smoother.

*

Monday morning: it was sunny and bright, but not too hot, I cycled to the office in good time arriving at 9:40. My first appointment was with Katy Porter at ten o'clock.

I was folding up the bike to take inside the office when out of the corner of my eye I saw a group of people descending on me. I recognized the man ambling along with three kids, it's Earl Porter from Mayne Island.

"Good morning, Earl," out of habit, and male operant conditioning, I stuck out my hand for a customarily business-like handshake.

Earl smiled but declined the handshake in favour of a raised palm up wave, COVID habits, "You must be Dr. Reilly."

"Yes," I nodded with a smile.

"I recognize you from the Google photos my granddaughter was showing me. Nonetheless, you do look rather familiar. Have we met before?" Earl asked.

"Yes, we've bumped into each other at the Farm Gate Store on Mayne Island a couple times."

Earl nodded, "Indeed, forgive me, it's a small island, and my memory is not what it once was."

"Yes, I know how that goes." I knocked on my bike helmet with a mental gesture. "Quite a posse you have here, Earl."

The young redhead boy replied for Earl, "We're Katy's entouragé, *not* a posse. We don't say posse because it's pejorative."

"Oh, well, that's good to know," I winked. "Always helpful to have your entouragé with you in the big city."

Earl smiled and introduced the respective entouragé members. "These are my grandchildren. This is Elaine, Clifford, and Katy."

"Great," I motioned to the front door of the office, "would you like to come inside, or are you dropping Katy off?"

The redhead boy, Clifford, looked confused, "Aren't you going to ask us all questions?" He pointed to the tall teenager, "Elaine says we're *collateral* informants for Katy."

Elaine gave him a shoulder grip squeeze, "Clifford," she whispered, "Manners."

I smiled, "Yes, that's true, but maybe today I'll just meet with Katy."

Earl nodded his agreement, "How much time do you need with Katy today? When should we return?"

"Any time after one o'clock will be fine for today," I suggested.

"Three hours until lunch," Katy sighed.

Earl scoffed, "Katy, you just finished a big breakfast. I'm sure you will be just fine."

Everyone seemed to give a faux chuckle about lunch. I could sense some of their apprehensions. Katy shot her father, and now she needed a psych assessment for the court, social workers, and juvenile government authorities. That's all quite stressful.

I took a look at my watch, "Well, okay, shall we go inside and get started, Katy?"

"Sure, let's get started," Katy fist pumped the sky, or something.

We waved goodbye to the entourage. They were off for errands.

I picked up my folded bike and we went inside.

Psych evaluations for children are quite different than those for adults. However, regardless of the patient's age, the ice has to break, and the process gets started.

This isn't the dentist.

Puzzle pieces.

Psych Assessments and Courts

I've held a British Columbia provincial license to conduct psych assessments for well over thirty-two years now. Long ago, when I was young, just starting out, I was way, way more confident of my diagnosing acumen than I am these days. Nowadays I'm a bit humbler about the human condition than those early psych days. I sometimes have more questions than answers. Predicting is precarious.

Back when I worked at the hospital we would do differential diagnoses diligently, but always under some level of time pressure. Physicians sent kids from all over the province by plane, train or car to our clinic. We were the provincial pros. If we didn't know what was wrong with the kid, who did?

The supervising director of the hospital's psychology developmental diagnostic clinic was a kind scholarly lady. She was always busy and working hard. One day I was shuffling by her open office door holding a freshly brewed industrial coffee from the cafeteria, "Excuse me, Dr. Reilly," she said softly. "Do you have a minute?"

"Yes, certainly, of course," I said without any hesitation. If the director wanted a word, we dropped everything and complied. Even the prima donnas and divas cooperate with the director. That's because she was a very nice scholarly lady. And she was in charge. "How's it going, Dr. Kovanski?" I asked.

"Fine, fine, thanks for asking," she waved her hand. "Come in, sit down, maybe you could close the door."

Closed doors and open doors were understood signals at the hospital. Of course, this was decades before COVID-19. A wide-open office door indicated guests and comments were cool. Closed office doors meant working – leave me alone. Privacy.

Dr. Andrea Kovanski's closed door meant a *confidential* discussion.

"How are you doing Randal?" She asked with a smile. "Hope we aren't working you too hard."

Truth was I was by far the youngest shrink on staff. Dr. Kovanski hired me when my friend from university, Jeanine, went on maternity leave. Jeanine Harpender had told Kovanski she thought I'd be a good fit for the department. "He's quirky, but a skillful clinician."

I needed the dough and documented hospital hours for the psych license prior to independent private practice privileges.

I gave Dr. K the thumbs up sign, "No, not at all. I'm enjoying working here, thanks." I gave her a small shoulder shrug, "Compared to when I worked in the asbestos mine shovelling rocks, this hospital job is sweet."

Dr K wiggled her eyebrows, tilted her head, and asked, "What were you doing in an asbestos mine?"

"It was a four-month summer student job at the Cassiar Asbestos Mine. I earned some big bucks and didn't need to take out too heavy a student loan for tuition in the fall. No trust fund here."

She smiled, "Me neither, but asbestos, I thought it has been established as carcinogenic?"

"Not that we knew. They called asbestos *white gold*. The mine originally opened in 1952. After some forest fires they discovered that birds' nests didn't burn. The nests had been built with asbestos fibres. And that was the beginning of asbestos mining in the north."

"Well, be that as it may, getting back to our business here at the hospital, I understand you had an interesting case conference with Dr. Helena on Monday."

"Yes," I knew she was going somewhere with this thread, closed door and all, but I wasn't certain. "Every case is interesting here at the hospital," I replied.

"Yes, that's generally true, some more so than others," Dr K tapped her pencil on the desk. "Dr. Helena reports your case conference diagnostic delivery skills are somewhat innovative."

"Okay, is that good?" I was confused now.

"You diagnosed the patient as a GORK?" Dr. K asked with a sigh.

*

Dr. K reminded me how things work here at the hospital. Kids from all over the province are sent to our program so the multidisciplinary pros can assess the patient and develop some answers, strategies and interventions to address the referral questions.

(Recently, after I had moved on from the hospital's employ, they changed the program's name to the *interdisciplinary* team with the idea that the pros were *integrated*. The old multidisciplinary moniker suggests each discipline stands alone. Interdisciplinary indicates everyone works together. Semantics, maybe, still Worf (1929) says language is *everything*.)

The child arrived early in the morning and was assigned a schedule. The team's social worker coordinated the allotted time slots, travel, and social work stuff. The speech and language pathologist got sixty minutes to assess the kid. The physiotherapist saw the patient. The shrink got time with the kid to do an assessment. And the last stop was the department's paediatrician for a medical evaluation. Didn't call her the 'cleanup hitter' because she was not into baseball, and it would be seen as a slight. She was okay, a bit uptight, but she was okay.

After all the respective pros had spent time with the patient, analyzed their notes and collected test scores, then there was the formal cumulative case conference at four o'clock. This is where everyone sat around the big table in the conference room. Often there were lots of people involved. Parents *and* step-parents sit at one end of the table and the rest of us filled in the other seats.

*

The hospital scheduling administrator and our department team's social worker assigned me the task of conducting an assessment for eleven-year-old Anjanue Baines early on a rainy Monday morning. Anjanue and her parents had flown in from Poucé Coupe (a small village in northern British Columbia, just west of Dawson Creek) the previous evening. The referring physician, school, and parents were all concerned with Anjanue's educational progress, personality development and social skills.

I was allotted two hours to see Anjanue. Then she would meet with one of the speech and language pathologists, followed by one of the occupational therapists for fine-motor skills evaluation. Dr. Helena was the designated paediatrician and case manager. Dr. Helena was responsible for the official hospital signing off on the file.

8:42, I arrived at the hospital with plenty of time to spare before Anjanue was scheduled. I stopped in at the cafeteria to pick up a freshly brewed industrial coffee. Then I scampered over to the file room to sign out Anjanue's file for review in my office.

It wasn't a thick file or a thin one. It was in between. A Goldilocks file. At the hospital, generally, a thick file indicated lots of attention had already been paid to the patient. A variety of people along the clinical road had written reports and those reports had been *filed*. Records. Thick files are good.

A standard file review meant reading most of the previous psych reports, physicians' notes, school report cards, counselling comments and whatnots they all previously reported. Some stuff was pertinent, others not so much. Documentation has become a big deal these days. "We're all accountable."

Thin files, on the other hand, indicated not much has happened with a kid. That could be good, or bad. It would be bad if the kid had fallen between the cracks in the system. It would be good if the issues were recent and currently being addressed. Early intervention is the rhetorical darling in the mental health community. However, it's important to note, some concerns do not arise until adolescence.

At 9:02, don't keep them waiting too long because that is rude, I ditched the coffee, ate a breath mint since nobody needs my coffee breath exhales. I strolled over to the waiting room to meet Anjanue. She was sitting with her parents reading a comic book. "Hello, you must be the Baines family. I'm Dr. Reilly." I stuck out my hand to shake with the parents. We did greetings and salutations, and then I turned and said, "You must be Anjanue?"

"Yes, I am," she gave me a wave.

"Do you want to come to my office and get started?" I asked.

"Do I have a choice?"

"Yes, *of course*," I assured Anjanue. "You never, ever have to do anything you don't want to do!"

"Ha, really," Anjanue snorted, "Every day I *have* to do things I don't want to do," she shrugged. "I had to come here today."

I smiled with a diffusing gesture, "Yes, I understand, gotcha." I glanced over to her parents, "but seriously, I'm telling you the truth." I raised my palm up in the air, "You don't have to come with me if you don't want to."

Mrs. Baines seemed to gasp and inhale, "Anjanue, we've come all this distance, I think you should go with the doctor."

"Okay." And with that Anjanue waved to her parents. "See you later gator."

Consent is a *big* deal in psychology. There is parental/guardian consent and then there is the child's assent. If you don't have it that's a problem. Psychological duplicity and tricks are bad. You'll get in trouble for that type of bad practices.

We walked down the hall to my office and started the assessment.

Anjanue, at age eleven, was conventionally considered at the early adolescent stage of development. She was not a little kid, but not a teenager either. She was eleven. Still, she seemed confident and competent for her age. She was referred to our hospital's program for an assessment by the community local physician and school because they suspected developmental difficulties, academic problems, and social skills. Someone suggested she fell somewhere on the autism or Asperger's spectrum.

I read that notion and smiled, "Right, yes, of course, everyone is on some spectrum these days."

Psychology is a soft science. Our colleagues down the hall in the acute care medical clinic had x-rays, MRI machinery, and an assortment of high-tech equipment. Nevertheless, from an interdisciplinary perspective we all generate hypotheses, we all ruled things out and we ruled things in trying to uncover a differential diagnosis. Some situations were complicated. It's hardly ever just *one* issue. Co-morbid, concurrently, and concomitant issues arose in the patient's clinical profile.

Psychology doesn't have x-rays. It has standardized tests. Some tests have a bad history of bias and discrimination. These days there have been improvements with stratified standardization samples. We use Canadian normative data. Some constructs can't cross the border. American education and school curricula are different – politics notwithstanding.

While remaining sensitive to the often-noted negative image of standardized tests, I explain my position by stating that *everyone* is a unique *individual*, and that's a given. However, there are some situations where it is worthwhile to measure where one student stands in relation to other students at the same age and grade level. Is he or she reading above or below grade level expectations when compared to the *average* Canadian student? Is there a delay – room for remediation?

I administered some standardized reading, mathematics, spelling and writing tests to Anjanue. On all those tests she scored at or above grade level expectations. Then I administered a battery of cognitive ability tests. In the old days they were called *intelligence tests.*

*

In 1905 the French government needed help with educating children. They asked Alfred Binet to design a test to help educators stream low level students *out* of the classroom. Those students impeded the progress of others. Americans developed the Stanford-Binet IQ test. "You can't look at someone and determine their intelligence." A test was needed.

A hundred years later, educators began to question what was so special with *special education*. Normalized education in neighbourhood schools was a student's right. Thus, the move to *integrate* all students into local classrooms was established.

*

Someone along the way had suggested that Anjanue's aptitude may be lacking. Consequently, I gave her some ability tests. Her test scores fell in the above average or well above average range for verbal reasoning, memory, and nonverbal information processing. No deficits or difficulties with her comprehension, verbal expression or receptive language skills.

Projective personality tests are somewhat akin to psychological Freudian fishing. I asked Anjanue if she could have three wishes what would she wish for? Then I asked what makes her sad/glad/mad/bad. We tried Rotter's Incomplete Sentences to no clinical avail.

Anjanue presented as quite normal. Nothing was abnormal or of any clinical concern. Although psychologists are accused of *labeling* or attempting to pigeonhole a person into a category, I tend to think of the process positively with a view to identifying or diagnosing a problem for treatment purposes.

The clock kept ticking and our two hours together was running out. *None* of the tests, inventories or scales showed anything *wrong* with Anjanue. She was normal in every way I could measure. You see, someone could be labeled as *eccentric* when they are over a certain age, and no one would think it as pejorative. Children, on the other hand, don't receive such latitude. Maybe she'd be eccentric when she was older. I didn't have a crystal ball, so I didn't know.

Thus, I explained to Dr. Kovanski that *none* of *my* measurements produced a definitive diagnosis. So, consequently, at the four o'clock case conference I claimed **G**od **O**nly **R**eally **K**nows (*GORK*) what's wrong with Anjanue because I don't. I gave her all those tests and I couldn't find *anything* wrong with her. Maybe God knows.

Just then Dr. K's landline started ringing, she nodded to me, "Okay, I understand, Miss Baines is a GORK." She pointed to her phone, "Sorry, I have to take this call it's scheduled. Let's go for lunch someday soon."

"Yes, sure," I gave her a thumbs up signal, "lunch would be great."

As I was leaving, she put her palm over the phone's speaker, "One more thing Dr. Reilly."

I turned back towards her, "Yes."

"Keep up the good work." She gave me somewhat of a salute signal or something and then waved me out of her office.

"Close the door, please."

Closing the door I smiled, thinking to myself, did Dr K. give me a compliment? She's not known for that.

Whatever, I had over an hour before my next case was arriving. I went and refilled the coffee cup and reviewed the next file.

✳

Shortly after I had passed *all* the required examinations, accumulated enough supervised intern hours, I left the hospital and went into full time private practice. Another intern replaced me and that's the way it should be.

Some twenty years sailed past, I was watching a CBC television news interview with a Dawson Creek veterinarian, Dr. Anjanue

Baines who was describing the problems with pesticides and grazing horses. "Pesticides are not worth the ancillary problems!"

That vet looked familiar and then I remembered Anjanue from all those years ago.

Looks like she turned out just fine.

Pesticides *are* a problem.

Go get them, Anjanue.

I'm proud of you!

Boomtown Rats

In 1979, Sir Bob Geldof, of the Irish rock band, Boomtown Rats, wrote the song "*I Don't Like Mondays.*" The song was about sixteen-year-old Brenda Ann Spencer who fired thirty bullets at a San Diego elementary school across the street from her house. She killed the principal and school custodian. Eight school children and a police officer were injured during the shooting spree.

Before the police were able to take Brenda into custody, a news reporter contacted her by telephone and asked why did she shoot those people?

Brenda's response was "I don't like Mondays."

Katy on Monday:

"Nice to meet you, Katy," I said, as we settled into our seats across the interview table.

"You too," Katy gave me a small wrist wiggle wave.

"Thanks for coming in early on a Monday morning to see me. I appreciate it."

"Ten o'clock is not too early. My old school starts at eight thirty and *that's* early. I don't think I had a choice about coming here to see you. It's expected of me."

"Says who? That is not true," I put my palms up in the air. "You certainly have a choice. You don't have to do *anything* you don't want to do."

"Well, that's what *you* say," Katy shook her head. "Everyone is already awfully angry with me. My mother has gone crazy angry with *everyone*. My father is still in the hospital. Yesterday my two cousins and grandfather arrived here in Vancouver. I ruined Cousin Cliffie's first trip to Seattle. That was them you met outside. The redhead, that's Cliffie."

I smiled, "He seems nice."

"Yes, Cliffie is cool. His mother and sister got killed in a car crash. He had some problems before that and then he got messed up more."

I nodded my head in agreement, "Yes, that is never easy for anyone."

"So, you know my gramps?"

"Yes, we have met before. I've got an old cottage on Mayne Island. On the island we all go to the Farm Gate Store for groceries. I've met your grandfather there a couple times."

"Oh, that's sweet. I spent the *whole* summer on the island."

"How was it?" I asked. "Some people find it too quiet and a bit boring."

Katy softly whistled, "Best summer ever!"

"It sure got hot for a while this summer on the island." I made a fanning motion with my hand.

Katy gave a small snort, "Naw, not hot for us. We were swimming, kayaking and biking everyday *all* summer. It gets hot in the city because of the concrete and pavement, but not on the island. We live at the edge of the island on the waterfront. I think it might get hotter up the hill inland away from the water."

"Yes, it's the opposite in the winter," I noted.

Katy squinted at me, "How so?"

"Well in the winter the ocean's moisture keeps the coastline warmer. When you go inland the temperature falls and it gets colder because it is farther from the ocean."

Katy whistled again, "Wish I was able to stay on the island for the winter. My cousin Cliffie is likely gonna be there this winter due to his mother's death. His dad had a nervous breakdown type thing. So, Grampa looks after Cliffie now. Besides, Cliffie had some personal problems before his mother died. Afterwards he was lost for a while."

"Oh, how so?" I asked.

"He's on some spectrum."

"What kind of spectrum?"

Katy smacked her lips, "You know, I don't really know all the details because it's no matter to me. My cousin Elaine told me. She knows stuff because she's a *brainiac*."

"She is?"

"Ya, but you wouldn't know it, she hardly shows it. For real, she is the sweetest person ever. Elaine is sixteen *and* she drives a car."

"So how do you know she's a brainiac?"

"She's in some University of Washington accelerated program for genius people. Besides that, she is awesome. She talked to me about you. She's coaching and guiding my attitude."

"Oh, what did she say?"

"She showed me the digital footprint history on you. That's how we knew who you were when you were folding up that weird looking bicycle."

"You don't like my bike?"

"It's okay, but you gotta admit it looks weird."

"Bike thieves are bad in Vancouver."

Katy made a raspberry noise, "Oh yes, that's the truth." She looked around the office, "You got a camera going?"

I shook my head, "No cameras here."

"Voice recording."

"No, notes by pencil and paper."

"When you gonna start asking me questions." Katy wondered.

I smiled, "We started a while ago."

"We did?"

"Yes, we started when we sat down at the table."

Katy nodded, "Elaine talked to me about psych assessments. She said you would ask all sorts of questions *with* validity checks."

I scoffed, "Validity checks."

"Ya, she said you are going to ask lots of questions. You will ask a question one way early and then ask the *same* question a different way later as a validity check to see if I'm telling the truth the whole time consistently."

I gave Katy a thumbs up signal, "Elaine knows her stuff, eh."

"For sure, she's a brainiac. Her father is from the Punjab. He met Elaine's mother at a big California university when *they* were teens on scholarships. Elaine says that Stanford is a big deal type school. Gramps says Elaine's brains are from her parents and because she eats broccoli."

That made me smile. "What else did Elaine say about today?"

"She said even though she doesn't know you directly, she knows you are a nice man because that's what your digital footprint history shows. She says I'm supposed to take everything very, very seriously, not goof around, or say crazy things."

"Crazy things like what?" I asked.

Katy wiggled her nose, "Dunno, but I'll tell you, when Elaine is acting all serious and looking grim, we don't do anything to interrupt or be silly. She doesn't like it."

"Who's the we?" I asked.

"Cliffie *and* me," Katy said. "On the island, Gramps is theoretically in charge, but Elaine runs the place. She's supposed to make sure Cliffie and me don't get hurt, break stuff, get lost, or cause trouble!"

"What kind of trouble can you get into on Mayne Island?'

Katy laughed, "Ha, all of the above and more."

"Getting lost sucks," I lamented.

"Getting stranded sucks more," Katy said with some authority.

"What's the difference?"

"Getting lost means, you don't know where you are. Getting stranded means, you know where you are, but can't get to where you want to be."

"Hmm, I see."

"Ya, one-time last spring I took one of the light weight kevlar kayaks out for a *short* paddle before dinner. I made a mistake. The tide was high when I left the dock, but it *turned* on me, and the current was too strong for my paddle strength. I was paddling hard as I could, but the current kept pushing me backwards the *wrong* way. So, I was stranded off the channel between Curlew and Samuel Islands. My Gramps had to come and get me in the skiff. He wasn't angry or anything. He said it was a teachable *moment.*"

"Sounds scary to me," I said with a grin. "Glad your grandfather was able to rescue you."

Katy snorted, "Ya, he wasn't mad about the kayak mistake, but he's pretty unhappy right now."

"How so?" I asked.

"I shot my father," Katy shrugged. "Gramps doesn't like guns. He's not happy with anything right now. Actually, I shouldn't say that because he's happy I'm coming here to see you. His daughter, who is my mother, went to lawyer school with your sister or something like that. Elaine says that's the six degrees of separation thing."

"Yes, it's a small world."

"Dunno, I didn't understand what it was about, but I knew I could ask her to explain later. Elaine's a good explainer. Breakfast with everyone around the table during tense times is not so good to be asking too many questions. Just keep it light and quite polite."

"Why were things tense at breakfast?"

"I shot my father."

"Right," I nodded, "yes, that's going to create some tension. Have you gone to the hospital to see your father?"

"Yes, my mother took me last night, but he was sleeping, so we went home. Nurse said he's sedated and we can't wake him. He had some surgery to fix the gunshot wound. Kinda freaked me out seeing him so messed up. Ma says we will probably go again sometime today. I'll be bringing Gramps with me this time."

"What are you going to say to him?"

"Who?" Katy wondered, "Gramps, or my father."

"Have you not yet spoken with your grandfather? He accompanied you here this morning."

"Yes and no, we have not talked too much. Elaine says Gramps is certainly upset. We want me to live with Gramps, but Elaine says timing is everything. He's not so much mad as he is sad. Bad, too, he feels bad about the whole thing."

I understood what she was saying. "When you see your father, what will you say to him?"

"Sorry," she rolled her eyes, and tilted her head back. "I'll say I'm sorry to him and everyone because I really am truly sorry. I wish I hadn't shot my father with his own gun. I wish this had not happened. I wish my parents weren't getting divorced."

"Divorcing is difficult," I placated.

Katy sighed, "Yes, that's the trigger."

"What does that mean?" I asked.

"Well," Katy shook her head, "when they told me about the divorce I got a bit upset. I think we tried to talk about it. They both said not to worry we'd still be a family, but my father was *moving* out."

"Must have surprised you to hear about the divorce."

"Yes, I guess, I don't know." Katy threw her arms up in the air, "I went to my room, kicked the bed and threw things around. I heard my father stumbling about in their bedroom. He was packing clothes and photos. I walked in their bedroom went over to his nightstand; I knew that's where he kept the gun. I pulled it out and shot him. Everything was loud and crazy after that. Lots of blood gushing out. My mother was screaming. I went back to my bedroom and sat on the bed. Next thing I know there are loud sirens, police, firemen and ambulance people all *yelling* at me."

"I assume the noise from the gunshot was loud."

"No, well, yes, I don't know, maybe," Katy wrinkled her forehead. "I was back sitting on my bed and guess I was still holding the gun. Everyone was yelling at me to drop the gun on the floor and put my hands up."

"Yes, that's what they do," I confirmed. "A girl with a gun gets everyone nervous."

"My mother pushed past the policeman at the door and dove on top of me. She was screaming, but not making any sense at all. She thought the cops were going to shoot me. Lots more yelling after that by lots of people."

"Yes, I'm sure your mother was upset."

"Yes, guess so." Katy pointed to the clock on the wall, "So, I think it must be close to lunchtime soon, eh? You told my Gramps to come back at one o'clock. It's getting close to that now, huh?"

I agreed, "Yes, you are right Katy." I pointed to the window, "I'm sure he is likely outside waiting."

"Wanna look?" She asked.

"Sure."

Katy walked over to the window facing York Avenue, "Hey, they are all there." She tapped the window and waved to what we fondly called her entouragé.

I joined Katy at the window and gave the thumbs up signal. The entouragé waved back with big grins.

"Okay, well, thanks for coming to see me today, Katy. Might I persuade you to come back tomorrow morning at ten again?"

"Sure," she nodded, "I'll first have to check with Gramps, but he wants this thing with you to happen. Elaine says you have to meet with me at *least* a couple times and write a report to the various *authorities*. If you say I'm not crazy that will go good for our side. If you say I'm not crazy and I go and shoot someone else, *you* will get in trouble."

"Are you going to shoot someone else?"

"No!" Katy frowned. "They took the gun away."

"Okay," I raised my index finger to make a point. "If you had another gun would you shoot anyone?"

"Oh no, *never* again," Katy rolled her eyes, "I'm done with dumb impulsive stuff."

"That's good, see you tomorrow."

Katy started walking to the door to leave, turned and asked, "Dr. Reilly, do you like Mondays?"

"Sure, Mondays are fine with me." I replied.

Katy pointed to the window, "My cousin, Elaine, says she *loves* Monday. It means she's got the *whole* week ahead of her to get things done. She says Friday sucks because sometimes she didn't get *all* the stuff done that Monday said she should. It's a Monday to Friday world out there."

"Yes, it is," I agreed. "I love weekends on the island. Especially when it's sunny."

"Ya, that's the truth," Katy chuckled. "Monday comes after Sunday."

"Gotta start somewhere."

"That's true."

Imbecile, Idiot & Moron Cretin

After a face-to-face assessment evaluation has occurred, the psych report is written.

The report *must* be able to stand professional peer review scrutiny. There are conventions and standards to be followed. An unconventional psych report won't be well received. Also, and notably important, the report *must* be written so the average layperson can understand the contents and conclusions. Too many technical terms with professional jargon are to be avoided. User friendly reports are required.

Imbecile, idiot and moron were all well-often used psychological terms applied to describe a person's cognitive intellectual information processing abilities. Popular parlance and vernacular speech adopted the terms and psychology found alternative diagnostic identifications. Imbecile, idiot and moron became unacceptable psychological terms.

Up until 2013, in British Columbia, the term *mentally retarded* was required by the government agency, Community Living BC, in order for a person with an Intelligence Quotient (IQ) below a certain cutoff to receive agency services. The labelling term, mental retardation had fallen into disfavour with the profession. Nevertheless, the government agency forms required a licensed psychologist to certify the American Psychiatric Diagnostic Statistical Manual's definition was met.

In 2014, the term intellectual disabilities replaced mental retardation for the government's category.

*

Back when I worked at the hospital, report writing was an important part of documentation and accountability in developing the patient's file.

First, the patient received a clinical interview, followed by a battery of tests. Next, the tests needed to be analyzed. The final step was the submitted written psych report.

The rotating case manager was assigned to the file and assembled the respective reports from the psychologist, social worker, speech and language pathologist and paediatrician. The filed report contained the multidisciplinary team's conclusions and recommendations.

The hospital is a public institution financed by the provincial government. Hospital psychologists are paid a salary.

Canada has socialized medicine. Hospital patients are not invoiced for services. It doesn't cost money to see a hospital psychologist.

Private practice psychology is different. Patients are self-referred, physician referred, and sometimes *spousal* referred. That's when a spouse says, *"You* have some problems. I will stay with you a while longer, but *only* if you go for counselling."

Unlike the hospital, private practice psychology services costs money. Similar to dentistry, some patients are covered through employment insurance plans. Private practice psychologists do their own invoicing. Some use a sliding scale for patients with limited income. Some do pro bono work. Rich people don't care. They just pay the fees. The psych licensing board says it's okay to use a sliding fee scale for folks with limited resources. It's *unethical* to raise your normal fee schedule for rich people. This applies to therapy and assessments.

Ambitious independent private practice psychologists might take on many files, maybe too many. It means many interviews to conduct and reports to write. Of course, my motto has always been:

know your limit and stay within it. My sister's *do me a favour* referral notwithstanding, nowadays I am a seasoned shrink with some many years under my belt, I'm confident of my competence with stress and time management.

Psychological statistics suggest *confidence* and *competence* stand as covariates. Ideally, one wants them both to surge, but if one lags the other can pick up the pace for a while. When both sag at the same time that can be a problematic patch.

1971, Sir Richard Starkey (aka Ringo Starr) released the song "*It Don't Come Easy.*" It was his first single since the Beatles broke-up.

A mantra of sorts for some – It don't come easy.

Shrinks & Celebrity Patients

Referrals for my psychological services arrive from a variety of sources. I've never advertised, I don't have a website, but always seem to have a more than steady stream of patients, spouses, and agencies requesting therapy, assessments, consults, and/or co-signing supervision. Word-of-mouth seems to be a frequent referral source. Typically, it's similar to this:

Voicemail ~ "Hello Dr. Reilly, I got your name and number from so-and-so, and she suggested I give you a call to schedule an appointment."

*

When we were in junior high school, we had a rock band called the *Peers.* We had some small gigs here and there. Played at some sock hops, school gymnasiums, and one time we did a co-ed dance at the YMCA. For a short while, we were junior high celebrities.

Cameron Tomlinson, the bass player, moved to another school. Jimmy Davis was recruited by the *Spiders* to pound drums for their band. Teddy's mum, a devout Catholic, didn't think devil worship via rock and roll was a good thing. The band broke up and we went separate ways. It was fun while it lasted. My mum was the best roadie ever!

A few years later Ronnie and I played the college coffee shop concert circuit. We had transitioned from Fender electric to acoustic guitars. Susan Spaulding sometimes sang backup vocals. Life rolled along, we all got degrees and graduated.

Backup singer Susan became a lawyer. A few years passed since college and one day out of the blue aether she left me voicemail, "Hi Randal, this is Susan Spaulding calling. I am representing a celebrity client. Unfortunately, she's developed a *severe* case of stage fright. Please give me a call. We need your help. I know this is an area of your expertise. Thanks, talk soon."

Since COVID-19, formal psychology conventions and customs have changed. Some of my colleagues still stay with Zoom therapy sessions. Shrinks like it, patients like it, and the licensing board still says it's kosher. Traditional assessments are pretty much impossible over the computer. Evaluations can be done that way, but I can't do them over the computer.

Out of courtesy, I called Susie back without delay. Couldn't leave her in the lurch. I had too many patients already and didn't need to be stretched further. That's what I was planning to tell her. Even without knowing the details, or the level of celebrity, I didn't need another file.

Susan Spaulding is certainly the type of lawyer you would want advocating for you. She doesn't take no for an answer easily. "What? You are saying no thanks and I haven't even told you who my client's name?"

I groaned, "That's the point Susie." I tried to explain. "My current caseload is too taxing. I simply cannot take on another file."

"Ha," Susan snorted, "I remember you saying if you want to get something done, get a busy person to do it. There's a reason they are busy, and the others aren't."

Marie Palmer is a fairly famous singer. She was formerly the leader in the band called *Wirlu Devenish*. They had a few successful albums, but when Marie dropped out, the band dissolved. I liked their music. They were a good band.

"Randal, whatever your fees are we will pay triple, plus expenses, and whatever you want. Write your own ticket. We need your help. Can you clear your schedule and fly to Malibu in the next few days?"

"No Susan, I don't hold a California psychologist license!"

"You don't need one," Susan insisted.

"Yes, I do!" I guffawed.

We bantered back and forth. Susan said she could get the California psychologist licensing board to grant me a temporary visitors license. She's done it before.

So, I said, "If you've done it before then re-hire that psychologist."

"Would if I could," Susan smacked her lips, "she's dead. Motorcycle accident."

Anyhow, long story made short, I ended up flying to California. Marie and I worked together on her anxiety and stage fright. I flew back and forth a few times until I felt like Marie had progressed to a point that my direct services were no longer required. She would have been content to continue indefinitely.

Marie was familiar with groupies and service providers, but in due course she understood it was time to let me go. Our work together did not need to go on indefinitely. She had improved, started touring again, doing concerts in sold out venues. She was confident of her competence.

Marie and her full five-piece band travelled up to British Columbia to perform a sold-out concert in Vancouver's Queen Elizabeth Theatre. Marie got my wife and me great seats in row two, backstage passes, after party invitations and gifts. I was pleased to see Marie's anxiety and stage fright were well under her control.

Just before her penultimate musical number, followed by the requisite encore, Marie *always* introduces all the members in the band one by one, sometimes roadies, too. It's her standard procedure.

The night we were there, she slowly walked to the edge of the stage, "There is someone else here tonight that I need to say a huge thank you to." She smiled, shook her head, "You know, I would not be here tonight if it wasn't for the best shrink I have ever had the good fortune to meet, Dr. Randal Reilly. Last year I was in rough shape. Some days I didn't want to get out of bed, let alone leave the house. Dr. Reilly got me back on my feet. He's the *best* therapist ever. Now, I'll tell you, he always makes a *big* deal out of patient confidentiality. According to British Columbia law, *he* can't go around talking about his patients. But I can. He says confidentiality is *my* privilege. Whatever, anyhow, he's here tonight." Marie points to me, blows a kiss, "That's him, right there, c'mon, stand up, take a bow, don't be shy. I owe you the world! You the man!"

I wasn't going to stand up. So, I simply stuck up my hand and waved to Marie, and the audience. I blew her a kiss and gave her the universal time-out signal with my hands in an attempt to get her to move on to the encore. She smiled and started singing one of her hit songs a capella. One by one the band started joining in. That was the encoré. It was a great concert.

Psychology has lots of rules like patient confidentiality, boundaries, dual-relationships and ethical standards. I always follow the rules. Over the years I have had some celebrity patients, wealthy patients, and those deemed as important people. Mental health doesn't discriminate about one's station in life.

I tried explaining to Marie the importance of the therapeutic relationship. We can't become friends. Boundaries are established for a reason. Maybe she might want to resume therapy some day down the road.

Marie didn't care. Her hearing is fine, listening is another issue.

Some celebrities are like that.

Marie can sing.

*

Jackson Browne's 1980 song, "That Girl Could Sing," was a big hit. It was about backup singer Valerie Carter (1953 – 2017). Valerie could sing. However, she always preferred a backup singer's role compared to centre stage. Valerie had difficulties with drugs. Singer James Taylor attended her 2011 drug court graduation ceremony. Good friends stand up when needed. Valerie died from heart failure six years later.

My Professional Opinion

"There is no right way to do a wrong thing."
~Dr. Perry T. Leslie (1944 – 2017)

*

As an independent practicing psychologist my professional opinion is developed from multiple measures *with* multiple methods. That's the conventional definition for the acquisition of empirical convergent validity. When measures and methods converge you feel confident of the construct. Divergence means you must look further for an explanation.

A competent shrink must interview a number of people involved directly and indirectly with the child's file. One interview with one person is not adequate. A thorough review needs interviews with various family members, some may show biases. Additionally, it's important to interview schoolteachers, past and present. That's the industry standard.

Similarly, direct assessments with the child require psychological test measures that include objective and subjective self-report sources. Scales and inventories are imbedded with lie detection and faking (good or negative) subscales. These are needed for reliability and validity checks.

Anything less is shoddy, and rightfully scrutinized by peers pejoratively.

Personality assessments are complicated.

*

Altogether, I met with eleven-year-old Katy Porter over three separate sessions on different days.

I interviewed her mother. Her father said he'd talk to me when he felt ready to do so, and that might take time. He has become a hospital outpatient. He needs physiotherapy.

I saw her grandfather and cousins separately, and together.

I met with Katy's teachers and the school's counsellor.

*

If Katy's parents could jointly agree, Earl Porter would continue informal guardianship of Katy. If parental access presented as a problem. Family Court would decide Katy's custodial living arrangements. Maybe it would be Earl, maybe the aggrieved petitioner, the court would need to decide.

For formal legal proceedings the court will require my psych evaluation and written report. Although I prefer to *not* testify at these things, I do so as the court requires. Some psychologists like testifying, it's their time to shine. Adds more money to the bill, too.

I prefer backstage.

*

After seeing Katy for two sessions, I started interviewing important people in her life. Her grandfather was at the head of the line. I wanted to speak with some significant people in her life before my third sit-down assessment session with Katy.

After a couple cordial introductions, the first thing Katy's grandfather said was, "Good thing Katy's a bad shot."

I smiled back at him because I did appreciate the levity, "Yes, that's true, I suppose, but it's never good to shoot your father."

"Yes, however, if Julian died from the gunshot wound, we would be talking about second degree murder or most likely manslaughter. Katy meant to shoot him, but it was not premeditated. In my mind it was more like an accident. Children should not play with firearms." Earl dipped his chin, shook his head, "I don't know what Julian was doing with a loaded gun in the bedroom in the first place."

Earl Porter, by any number of measures, is an important person, yet you wouldn't know it from his presentation of self. He comes across quite folksy and friendly.

While it is true that this situation would undoubtedly be much worse if Katy's aim and subsequent gunshot had indeed been fatal. Nevertheless, the fact remains that Katy *did* shoot her father. That in and of itself is troubling.

"True, no disputing that."

Although I could never personally afford to retain someone like Earl Porter, his consulting fees are quite high, he patiently sat with me presenting a detailed explanation of his interpretation of what's currently going on with Katy in general, and specifically the night she shot her father. He had spent the summer with Katy and her two cousins. Earl's sample of her recent behaviour was based on day-to-day discussions, and summer activities with Katy and her cousins. It was obvious that Earl's early legal training has lasted. On my intake confidentiality conditions form, he lists his occupation as a *financial consultant.* Earl is a self-made man.

We both agreed that Katy's sincere remorse about the shooting represents a positive point. Katy feels terrible about shooting her father. "Remorse is a good thing. I've met many people who've made mistakes, but they don't feel *any* remorse or responsibility for their misdeeds. They are sociopaths," Earl reported. "Katy's always been impulsive. She's a ready, fire, aim, sort of person," Earl explained.

"Mind you, we must remember, she's *only* eleven years old. She's certainly immature on some levels, but she's not a sociopath. She's just impulsive and immature."

I agreed, "Developmentally, eleven-year-olds sit in that grey zone of maturity. They are not simply little kids with diminished capacity, but they are not complete cognitive physical adolescents, either."

Earl and I discussed the *aging situation*. I asked how he felt, at age seventy, taking on the guardianship and parenting of eleven-year-old Katy. "When she's twenty, you'll be eighty," I noted.

Earl replied, "Be here now. That's what we're doing. Katy needs me *now*. Down the road math doesn't matter at this juncture. Predicting the future is immaterial at this point."

"Yes, I understand."

*

Next, I met with Katy's two cousins, separately, and together with their grandfather. I was interested in hearing their perspectives on Katy and the shooting. I was putting pieces together for the file's eventual report for the court.

In unison the two cousins claim, "We're a family, and that includes Jaspar."

"Jaspar?" I ask.

Earl chuckled, "Jaspar is our Labrador retriever."

"Jaspar is seventy-seven years old in dog years," the redhead, Clifford, explained. "but he's only eleven years old in Canadian years counting. Both Jas and Katy are eleven."

Both cousins were gobsmacked when they heard about the shooting. Clifford explained, "Elaine and I were in Seattle when it happened. Everyone *except* Katy knew her parents were getting divorced. But I was told it was not my prerogative to tell her. It would be bad manners. Elaine and I are scientists, so we know nothing about *business,* but I know what it means when they say *mind your own business.*"

"What type of scientist are you?" I asked.

"GP," Clifford responded with authority. "We're General Practitioner Scientists. Elaine says we don't declare our major until we are required. No one pigeonholes us."

"Who would require a declaration?" I asked.

Clifford seemed to think about it, then he sighed, "Probably the University of Washington and the folks funding us, I guess. We don't care about awarded degrees and such, but we want their collaborations and resources."

"Tell me more." I encouraged Cliff. "Certainly, sounds interesting."

"Ya, well, I used to go to the Dunbar Beach School here in Vancouver. When my mum and sister died in the car crash, and my dad had the breakdown, I went to live with Grampa Earl on Mayne Island. Katy was spending the summer there, too. Gramps said me and Katy couldn't just goof around all day and we had to do school stuff for a *spot* of everyday. We could decide the time slot, but mornings are popular. He and Elaine were our sponsor teachers. Then when summer was ending Katy had to go home. That's when I joined Elaine and became a University of Washington online auditing student. We went there to meet with people Elaine knows who sit in endowed chairs. She told them I work with her as a research assistant."

"That's pretty cool!" I nodded. "What work are you doing?"

Clifford sat straighter and started explaining, "Well, currently, we collect primary data samples, test theories and run some experiments where the CPU generates secondary data time series models. Then we do the analyses and report writing. But, right now, we're taking a bit of a break until all this stuff with Katy gets settled and sorted. Elaine says I'm not to worry or cry about these things because it's going to all be okay."

I gave Clifford an affirmative nod, "That's good."

"Ya, well, it's not good that Katy shot her father, but she didn't kill him, and he shouldn't have had a gun in the house anyways. Elaine says Katy's not going to jail or anything. Nevertheless, her parents are still getting divorced. Elaine says not to worry because most likely Katy will come back with us to the island. Katy's parents are messed up."

"Why does she say that?"

"Because Katy is only eleven and eleven-year-olds can't go to jail. That's illegal in Canada and we would file a lawsuit. The laws are different in Seattle, but it happened in Vancouver. So that's the deal."

"Yes," I reassured Clifford, "Elaine's correct, Katy is not going to prison."

We pleasantly spent the rest of our session with Clifford explaining *mind* over *matter* molecule shifts, bio-sociology, and cloud computing. He explained how their work was different from the mainstream artificial intelligence groups because they are using the cloud source independently.

I nodded, "Mind over matter sounds fascinating."

Clifford pointed his index finger at me, "You remember back in the middle of August, when it was heat dome hot weather? Well, we had a giant eagle fall out of our front arbutus tree. Americans call them madrona trees. Anyway, what happened was the eagle had eaten a rat. The rat had eaten poison planted by one of the island's farmers. The eagle didn't know the rat had been poisoned. The poison was not diluted and was transmitted to the eagle's brain which causes a neurological spike in the wrong direction and that's why the eagle fell out of the tree. No gyroscopic bird balancing ability due to *brain* poisoning."

Clifford shook his head, "My dad is different because his *mind* took a turn downside on him. In the beginning his brain was basically okay, but as Elaine explains, *everything* is neurological in the sense that his mind misfired synapses and that causes problems. So, maybe, it wasn't neurological in the *beginning*, but it certainly is now."

"What happened to the eagle?" I asked eagerly.

"Sandra and Ed Brooks from the mainland Orphaned Wildlife Rehab Society (OWL) flew from Delta over to our beach in a little helicopter. Sandra told us to all join hands and make a circle around the eagle. Then she threw a Hudsons Bay Co. (Here Before Christ) blanket over the eagle. She picked up the eagle, gave a web card coordinates to Elaine, and ran back to the chopper. We've been following the eagle's rehab over the webcam. The eagle didn't die, but the poison is bad. When the eagle is good for release, we are all going up to Brackendale to do it. Gramps gave them a donation to cover recovery costs."

"That sounds encouraging about the eagle's recovery. How about your father? How's his recovery coming along?"

"Ah, ya, he's not recovering in a linear slope. He's all over the recovery map. Uncle Julian brought dad over to the island to visit. Dad's dad is my Gramps. Elaine says we should be patient because this might take some time. So, we don't know everything, but remain hopeful. It could be worse, but I don't know. I think I get my crying spells from dad's genetic contribution to our family tree."

I nodded my head, and suggested, "You've been through a lot in the last little while. I'm sure it's been difficult."

"Ya but being with Katy's been good." Clifford pursed his lips together, "Katy's gonna be okay. She's certainly different, but in a good way."

*

I met with Elaine next. She is indeed extremely intelligent, and incredibly mature for a sixteen-year-old. At first, she was quite guarded with her comments to me, but eventually opened up and explained the dynamics of living with her grandfather on Mayne Island. It's an arrangement they have been doing for a while. Elaine went to Mayne after Ellen, Earl's wife, died.

Elaine's parents are busy in Seattle. They visit as often as they are able. At any rate, everyone seems happy with the arrangements as they are structured. Seems it's favourable for Elaine and her grandfather.

Elaine explained she doesn't really see herself as a caregiver companion for her grandfather or the cousins. "He's quite tough and together." She thinks of herself as her grandfather's assistant. "Cliffie, on the other hand, requires a lot of attention. But he's worth it. We're making progress. Clifford is a fast learner with excellent splinter skills for programming. He's been helpful with the computer modelling simulations we are developing. He's going to be okay. It's going to take some time. And, you know, we've got the time. He's only nine, yet some ways he's going on forty. Cliffie's sort of like an old soul in some ways."

I enjoyed spending some time with Elaine. I learned a lot from our interview.

*

Although the profession does not have a set established standard formula or template for completing all the components of one of these assessments, I felt as though an adequate file had been assembled to complete my written report. I could withstand peer reviews. I had completed direct assessment measures with Katy, along with a broad number of collateral interviews with relevant people in her life. It was time to start writing. Put it in plain language – bottom line.

Psychologists are asked to predict the probability of future behaviour. Of course, we all know that the *best* predictor of future behaviour is past behaviour. Predicting *dangerousness* is not that difficult for some people. That is, you just know some people *will* reoffend. Leopards do not change spots. Some people are the way they are and will not change.

Some people do not show any remorse. Some people show *faux* remorse. Katy's remorse was sincere. To that I had no doubt.

In the end I wrote that it is my professional opinion that the likelihood of Katy repeating violent behaviour was low. I wrote that it was my professional opinion that Katy would do well to live with her grandfather. He would be an excellent guardian of Katy's best interests. I could not see any reasons why it would not be beneficial for everyone involved.

Of course, Katy's parents could always petition the court asking for changes with the custody and access arrangements. That is their right under law.

I always end with the statement: "If I can be of any further assistance, please do not hesitate to call."

Part Five

Prime Numbers

Not everything that counts can be counted and not everything that can be counted counts.

~Albert Einstein (1879 – 1955)

Elaine and Gandhi

"We are our choices." ~Jean Paul Sartré (1905 – 1980)

*

According to Clifford:

Elaine and Mahatma Gandhi were both born on October 2.

Elaine is going to be seventeen next week. That's a *prime* number. Katy's eleven, that's also a prime number. But she'll be twelve in November. That's *not* a prime number. Twelve is divisible by one, two, three, four *and* six.

Gramps will turn *seventy-one* in June. That's a prime number.

Elaine says I'm not supposed to *perseverate* on numbers or other OCD things. Of course, I didn't even know about these obsessive-compulsive doings until Katy explained that was what I did *too* often. I told Katy, "If I don't know I'm doing it, it's hard to *stop* doing it."

Katy put her palm up in the air and replied, "Cliffie, don't worry about it. I gotcha. It's no big thing, we'll work on it. Nothing happens overnight."

Whew, gotta say it is great to have Katy back again. Things were not too good for a while, but we think it looks like we're going to be okay now. Things are settling. The government's shrink filed his report on Katy. I guess it was favourable enough to keep Katy out of juvenile detention. Looks likely Katy is going to be able live with us.

It takes time, they say, to complete the unofficial and official requirements correctly. Gramps is working with the required aspects of the whole thing. Elaine says Gramps is good with these things. I don't know much, other than things were tense. Tempers were flaring. Katy was mad, her dad was mad, and the whole thing just seemed sad to me. I have cried more than a couple times about the sadness of it all. I miss my mum and sister.

Everyone was quite upset after the shooting. Emotions ran high. Amends were hard to make. Katy was still mad at her dad. And she shot *him* with his own pistol. She and Gramps went to meet with her dad to talk about the shooting. Katy was coached to sincerely say sorry. Then, Katy was not talking to her mother because her dad said that he was moving out of their house *because* of her mother. "Ask your mother," was what her dad said. However, Katy's mother tried to mollycoddle saying that she didn't want to talk about it just yet. Maybe later. She's living with a new man now. I haven't met him. Katy met him but it didn't go well.

Gramps and Elaine seemed to understand what was going on. They said Katy and me were too *young* to understand. Katy, of course, doesn't take too well to that sort of an explanation. After all, she almost *twelve*. Soon she's a tweenager.

Katy made a face, burped, and belched loudly, "So, my parents are getting divorced. Both of them keep saying it's *not* my fault, but neither will say who's at fault for this thing. My mother makes like my dad did something and he says he's moving out because of her. So, I don't know nothing other than the old family is done. And now they are saying we are a *new* one. But we aren't all going to live together anymore. Whatever, it is actually fine by me. I like living with Gramps. Even though sometimes he is a grumpy, gruff, gramps.

"I think you shooting your father made Gramps grumpy," I said shaking my head with a finger pointing at Katy.

This afternoon, just before we climbed into the car's back seat, Elaine quietly told us to cool the complaining for a little while. I said, I wasn't complaining, but she gave me a side eye squint, so I stopped saying anything. Thumbs up signal, no problem with this here goblin.

"I'll explain what's going on later when I get a green light from Gramps. Just be patient, okay," Elaine whispered.

Katy is not normally a patient person. Yet, she listens to Elaine, and I know she's happy to be back living with all of us. "Fine, later gator, we can candlelight talk tonight."

Candlelight talking is what we did late at night while watching stars on the island. We didn't use candles rather we had flashlights we presumed as candles. There is too much light pollution in the big city for stars. Now we are staying at condo penthouse apartment place that Gramps uses when he's in Vancouver. We are all looking forward to getting back to the island, but it's not time yet, evidently. There's *more* business to do, or something.

The condo is modern, made out of concrete, it's nice, I guess. The front part looks out at Vancouver's Locarno Beach with giant freighter boats mooring all over the harbour. Sailboats seem so small scooting between the big freighters. We drive the car deep down into the underground parking and take a private elevator to the top of the building. Other people use the other lobby elevators and parking spots. We don't mingle much with the other people in the building. COVID-19 changed everything.

We know *all* our neighbours on the island. We know no one in the condominium building. Elaine says deindividuation is the deal in the big city. "The island has *quality* of life, and the big city has *quantity.*"

These days we like to get interesting restaurant food that's take out curbside pickup and delivery here in the big city. Nothing like that happens on the island. No fast-food restaurants there. No curbside pickup, neither. Mayne does have some nice restaurants and bistros that we like. The city is different.

Here at the Vancouver condo apartment place, we still do candlelight night talking sessions. We sprawl about on the floor's Indian weave carpet after the big screen video television is turned off. Gramps doesn't want us watching video stuff all night long. He does work and phone calls at the other end of the condo. He clunks down the hall in his Birkenstocks to check on us periodically. Too noisy is not too good, and too quiet raises suspicions. Gramps likes Goldilocks noises from our section.

"So, Elaine," Katy mumbled, "you get a *green* light to tell us what's going on?"

Elaine exhaled, "Yes, I wanted to be certain about the situation before blabbing about it to you two. Gramps says *both* your parents, Katy, have agreed you can live with us. No court proceedings needed. Uncle Julian is moving to London for a while. He doesn't want to live here right now. Auntie Esmae is going to live with her new man. They are in love."

"Who is in love?" I interrupted Elaine's speech, which I know I'm not supposed to do, but I had to interrupt. I was getting confused and couldn't help myself.

"My mother," Katy moaned, "that's who is *in love*."

"Oh, okay, I don't know how these love things work, do you?"

Katy moaned, "Who knows, I *don't*. Do you, Elaine?"

"What do you need to know?" Elaine replied.

I, of course, again, could not keep quiet, "Oh, is *this* the thing about needs and wants analysis binary business?"

Elaine guffawed, "Yes, precisely. That's the truth!"

Katy snorted, "What are you two talking about?"

"*Love*," Elaine sighed.

I chortled, "That's what we are talking about, *love*?"

Elaine smiled, "You know how Gramps often says that this isn't a dress rehearsal, it's the real deal."

Katy sat up, "Ya, why does he say that anyway? Makes no sense, but you two just always nod your heads like you agree or something."

I rolled over on my side, flashed Katy the peace sign, "Ya, I do because I go along to get along. Doesn't mean I understand stuff, just staying out of trouble. Also not making people mad at me."

Elaine laughed, "I'm so proud of you Cliffie! You're showing such progress. And, by the way, *I love you!*"

"Thanks," I smiled, whistled, "Elaine, I love you too."

Katy thumped the floor, "Hey, what about me?"

"Ya, Katy, for sure, I love you for lots. We were worried we were going to lose you to the system or something," I croaked. "Gramps told me so."

"He did?"

"Ya, he was massively upset about everything. Your mum is his daughter."

"What," Katy rhetorically asked, with sarcasm, "you didn't know that?"

"Katy, you know I get confused when the air gets fuzzy," I explained with a sigh.

"Fuzzy," Katy asked, "you see *fuzzy* air?"

"Ya, you don't?"

"No, I don't!"

Elaine whispered, "Cliffie, I do too."

Katy moaned with exasperation, "Oh you two are just messing with me. I'm *serious* about the love bug. My mother got bit and now everything has fallen apart. I don't understand *why?* Makes no sense, *why* would she *choose* to do this?"

"The thing about *love*," Elaine began, "as I understand the concept. People fall in *and* out of love. For instance, Katy, you *loved* that sugary breakfast cereal with bananas. Now, you don't. You grew out of it."

"She morphed," I added. "You are evolving, Katy."

Katy moaned, "Food is not the same thing."

Elaine clicked her tongue and made the tongue noise, "Yes, it is the same. Except, maybe the sex part of love. Your mother fell *out* of love with your father and fell *in* love with the new guy, Arnold."

"His name is Arnold?" I asked.

"Arnold, Arnie, douchebag, it doesn't matter, they are synonyms," Elaine explained.

"Either way, I *hate* him!" Katy whisper shouted. "He messed with a married woman. Wrecked my family."

"Thought you blamed your mother," I wondered out loud.

"I do," Katy hissed, "I hate her too. Betrayed us!"

"Well Katy," Elaine exhaled, "this is where the theory of love gets complicated. You see, Gramps, well, he loves us *unconditionally*. Doesn't matter what you do, Gramps loves you. And that's even after you shot your father. On the other hand, both you and your father have *conditions*. Your mother strayed, coloured outside the lines, and fell in love with someone else. So, once you crack the egg open, you can't get the yolk back in."

My sister, Sandy, said, "You can't get the toothpaste back inside after squeezing it out. So, you live with the consequences."

Elaine nodded in agreement, "Yes, same thing."

Katy yawned, "Maybe, when I think about it, I don't *hate* my mother, but I am awfully angry."

"Ya, well, at least you still got a mother, Katy. I really miss my mum. She was the best."

"Your mum certainly could sing," Katy whistled.

"And dance," I added.

Elaine was quiet, didn't say anything, but sorta snored or something. Katy looked at me pointing with her index finger over her mouth which means, be quiet. Then she mouthed, without speaking, "Elaine's sleeping."

I have been learning how to read lips. Katy mouths words.

Katy gently covered Elaine with a blanket, and we snuck out down the hall on tip toes quietly. When we were far enough down the hall, Katy whispered, "She'll be fine. Good night Cliffie, see ya tomorrow." Then she *kissed* me on my forehead.

"Good night, Katy." I didn't kiss Katy back, but I held up my palm and waved.

My bedroom is across the hall. Not far to fall.

Hearing & Listening

"We hear what you are saying, but we are watching where your feet go." ~Dr. Sally Rogow (1930 – 2012) Professor of Visual Impairments

*

Elaine has hyper hearing. Seems like she hears stuff before it has happened.

Katy's hearing is adequate, her listening is *not*.

Gramps is old, his hearing has deteriorated, but he's the best listener around.

My hearing seems to be okay. There are twenty-six letters in the alphabet. I've got the English sound/symbol relationship with vowels, consonants, and diphthongs mastered. Spell checker is a good thing. My new computer has giga power exponent counter. Reading between the lines is complicated.

Music is a different deal altogether. The music written language has twelve main notes with five flats and sharps in between. Elaine has shown me how to draw notes on the paper, or electronic screen. Three notes to a chord, at a minimum.

Katy likes music. Of course, *everybody* likes listening to music, but not everyone has a theoretical fascination. Katy says theory is boring. So, she does the visual arts as a substitute subject. She has to cleanup whatever mess she makes. She's good at making messes, slags on the cleanup. I help her when I can, I'm a good cleaner.

Elaine started me with the standard 88 note piano keyboard. It's a *baby* grand, but I don't know the difference. She does. At first the theory was confusing, but I kept listening until I was able to identify the mechanics with corresponding sounds. With my eyes closed, when a note is struck on piano, I can name it, sharps and flats notwithstanding. Currently, we are working on seeing the note on paper or tablet screen and then transposing it to my brain. My mind is what creates the music. I got those genes from my mum. She was pitch perfect.

Katy's attention span is not suited for this stuff. However, it's strange because she can sustain attention infinitely while playing video games. Elaine says Katy has impulsiveness problems. She needs to develop her skills.

"That's how Katy gets herself into trouble. She's too impulsive."

"Gramps says some spontaneity is good. He who hesitates is lost."

"That different."

"Okay."

The Sound of Science

1940 – Hans Johann Asperger (1906 – 1980) was the director for the University of Vienna Children's Clinic. The autism spectrum disorder Asperger's Syndrome is named after Hans.

1949 – The Refrigerator Mother Theory: Bruno Bettelheim (1903 – 1990) director of the University of Chicago Orthogenic School for Troubled Children claimed it was something the mother did or didn't do that *causes* autism.

1994 – Asperger's syndrome was added to the American Psychiatric Association's Diagnostic and Statistical Manual of Mental Disorders.

2013 - Asperger's syndrome was subsumed into a broader category within the autism spectrum. Asperger's syndrome was no longer a separate stand alone category.

*

In the big city it is quite quiet *only* if I keep my bedroom windows closed. There is some soundproofing with these thick windows which guarantees no noise at night.

Otherwise, we hear horns honking, sirens, and loud city noises.

Elaine says our apartment has significant air filtered conditioning to keep the heat down and capture negative ions as well as carbon particles. That's a big thing in the city because the concrete, pavement and all the glass generate and retain heat. The heat dome effect is a problem with city pollution. If I open the bedroom windows, I get fresh air but that defeats the air conditioning filtre system. Also, open windows let all the street noise come inside. Gramps complains about the Vancouver traffic. Elaine says it's nothing compared to Seattle traffic. There's no traffic on the island.

On the island we don't have air conditioning. The ocean and trees keep the temperature down and cleans the air. Open bedroom windows lets all the bird songs and ocean noises come inside. In the morning it is sorta nice. No honking horns from cars to hear. On the island I can hear the sea lions lounging on the rocks honking. They can be loud because sound waves travel on the water. It's not an annoying noise or anything. Yet the lions are loud at times. Katy says mating season makes the males loud. Mind you, Katy is quite loud sometimes. That's just how she is and I'm starting to adjust. She's not too annoying or anything, just loud. Her voice is distinctive.

Elaine got me another new tablet electronic computing machine. The other older one's coprocessor was not strong enough to adequately calculate and run our new algorithms. Running algorithms successfully, that is my main responsibility. Inputting equations and running the simulation files takes careful steps. I'm good at crunching the data. Then I layout the spreadsheet summaries for pattern searches.

Elaine downloaded all my mum's videos and songs from the previous device onto the new one. It's good, I like it. My mum could sing. Hearing her voice is soothing. When I needed to get calm or sleep, Elaine taught me to keep reciting the alphabet backwards. Now all I need is listening to my mum sing.

I told Elaine that I was feeling sad about my current memory decay. I can't really remember my sister Sandy's voice. "I remember how Sandy looked because I got all these pictures, but I'm struggling to remember her voice. I know it was soft. I remember that part."

Elaine told Gramps about my memory decay thing. So, Gramps made an appointment with Sandy's old school principal at the Dunbar Beach Middle School. I had forgotten that Sandy was in the school's play called *Wizard of Oz*. Sandy played a character called Dorothy Gale. The school had a video of the play. Gramps got a copy. And then the school put the word out and all sorts of parents started sending in their various videos of Sandy singing in the school plays, but they also had videos of Sandy pitching softballs, soccer and stuff. Jackpot.

Sandy and Charmaine Donnelly were in the same dance school class. Charmaine's mum sent Gramps some videos of the girls dancing Irish jigs. We aren't Irish, but somehow Sandy got involved with the dancing. If my mum was here, I could ask about the Irish.

The *Wizard of Oz* video was the best! I started crying and couldn't stop when we watched Sandy singing *Somewhere Over the Rainbow* song. I know the crying thing upsets other people, but holy -crappo-li, Sandy could sing!

Katy started crying too because she says crying is contagious.

Elaine installed it all, on my cell phones, new computing tablet and desktop devices. Now we got Sandy singing through the quad speakers. Katy turned the volume dial up to the top. It was so loud the vibrations made glasses shake. Gramps didn't like that, he came thundering down the hall, and it got turned down to a *reasonable* level.

Elaine says we gotta do more work on the crying thing.

"Okay," I wiggled my nose, "that's probably a good idea."

She smiled.

Reliability and Validity

Under the auspices of "Nobody tells me nothing," today I found out that Katy is under some kind of government probation agreement situation. This morning Katy and Elaine left early, around nine or so, to go downtown in the little car to meet with the *supervisor.*

Katy's mum meets them there. Auntie E's a lawyer, but certainly she's cooperating with the authorities to keep Katy out of the system and the trouble that goes with the system, according to Elaine. She knows how it goes. I know nothing.

Gramps tilts his head, looks at me and says, "Katy shot her father. There are consequences when that happens."

"Ya, but Katy's only eleven years old," I held up both palms in the air.

Gramps shook his head, "Doesn't matter, shooting someone is not good."

"Does it matter that it was his firearm?"

"No, not really."

When the girls are out, Gramps stays home. He doesn't like leaving me home alone. I said it's not a problem for me. Jaspar is here. However, Katy says it's against the law to leave a nine-year-old home alone. Katy has become a legal authority these days. She has increasing legal experience.

So, at eleven in the morning, Gramps comes heavy tromping down the hallway, leans on my bedroom door frame and asks, "Whatcha doing?"

"I'm running raw data batches that Elaine programmed before they left." I held up her instructions, "Seriating and correct sequencing is important for these sets."

"That's good," Gramps nodded his approval, "you gonna be ready to leave for lunch in thirty. Trousers, no shorts, and a shirt with buttons."

"Yes, 11:30," I gave the thumbs up signal, "Elaine said these clothes are the ones that I should wear for the restaurant." I pointed to the chair by the window.

Gramps seemed pleased, "Good, I'll be back to get you in thirty."

"Yes, got you, I'll be ready." I assured him. Katy's reputation for dawdling has spilled over to my side of the hall. Truth is, I am good with a time schedule, never late unless Katy messes us up. "You can count on me, Gramps."

He smiled, "Yes, I know," he pointed his finger at me, "you are a good boy, Clifford."

"Thanks," thinking to myself, I didn't know there was doubt about my behaviour, but good to know I am in the clear. Consequently, I got dressed and ready to go early. I sat by the elevator with my hand held cloud computing device waiting for Gramps. I have now learned how to run the data from a remote cell phone satellite input. Sometimes it is slow but works well otherwise. Co-processors are key.

Last night, I explained to Katy, "The data processing we are currently doing is like a car, you should never run out of gas because that causes more problems than those solved in the first instance."

Katy shrugged, "Whatever, sounds boring, and it's not my thing."

Time wise, right on the button, Gramps came trotting down the hall wearing his clickety heel shoes. And he was in a fancy suit. He had the pinstripe fancy one on because we were lunching with his old friend, Dr. Joe Moriarty and Joe's wife, Peggy, at a fancy restaurant.

Elaine coached me last night about the expectations. Elaine reminded me *not* to talk like a robot, no high-pitched noises, and try to *listen* more than speak. "Remember, going to a restaurant with Gramps is a big deal. Don't blow it."

No pressure for me with these things. Other than Gramps driving in and out of traffic lanes. Using self-hypnosis, my car phobia is getting slightly under control. Elaine is a much better driver, and she doesn't need to cuss out civilians. Gramps likes to honk the horn, and mutter expletives. Turns to me, and says, "Excuse my French. Don't want to be late."

"Ya, never good to be late," I agree.

Turns out, in the end, we were early. I think Gramps was speeding. Valet parking is quite cool. We just pull up to the place, Gramps gives the girl the keys, and we march into the restaurant.

Seems like everyone in the restaurant knows Gramps. Lots of people always try to shake his hand, but COVID-19 changed that. Gramps doesn't hug or shake hands with hardly anyone. Evidently, in this restaurant, he has a special table. He says that is not so, rather it's his *favourite* table. Guess there is a difference. That's what Elaine calls semantics. Katy is more semantic than anyone I have ever known.

Shortly, Dr. Moriarty and his wife are escorted to our table by André, the maître de. We stand up quickly because that's good manners. Then we wait for André, the maître de, to seat Mrs. M before we sit down. Gramps nods his head at me, approvingly, "Good manners are important, Clifford." He says stuff without words.

Gramps clearly takes charge, ordered wine, and a *bottle* of Coca Cola for me. "Nice to see you two," Gramps semi-salutes, "this is Clifford, my grandson."

I gave them the namasté two palms together sign, "Hello," with a soft voice.

Elaine's been teaching me French, Spanish, and *small talk*. We practice with auditory repertoire and visual screen input/output formats. "Small talk is like reading *between* the lines, extrapolating, interpolating, and inferencing."

We have an algorithm for recording facial recognition, gait and respiratory rates, which we use with cloud support to categorize for macro analyses. It's been working well, but it's not small talk.

I remembered, in my mind, Elaine putting her hand on my shoulder, "Remember, weather, always small talk *weather.*"

Dr. Moriarty is a distinguished cardiac surgeon. Previously, I explained the physician and surgeon dichotomy to Katy, "It's like the legal solicitor versus barrister business." Katy cares more if the explanation has a legal anchor grounding.

In addition to lunch, Gramps and Dr. M were signing stuff for their philanthropy project. They have some financial involvement with heart transplant machines at the BC University Medical Centre.

Elaine says we're not affiliated with those folks, we're with UW Med. I, of course, really don't know the difference.

Mrs. M speaks with a soft melodic voice. She teaches art and music three days a week at the Emily Carr College. "Clifford, I understand you are doing impressive home study courses with your grandfather," Mrs. M smiled at me quizzically.

Fortunately, Gramps splits off from his deep discussion to jump in and say, "Yes, Peggy, Clifford is doing very well with his studies, but full credit goes to my granddaughter, Elaine. She does most of the work. I merely sign some supervision forms.

"Oh my," Mrs. M pursed her lips together, "that sounds marvellous. What projects are you working on now?"

Gramps raises his hand in the air and waved, "Oh don't get Clifford started, Peggy, because he can speak at length about their cloud computer research projects."

I looked at Gramps, not sure how to interpret his cue, and I looked at her and she was all smiles, "I'd *love* to hear about your projects, Clifford. Please, tell me all about what you are doing."

I looked at Gramps, and he waved me on, "Well, I'm not supposed to dominate the conversation at lunch, but I can give you a synopsis," I suggested.

Dr M shook his head, "*Who* says you are not to *dominate* the discussion."

"My cousin, Elaine, says it is bad manners if I ramble on about things that others are not interested in hearing. I'm supposed to be a better listener and engage appropriately."

"Oh my, but your cousin sounds smart," Mrs. M smiled. "Nevertheless, I'd *love* to hear a synopsis."

Again, I looked over towards Gramps.

"Yes, yes," he waved his hand in the air, "of course, a *short* synopsis, Cliffie."

"Okay," I thumbs up signalled Gramps, turned to Mrs. M, "well, we are running three projects concurrently."

"Three *concurrently*," Dr M interrupted and gave a soft whistle. "Why not one at a time?"

"Well, both Gramps and my cousin, Elaine, say that one should not put all their research eggs in the same basket. It's not fear of failure or anything, it's more a matter of momentum. When one lags from unforeseen events, then the other picks up the slack until the resolution is developed."

Gramps nodded approvingly, did a hand gesture, "That is correct, Clifford, keep going with the *short* synopsis."

"Lag time also dictates the project planning process," I explained. "Sometimes when we are running a data set for analyses it will stall in the cloud's line up."

"The cloud has a line up?" Dr M asked.

"Oh yes," I nodded my head, "There is *always* a line up to run the data in the cloud processing queue. Sometimes we circumvent the lag, move to the front by purchasing processing space with crypto currency or traditional standard physical finances. Right now, we have been having problems with results showing inadequate reliability coefficients and that leads to the inherent validity problems. We had a small data set with one thousand people. It's not easy getting one thousand Alzheimer peoples' data. That cohort worked well, but we knew our reliability coefficients would increase if we increased the number of respondents. The trouble there was a couple of crashes because our coprocessor couldn't carry the load. So, we merged our set with the public domain cloud responders. More problems because the validity became questionable. You see, just because the reliability looked good that didn't mean validity was acceptable. The best social science example I can give you is when they said African American black people were not as smart as whites. Their tests were *reliable*, but *not* valid. Biases notwithstanding, sociological explanations were stronger than the psychometric ones. Ten out of ten administered measures may be consistent, but without validity you have *nothing*. Thus, reliability must be consistent, yet validity is the truth. Next week we are going to UBC to meet with Professor Bruno Zumbo. He has developed a modern method to manoeuvre around the macro data set crashes to keep the cycle floating. We don't know how to do those analyses, but he does."

Just then two waiters approached our table with *snails*. These are called escargot appetizers. Last night, Elaine told me that for sure Gramps would order the snails because he *loves* eating snails. I looked at Gramps and indeed did he ever look pleased. So, I knew it was time to yield and *not* talk for a while.

"Thank you, Jacques," Gramps looked up at his friend the head waiter man, "These escargots smell marvellous."

Everyone seemed to agree and started eating straight away. The snail comes in its shell and with a special fork you dig it out to eat. It did smell good. I'd never eaten snails before. Who knew snails as a snack?

Dr M pleasantly pointed his finger at me, "You know Clifford, I was thinking about what you were explaining about research reliability and validity problems. It reminded me of baseball."

"Baseball," Mrs. M scoffed.

"Yes, baseball," he continued, "Clifford, what do you think is more important good *pitching* or better batters?"

"Ah, that's easy," I put my escargot special fork down, "batters, because you can't win a baseball game without scoring."

Dr M smiled, "Yes, good point."

I nodded, gestured to the windows, "I hear it's going to rain tonight."

Small talking.

The Lions Gate Bridge

The Lions Gate Bridge first opened in 1938, connecting Vancouver's Stanley Park across the Burrard Inlet's first narrows to the north shore. It's always been a busy bridge. No more ferries between Vancouver and the north shore.

Before COVID-19, when my mum was alive, I went to school five days a week. She would wake me up quite early in the morning. I would eat breakfast, watch some cartoons, and then change out of my pyjamas into school clothes. No sense wearing good clean clothes while eating breakfast. She called it the spilled milk scenario.

Nowadays with Elaine, Gramps, and Katy, it seems like I'm doing school stuff eight days a week. We have projects. Truth is I like home school better than the physical school. No lineups, bells, loudspeaker announcements, and smelly toilets.

One of the custodial agreements Gramps made with Katy's dad (my uncle Julian), was that they would regularly report on her academic progress. Consequently, Katy spends lots of time with traditional middle school curriculum. I help her when I am able. Katy's room is across the hall from mine. She likes to knock on my door then run and hide.

Elaine simply says, "Katy is Katy."

This morning I'm just semi-dozing, lollygagging in bed. There's no rush to rise and get to school I'm not on a bell's schedule. Besides, I have a load of Wheatios cereal in Tupperware under my bed in case I get hungry. This way I can snack, not bother anyone, or need to go to the kitchen. Of course, milk makes it a better meal, but this is fine, too.

I can hear some scuffling and shuffling sounds coming from across the hall in Katy's direction. It is often suggested that she should *mind her own business.* I don't really know what business means or anything, but I know it doesn't need my involvement unless danger is happening. Gramps says we don't walk by something dangerous, and we won't ignore it either. Katy gets involved with lots of stuff all the time. Sometimes she shouldn't.

Elaine has shown me how to generate binary decisions into a mathematical formula based on omissions, commissions, false alarms and correct hits. It's actually quite a simple formula. We plot the graph to see patterns and progress.

"If you do nothing then no thing happens."

I could hear Gramps outside my door muttering something to someone. Then he did a soft tap, tap, tap, opened the door and asked, "Clifford, are you awake?"

"Yes Gramps," I sit up, "what's going on?"

He gave out a small sigh, "You best get dressed, come to out the west roof patio, we have people who want to talk to us."

"What do they want to talk about?"

"Just get dressed, and come out, okay."

"Ya, ya, no problem," I've been learning to read *between* the lines with prose text stuff as well as nonverbal cues. Thus, I can interpret that something is up with Gramps, and this is where we all comply and don't ask why.

Holding up my index finger, I asked, "Is the west patio same as sunset one?"

I had to ask because we have patios on the roof as well as three side patios. Katy taught me left from right with hand signs. Using your thumb and index finger the left hand makes an 'L.' I'm still not good with compass signs and subsequent directions. North, south, west, whatever, doesn't work for me. Sometimes I don't know which day of the week it is, but it seldom seems to matter much. I like Tuesdays.

Gramps sighed and smiled, "Yes, west is where the sun sets."

"For sure, I'll get dressed and be there straight away."

"Okay, thanks," he said softly, walking away.

Obviously, this is an information processing situation. Gramps seldom tells me what to wear or what is not appropriate. Last week when we went to the restaurant to meet his friends, he said shirt with a collar, trousers, not shorts, and something else but I can't remember now. No performance pressure, right.

Elaine says I must stop *overthinking* pedestrian problems. Which clothes to wear would be an example. If Gramps hadn't said get dressed, I likely would have just gone out in my pyjamas. Obviously, he wants appropriate clothes. Pyjamas are inappropriate, I guess. We have guests.

My sister, Sandy, still sits on my shoulder giving suggestions. Like Clifford get a wiggle on it, the clock is ticking, pitter patter you best get at 'er. It is rude to keep people waiting while you ruminate. So, I selected jeans, a polo shirt, and flip flops, but then decided against the flops and went with slip on sailing shoes.

Now I felt flummoxed about the situation, so I sat back down on the bed to reboot and figure things out. No need to rush was what I was thinking. Rushing never works well. Someone said, fools rush in, but don't know who said that originally. It was probably some over thinker. Maybe I am obsessive, when it is not helpful.

Although I now have a large number of electronic devices, including my new electric piano with headphones, the handheld pocket device is the one Elaine says I should keep with me and pay attention to messages. It was on my nightstand, vibrating, flashing and small beeps. Elaine has it programmed so I cannot mute or silence the device. That comes in handy when I misplace the thing. She was sending messages, "Do you need me? No overthinking, okay. Don't dawdle."

Immediately, I messaged back, "Okay, I am coming now."

First, I stopped to wash my hands and face. Elaine says hand washing is always a priority. I knew something was happening on the patio. I was sure it wasn't Katy, but you never know. Things happen.

I trotted out to the big patio where we watch sunsets over the ocean. Evidently, it's the west one. Since COVID-19, Gramps always meets strangers or non-family members outside on the patio, hardly never inside. There were two men and a woman sitting together in a line. They looked serious.

Gramps and Katy are both right-handed, Elaine and I are left-handed. Some people think this handedness thing means nothing, but Elaine and I are not convinced. Metadata might help at some point. Small samples are spurious.

While we were running data sets for facial recognition, gait, and posture analyses we also entered additional data to examine handedness and strong-arming effects. The hypothesis comes from photos of mothers, politicians and cops. A mother always keeps her kid on her strong arm side so she can grab him and pull him out from harm. Right-handed mothers kept the kid on the right side. Left-handed mothers had the kid on the left. We have pictures where politicians put their hand on the small of someone's back to guide with their strong arm. Of course, cops do the same thing.

I arrived at the patio and scanned the scene trying to determine where to strategically sit, keeping in mind the handedness hypothesis. I realized I had seen that man in the middle before. Facial recognition software is much more reliable than my memory, yet I knew something was wrong. Something is going down here and now. "Who is that guy I wondered? Why is he here?"

Gramps grandly gestured for me to come and sit down beside him. I sat to his right side. My left arm matched his right. We were copacetic. I could see Katy was now squirming, so that meant something, yet I didn't know what. Elaine was stoic, she nodded reassuring to me.

"Mr. Porter," the lady with the black hair, who seemed to be in charge, asks, "is everyone here, should we begin now?"

Gramps nodded and waved his hand, "Yes, please, go ahead, everyone is here."

All of a sudden, Katy stood up, "Sorry Gramps, sorry Cliffie, whatever we're doing I don't want to do it. I'm going to the bathroom. Come get me later, Cliffie." And with that she darted off.

Elaine looked at Gramps with a nonverbal should I go get her expression. Gramps just waved her off, "Katherine will be fine. Just leave her be."

Gramps *only* calls Katy by her birth certificate name, Katherine, if she's in trouble or something like that sort of thing. Maybe he was doing it for the benefit of these strangers.

The lady with black hair cleared her throat.

Gramps nodded, "Please, Dr Quan, continue."

All of a sudden, I remembered; I have seen that man in the middle before. He was one of the cops who came to the soccer pitch to tell us about mum and Sandy on the day of the car crash. I whispered to Gramps, "That man in the middle is a cop!"

"Yes, I know Clifford, they made a special trip here to talk with us. Let's let them proceed, okay."

Although Elaine insists, I am not stricken with panic attacks, rather it's really just an adrenalin surge, all of a sudden, I certainly felt uneasy. Something is going on. Gramps seemed to be not too concerned, and Elaine's nonverbal cues were uninterpretable. I didn't know what to think. This can't be good. Katy must have known something. Katy says she has *spiddy-sense* for these types of things.

Dr Quan smiled at me, it wasn't a faux smile, yet it didn't appear on the positive side either. "Yes, Clifford, your memory is correct, this is Captain DuPont from the Vancouver Police Department," then she gestured to the other guy, "and this is Constable Roberts from the West Vancouver Police Department. We are here to talk to you about your father, Erik."

"Ya, what about him?" I asked as politely as I could without the tone. Gramps disapproves of tone talking. He doesn't like *ya* and prefers I use yes, but I forget under pressure.

Gramps exhaled, didn't say anything, just patted me on the knee reassuringly.

Dr Quan continued, "Well, Clifford, I am the Administrative Director of Saint David's Hospital in Vancouver. Your father has been one of our patients for this past while. As you know we have previously given your father day and weekend passes in the past. I think he came to visit family on Mayne Island on one of those occasions."

I didn't know if she was doing what Elaine calls rhetorical speaking or what, so I answered, "Yes, Uncle Jules brought dad to visit. That was before Katy shot him."

Dr Quan looked at Gramps, "Katherine shot someone?"

Gramps gave a heavy sigh, "Yes, it's a long story, however it has been looked after and is not related to this situation."

"Ya, Katy shot *her* father, not mine. Sorry if my syntax messed you up," I clarified for Dr Quan.

She smiled, "No, not a problem, thanks for clarifying, Clifford."

The policeman from West Van looked at his wristwatch. I suspected this was taking longer than intended. He didn't say anything.

Dr Quan continued, "As I was saying, the reason we are here today is to explain recent events. Around forty hours ago, Erik William Porter, was given a day pass so he could leave the hospital and walk around the community. It appears Mr. Porter walked from the hospital to the Lions Gate Bridge. Witnesses state that he jumped off from the bridge around two in the afternoon. The ocean currents prevented a quick rescue and recovery. This morning a body surfaced and washed ashore at Ambleside Beach in West Vancouver. We are here to inform you that your father has died."

I sorta expected from this formal setup that bad news was likely coming yet didn't think it would be this bad. I thought it had to do with Katy and her legal problems, breaching probation conditions or something of the sort. I looked over at Gramps. He was quiet controlled crying. Not big tears and sobs, but he was crying. We always thought dad was going to get better. His son, my dad, was *dead.*

The grownups did more small talk stuff. I interrupted and asked if I could go to my room. Gramps said yes, Elaine would take me and check on Katy.

Elaine explained that dad's body washed up in the West Vancouver jurisdiction. Vancouver Police were involved because dad jumped from the Vancouver side of the bridge. Now they want Gramps to go to the hospital's morgue to identify his son's body. Although it seemed to me to be an unnecessary formality, Elaine said it was important. The cops would take him in an unmarked car and bring him back afterwards. Gramps was in no condition to drive by himself. He didn't look good.

Some people process information differently and faster that I do. I tend to look from unorthodox angles. I know it's not a good thing to be obsessive. Definitely, don't think I have recovered from my mum and Sandy's car accident deaths. The government shrink said it's not necessarily a recovering type thing, but rather coping and carrying on with my life.

Dad certainly couldn't cope, and he didn't want to carry on. Dad was heartbroken. Literally speaking and then it became physical. Instead of recovering he went deeper into despair. They tried meds, talking therapies and various combinations of both. Maybe he was marginal to begin with and the accident was the final stressor or something.

I asked Gramps if he would like me to come with him, but he said it was best he went on his own and I should stay back, "Look after the girls."

Of course, Gramps knows best, it's preferable to remember dad when he was strong and healthy. We have his baseball videos. My memory of mum and Sandy in the open lid wooden boxes still seems haunting. That wasn't good. They didn't look like my memory. I remember dad saying he thought the morticians did a good job.

I wasn't going to argue, but I didn't agree either.

Open caskets, that's what they were called.

Boxes with the lids open are caskets.

Anthropology and Ancestors

Gramps comes and checks on me a couple times a night and then again before he goes to bed. Standing at my doorway he shakes his head and mutters, "I'm sorry how things turned out with your father. We were always holding hope for the best with Erik. You know I don't think a nine-year-old should have to deal with these tragedies. We'll take things a step at a time. One way or another we will get to the other side. Trust me, we will get there. Remember, your father's story is more than these past few months."

"Yes, I know."

"And don't stay up too late, okay. You need sleep to grow."

"Yes sir," I saluted, "see ya in the morning."

"See you in the morning," he closed my door and shuffled down the hall, softly whistling some song from the sixties.

*

Sometimes I dream about my mum and Sandy. When I am dreaming, I forget that they are dead, until I wake up. I haven't had any dreams about dad. Maybe it's too soon. Katy and I rode our bikes to the Lions Gate Bridge to see where he jumped. It was quite a long ride, and when we got there, it didn't make me feel better but wasn't worse either. I didn't exactly know how to feel. It wasn't good. Still wonder why dad jumped.

Elaine says that's the sort of expedition thing where we ride our bikes across town is certainly something we should talk to her first *before* we do it. We said she was busy on a video link call, and we didn't want to disturb her. She was working. So, we rode away anyway.

When my mum and Sandy were killed there was a big ritual funeral ceremony at a majestic cathedral in downtown Vancouver. Lots and lots of people attended. I think I knew some of them, but many were strangers to me. Dad didn't want to talk about it. He said we'd talk later, but we didn't. Dad started spiralling down. He was never the same again after mum and Sandy died. In the end, I think dad just didn't want to go on living anymore.

Elaine says Gramps is planning something private and a much smaller service for dad, but now we are waiting for Uncle Julian to get back here from England. Evidently, they got a hold of him and soon he will be enroute. There are lots of things I don't understand. Katy's eleven and she says it's not any better being older.

Elaine says, anthropologically, different cultures deal with death in various forms and customs. "Life after death is a common thread with most religious beliefs."

Katy says the Porters are descendants of Vikings, but we can't put dad on a burning raft out to sea. "That's what the Vikings did."

Most likely we will do the same as with mum and Sandy. Uncle Julian will take us out on his boat, and we will put dad's ashes in the sea. This way the sea's currents take the ashes to the four corners of the world. So, I am told.

A lot of people bury the dead six feet underground. It's a standard grave depth. Originated during the 1665 London Black Death Plague. The other idea was six feet under could deter grave robbers or animals.

"Cemeteries take up a lot of surface land space," Elaine pointed her finger at us.

Katy says she heard that our ancestors are always watching us from above.

I'm not really religious. She isn't either, but she says that sort of stuff for whatever reason. Probably too much television isn't good for Katy.

Elaine rolls her eyes, shrugs and says, "Supernatural beliefs are strange."

Whatever, I do hope dad's in a better place or space or whatever happens after you jump off a giant bridge.

All in all, it's all quite sad.

We all are feeling bad.

Especially Gramps.

Jaspar ~ Bad to Worse

People always say that dogs belong in the country. That's where dogs have room to run and roam around in rural areas. They say the city is not a good place for a dog to live. Freedom is what we hear all the time, rhetorically speaking.

However, personally speaking, I've learned that's *not* true. Dogs don't get shot by rifles and shotguns in the city. They might get run over by a car or something. In the country a farmer will shoot a dog if the dog chases cows. Dogs get shot if they get caught *near* a chicken coop. A dog can get in a lot of trouble out in the country.

Having said that, Jaspar, our dog on the island stays on the island, and doesn't come to the big city towering apartment building where we stay. Keven Parker, our handyman caretaker looks after Jaspar when Gramps is in the city. He feeds our chickens, too. Gramps says the apartment is too sterile and confining for Jaspar. Barking is bad. Besides, constantly taking him outside to pee would be a problem. It could be done, but elevators, concrete and city stuff aren't well suited for Jassie. So, he stays on the island. He's better off there.

*

I was in a stage seven level of deep sleep, dreaming about something exciting when Elaine came into my room. She softly shook me awake. That's one thing, but the other is she was crying. *Big* tears sliding down her face, big time type crying. She was seriously sobbing.

Quickly I slipped out of my sleeping sense and ask, "What's going on? Why are you crying?"

"It's Jaspar," she sniffled, "he has died. Keven called Gramps to tell him."

I think to myself, this is not good. For sure, Jaspar is old, everybody knows that fact. Calendar years counting, he's eleven. Katy says that translates into eighty something in dog years. Evidently, Labrador retrievers' life span expectancy goes as high as sixteen calendar years. However, it's not unusual for a lab to die of old age at eleven. They say *natural* causes. The warranty was expired and now Jaspar is too. Eleven actually is reasonably old for a Labrador retriever.

"Have you told Katy?"

"Nope," she sighed, and cried some more, "thought I'd start with you first."

"Okay," I wasn't sure what to say to Elaine. I didn't want to say the *wrong* thing. Sometimes I am not too crisp when I first wake up. Takes me a while to process the magnitude of it all. It was only eight in the morning.

Elaine looked at me, gave me a hard hug, "I thought I was okay. I was confident I could tell you about Jaspar, but it's harder than I thought."

"Yes," I agreed, "Jaspar is the best dog ever! How's Gramps doing?"

"Bad, but he pretends he's okay."

"Ya, ya, I know, Gramps really loved Jaspar."

Elaine wiped the tears from her eyes, cheeks, and sniffled her nose, "I'm going to go check on Gramps. You tell Katy, okay."

I held my hand up, wobbled my head, "I think if Katy is sleeping, we should just leave her alone for now. What's that expression Gramps says? You know, let sleeping dogs lie."

"Yes, something like that."

"I will talk to Katy after she wakes up. Let's go get Gramps coffee and toast."

Elaine nodded, "Cliffie, I'm so glad you are here. You know exactly what to do and I don't. This has hit me hard." And with that she cried some more. "This is so *sad!*"

Well, now I know things have gone deep south because Elaine *always* knows what to do and I seldom have a clue. My forté is something else, but I'm not sure what it is other than data processing. I'm good at that. Katy keeps saying we will work on my *social skills.*

Elaine says, "Katy's a fine one to talk about social skill improvement!"

"Ya, she shot her father,"

Elaine sniffled, "Don't remind me," she scrunched out a small smile, "I'm trying to *forget* about Katy and her dad. Whoa boy, good thing we are close to getting on the other side of that stuff.

"We are?" I asked.

"Yes, Gramps says things are shortly going to be settled on that sector."

"That's good."

We went to the kitchen, ground coffee beans, brewed them up, poured a big carafé of java for Gramps. I toasted the bread and loaded everything onto a wooden breakfast in-bed-tray thing. I got partway down the hall, had to reverse and get the jam jars. Gotta have jam on the toast.

The door to Gramps' room was ajar, I used my foot to swing it open fully. I was careful not to spill because that would defeat the purpose. I didn't speak out loud, rather used my nonverbal communication skills. Sometimes words will wreck the mood. He was sitting upright in bed watching commercial network television news. He watches the news all the time on nine different channels. It's always bad news, but he watches anyway. I slid the tray over his lap.

"Thank you, Clifford," Gramps said as his hand thumped the bed beside him a couple times. That meant I was invited to join him on the bed to eat toast and jam. Katy and me don't drink coffee, but Elaine and Gramps guzzle gallons of coffee, morning, noon and late afternoon coffee *break*. Elaine is seventeen, old enough to drink coffee. Even though Katy and I hold Norwegian genetic heritage, and those guys drink coffee early, we don't like the taste. Elaine says we are not old enough at any rate.

Elaine had run reconnaissance to let Gramps know I was coming with the breakfast tray. Then she retreated to her room to do whatever she needed to do for a distraction. She works all the time these days. We are trying to get ahead of schedule, evidently.

"Little Buddy," Gramps mostly calls me Clifford, but lately he's been calling me his Little Buddy. Now, of course, Katy has started calling me her *Little Buddy.*

"Yes," Gramps prefers we, particularly me, reply with a formal *yes* rather than a sloppy yup or ya. He says, remember proper diction and enunciation are important.

"You doing okay?" Gramps tilted his head and asked with a soft-spoken voice.

"Dunno."

"Pardon?"

"Well, I am most certainly massively sad. And it's not just contagion from Elaine, yet some amount of explanation comes from her grief."

"Yes, I suppose that's so."

"Katy?"

"Still sleeping, I will speak with her when she's awake. Sometimes she is cranky when waking early."

"What do you prefer? Raspberry or blueberry jam?"

"Toss up."

"Suppose so."

"You think Katy might have a bad reaction hearing about Jaspar?"

"Without a doubt."

"Firearms?"

"None."

"We having something for Jaspar?"

"Of course."

"Cremation or bury?"

"Bury."

"Where?"

"Under the big Arbutus tree."

"Americans say Madrona tree."

"Yes, they do."

"You want the last piece of toast?"

"You take it."

"Split."

"Sure."

My pocket handheld cellular computer phone started vibrating, beeping, and Bach bars. Elaine has both Katy's and mine programmed so we cannot ignore one another's calls or messages.

"What's that noise?" Gramps snorted.

"Katy's up," I saluted, "that's her calling me walkie-talkie style."

"Oh, well then," he sighed, "go ahead and answer."

I wrinkled my forehead, "Nah, I am going to go see her in person. She's in the kitchen."

"Making a mess."

I smiled, "Probably, that's our Katy. She makes messes."

Gramps patted my head, "Thanks for breakfast, Little Buddy, it was grand."

I got up out of bed, organized the tray, and started to leave, turning around I said, "Call me if you need me."

"Will do, thanks," Gramps gave me a salute.

Although the meaning or purpose escapes me, saluting each other is our new thing. I think he likes it. His dad, my Great Gramps, who for sure, I never met, was in the Royal Canadian Navy (RCN). I've seen his picture. They look alike.

Katy was banging around in the kitchen, putting cereal in a bowl with milk and raspberries, "What's up?" Katy spilled some milk overshooting the bowl while looking up at me. "Where is everyone? I was calling you."

I said she should sit down, and I'd tell her what's happening. I spoke slowly and clearly describing the situation. Katy gasped, got glassy eyed and started soft whimpering, but basically, she was okay. One never knows how Katy might react to bad news. And this was bad news.

Katy pointed her spoon at me, "Does this mean we are outa Vancouver and going back to the island?"

"Ya, tomorrow."

"Good," Katy seemed pleased, "early or late ferry?"

"Dunno."

"Whatever."

"Ya, doesn't matter."

Two Ferries A Day

We were all travelling back to the island cavalcade style. No one left behind. The decision was made early not to travel with a *boys'* car and a *girls'* car. Consequently, that means Katy goes with Gramps in the beat-up truck, Elaine and me in the electro hybrid car. Mixed seating travel.

There are *only* two ferries a day leaving Vancouver to Mayne Island. One in the *early* morning, the other at night. Some of us are not morning people. Also, Gramps is not good driving at night. Something to do with his eyes, impending cataracts, and/or night vision. Even still, arriving at night, in the dark, stumbling around the trees, rocks, and driveway is an accident waiting to happen, according to Gramps. No one will argue on that account. We've all done it.

Consequently, we made a concerted effort to catch the early morning ferry. It's not easy getting everyone up and out, loading the vehicles and getting through the traffic and the Ladner tunnel on time. If you arrive at the ferry terminal late, (God forbid, Buddha and Zeus too), they will put you in the *standby* line. That's never good. Gramps is not a gambler, although Elaine says he's in heavy with the stock market commodities and bonds business.

"That's gambling, isn't it?" I asked.

"White collar calculations," was her reply.

*

Elaine changed lanes, smiled, and said, "I think it's sweet for Gramps and Katy to spend time together. Call it bonding time." Elaine explained as we whipped through the entrance to the Ladner Tunnel that leads to the ferry terminal. We were on schedule, making adequate clock time. No stress yet.

"Ya, hope so," I smiled wondering whether Katy might push the limits with Gramps too far. "He's pretty patient, yet there's a threshold. Katy sometimes pushes things too far. She can be annoying."

Elaine *only* honks the horn if it is necessary. Gramps honks incessantly. He curses, and then says, "Pardon my French."

However, Elaine said, "Gramps does not really speak French, but he does curse. And saying *pardon my French* sounds sort of racist in some respects."

"Dunno, but I got the French language learner app or the tablet. I'm doing well! Didn't take too long to get to level four." I smirked at her.

Elaine dropped her voice low, "Thanks for helping me yesterday with Gramps and Katy." Elaine turned her eyes from traffic to look directly at me, "I was severely stressed *and* sad about Jaspar. I've got too many irons in the fire right now. These are stressful days. I was a complete *mess*. Stressed to number eleven."

"Whatcha stressed about?"

"Oh, where should I *start*," she sighed. "Psycho-social stressors are the worst with a cumulative compounding effect. Jaspar's death was similar to the final straw that broke the camel's back."

"Does Gramps know you are stressed out?" I asked. "He'd say seventeen-year-olds shouldn't be stressed."

She smiled, "Yes, he'd be correct about that, seventeen-year-olds *should not* be stressed out. However, he's one of the reasons I am stressed!"

"How come?"

"He's *seventy*," she shook her head, "I've been looking after him for a while now. He's getting older, every day, slowing down, stubborn, and facing one crisis after another. When your mother and

Sandra died, that was tough for him. When Katy shot her father that was extremely difficult. Your dad, his middle child, jumping off the bridge has been a gut punch and a half. And now Jaspar's death has hit him hard. Don't know how much more he can take. This perpetual ongoing grief cycle is not good."

"Ya, never ending."

She whistled, "Don't know how much more I can take."

"What's the alternative?" I asked.

"That is the point," Elaine emphasized, "I don't know what's around the corner."

"No one does," I raised my palms in the air, "do they?"

Elaine groaned, "Remember, people don't plan to *fail,* they fail to plan."

"Cool," I gave her a grin, "you got plans?"

"Yes," Elaine pursed her lips together, "defending my masters thesis in *three* weeks."

"Ya, sweet," I saluted, "how do you defend a thesis? You got weapons?"

"Yes I do!"

Ya, like what weapons you gonna use?" I asked with a raised curiosity. "Katy signed a contract form saying she will not touch any weapons anymore."

"I know, I was there when she signed," Elaine smiled. "My weapons are mathematical models and artificial intelligence applications."

"Cool!"

"I have listed your name in the footnotes and acknowledgement sections because you have been a big help doing data processing and model mathematics."

"Cool, but you know I was happy to help. I had nothing else to do and I like the cloud work."

Elaine gave me a soft shoulder slug, "Cliffie, your computer cloud work is the best!"

"Ya, that prof from the university in Washington seemed to think we were on to a productive thread."

"Yes, that was Professor Hubert Blalock!" Elaine whistled, again, "he said we blew his socks off with the nuances in our work. When he found out that you are nine and I'm seventeen he couldn't believe it. That's when he started the video calls. Ordinarily, he has so many disciples the thought of more was not enticing until he read our work and saw our YouTube video link."

I shrugged, "You know Elaine," I whispered, "all those old guys look alike. I can't tell one from another except Professor Zumbo, from UBC, I like him. On the encrypted cyber circuits, he taught me modelling math making from nominal derivatives. He's quite cool! When he gets back from Italy, he promised to take us out to his favourite restaurant for spaghetti."

"That fantastic!" Elaine was impressed. I had forgot to tell her before because everyone was so busy. "What's Dr. Zumbo's favourite restaurant?"

"Dunno, we haven't gone yet. He's still in Italy on sabbatical."

"Yes, but did he tell you the name of his favourite restaurant?"

"Maybe," I wrinkled my nose, "I wasn't paying attention to that part because I had already split screened the nominal input data."

"Geez, Cliff," Elaine frowned, "you gotta pay attention to those details."

"Oh, now you tell me," I raised my hands to surrender, "last week you said don't be *obsessive* with too many details!"

"That's different!"

"How so?"

"We can take Gramps to Zumbo's favourite restaurant. It's basic restaurant probability theory."

"Mathematics?"

"Logic."

"Okay," I put my thumb up, "gotcha, if Zumbo endorses positively, chances are it is *probably* an excellent wager."

"For sure," Elaine thumped the steering wheel, "send him a message, get the name, and tell him about Gramps."

"What about Gramps?" I asked.

"Just tell him Gramps is old and we want to take him to an excellent Italian restaurant."

"Alright," I pulled out the handheld computing device, typed out the message to Prof. Zumbo, turned to Elaine and said, "Done."

"That fast, what did you write?"

"I told Zumbo my grandfather is old, combatting a variety of aging cerebral issues. However, he loves *good* Italian food. My cousin, Elaine, told me to ask you what's the name of a good Italian restaurant in Vancouver. She wants to make dinner reservations. Maybe you will be back by then and might accompany us to the restaurant. My treat. You will like our grandfather, he is erudite. Thanks, Clifford M. Porter."

"Geez, Cliffie, let me see that, did you type *all* that out so quickly?"

"Ya."

"That's too many words. Remember, you are supposed to keep insta-messages *short*."

"It's *not* an insta-message. I sent it through the encrypted communiqué application that Zumbo uses."

She *tried* to grab the device from my hand. "Nope, nope, no you don't. Not while driving. There are LEOs everywhere!"

"LEOs?" Elaine wrinkled her nose, asking with a tone.

"Ya," I saluted, "Gramps calls them *Law Enforcement Officers*. Although he says they are *our* employees. That's under the auspices of civil servants working on our behalf with the tax dollars he provides. Yet they are independent and autonomous. Gramps says there are a half dozen police departments in the lower mainland. VPD, Transit Cops, RCMP, Surrey Constables on Patrol, West Van, Port Muddy, and the Delta Cops. And, by the way, we are currently cruising in their jurisdiction."

"What," Elaine exclaimed with exasperation, "are you talking about? Jurisdiction?"

"Ya, we are currently driving in the Delta Cops' jurisdiction."

She nodded, "Okay, gotcha. When was Gramps telling you these things?"

"*All the time*, every time we drive anywhere, while he speeds above the posted limit. He talks lawyers, too. But that's a different tangent."

Elaine smiled, "Cliffie, you are one tangent, after another."

"Ya, but no more car phobia," I smiled. "Gramps fixed that."

"Thank Buddha, Zeus, and all the other gods! How did that go down?"

"Ya, well, Gramps said it was time for me to *shake off* some phobias. No pills needed. Pills stunt your growth. We would do it with talk therapy. First was the car crash problem. Gramps says I can't have PTSD because I wasn't in the car that crashed. Gramps said he'd make arrangements for me to talk to a shrink or I could talk to him. My choice. Either way, he wanted the car crash concerns to stop. You know when he uses that tone, the voice of authority?"

"Yes, of course, what'd he say?"

"He said, Clifford, you are nine years old and that is way too young to start packing around that type of brain baggage. Let it go. You must travel softer and lighter."

"What did you say?"

"Just said, okay Gramps, you got it." It was the least I could do. Dad had jumped off the bridge and Gramps was struggling with the whole thing. In exchange I asked if he could quit honking the car's horn *all* the time because it was embarrassing and made me jump unnecessarily."

"What did Gramps say?"

"He said he was sorry and would try harder."

"Good work, Cliffie, getting Gramps to compromise is an accomplishment."

"Ya, that's what I thought, too."

We arrived at the ferry terminal, *on time*. Our car got directed to drive onto the top deck.

We like the top deck best. The ferry's belly is where all the diesel trucks are loaded.

On the top deck we had a nice view with the water and the world passing by.

It takes two hours sailing time to get from Vancouver to Mayne Island because we always have to stop over at Galiano Island first for transfer traffic.

Elaine pulled out her computer and started working.

I reclined my seat, went back to sleep.

Sleeping to Dream

Katy seems to have some bad dreams. I don't, at least not that I am aware of, but maybe I do, and don't remember. Elaine says those bad dreams are called *nightmares.*

Mind you, if she can get away with it, Katy will stay up all night playing video games, watching movies, and basically goofing around. Katy is a *nighthawk.* She usually flakes out at some point or other. Runs out of gas and conks out for the count.

Elaine also will work late into the next day's morning, but she knows what she's doing. She calls it *sleep hygiene.* "Just like you cannot eat junk food all the time, you must have a balanced diet, sleeping is the same."

Elaine explained that sleep deprivation is bad for your physical health. If you don't get enough sleep your body breaks down. Just like recharging batteries, sleeping recharges the body. Growth, cell division and repair are correlated to sleeping.

Dream deprivation is bad for your mental health. "Dreams cleanse the mind, that's different than brain functioning. Likely they are correlated. It's not a Freudian thing."

"Okay," I nodded to show I was paying attention.

Elaine showed us some videos where real people volunteered to sleep in the laboratory. Their skulls were wired up so the researchers could monitor their sleep stages. Whenever their EEG reading showed that they were dreaming by entering REM (rapid eye movement) sleep stage, the researchers woke them. Then they made them fill out forms, answer questions and interviews. Often they were awfully irritated, cranky and did poorly on the tasks. They got adequate sleep for their body, but not enough dream time.

Katy said, "Whatever, I don't believe that stuff."

Katy can be stubborn. It's a personality trait. She's a *contrarian.*

*

Sleeping to Dream was a popular song performed by the Nancy Walker Band. My mum wrote the lyrics and music. We have a video of her singing it at the Queen Elizabeth Auditorium.

*

Musically speaking, there are piano songs that are structurally quite different from guitar songs. Big difference between them.

Progress is not something I think about. Doesn't matter to me. Linearity is a relative matter for me. Gramps, on the other hand, seems to think that parameter has merit. Consequently, he decided it was time for me to get an electric guitar. I've shown some good progress with the acoustics. Thus, meriting advanced equipment.

In my bedroom, at any time of day or night, I've been pounding the keys of the electric piano while wearing headphones. Don't want to disturb others or make an annoying racket. That's bad behaviour. I've also been strumming my mum's maple Jean Larrivée Parlour guitar. So, the idea of an *electric* guitar was awfully appealing.

Gramps favourite music store in Vancouver is called *Rufus Guitar Shop.* Evidently, he's been going there for forty years. He knows everyone. Gramps sends them a message prior to our arrival saying what time we will show up. That way the guys have a practice room and the equipment he wants to tryout ready and setup.

I tried out a Fender Telecaster, Stratocaster, a Gibson SG (solid guitar) and a blue Godin from Quebec. But when we plugged in the Collings 290, the deal was sealed. It was wonderful!

The guitar's name, 290, comes from the highway that passes by Bill Collings factory. We got the jet-black model with Tacoma's Jason Lollar pickups, Gotoh tuners, and a Kluson bridge.

It was love at first sight. "Thanks Gramps, I'm electrified!"

*

The place was packed. Mum's concert was going well. They were playing all her hits. The audience was loving it.

Then, after performing one of her popular tunes, mum walks up to the edge of the stage, "Andy, could I get you to raise the house lights for me," pointing to the audience. "There is someone here tonight that I would like you all to meet."

The audience started clapping.

"My son Clifford is out there somewhere," she put her hand over her eyes like a shielding visor. "Where are you, Cliffie?"

I raised my hand up in the air and waved to her.

"You know, Cliffie is a guitar player and a singer. He's written some beautiful songs." Mum waved to the audience, "What do you think, should we get Cliffie to come up here and sing us something?"

The audience started chanting, "Cliffie, Cliffie, Cliffie!"

I stood up, waved to everyone, and an usher came to escort me to the stage stairs. I had an inkling something like this was percolating. When I saw my Collings 290 guitar on a stand, I knew it was a setup, but it was cool!

Ronnie, one of the nicest roadies ever, handed me the guitar, and plugged in the transmitter. I was live. "You are good to go, Cliffie," Ronnie semi-shouted over the crowd noise, tapping me on the shoulder.

Mum was smiling, ear-to-ear, "Whatcha going to sing for us, Cliffie?"

I played a D chord, to check the tuning. Stepping up to the microphone, "Here's a new song I wrote called *The Theory of Love.*"

Mum put her arms in the air, "Well alright then, let's hear it."

I turned to the band and said, "I'll start off with some picking, you all just follow in whenever you like. Key of G."

Turning the guitar neck's pickup to 8, bridge pickup to 5, and tilting the microphone up, I started picking and singing, "The theory of love, oh it looks a lot like you. It's been scientifically tested, mathematically, been proven true." I ran the notes on the lyric true longer, did a short guitar solo before the next verse.

"Yeah, but nobody cares about the science,

Math doesn't matter, not too much."

I threw in another guitar riff, "Albert Einstein, he once said, not everything that can be counted really counts, And not everything that counts, can be counted. Oh, he should know, And he told us so. Now I'm telling you. Oh, you know it's true."

I gave them another small guitar solo riff followed by going back to the top, "Oh, the theory of love, looks a lot like you. It's true, a lot like you, a lot like you, a lot like you. It's the theory of love, it's love and it's you."

I finished with a flare and crescendo.

Mum was soft crying, nothing too serious, she had her own microphone in hand, "Cliffie that was wonderful!" She turned to the audience and asked, "Should we get Cliffie to do us another number?"

The crowd started chanting, "Cliffie, Cliffie, Cliffie!"

Mum was smiling, "Well, Cliffie, what do you say?"

I stepped back up to my microphone, "Sure, what would you like?"

Mum waved her hands, "How about *The Oxford Comma*? That's one of my favourites."

I quickly tuned the guitar's low E string down to D, and said, "Okay, here's *The Oxford Comma.*"

I was starting in strong with the first verse when all of a sudden, my shoulder was shaken, "Cliffie, time to wake up, ferry is docking." Elaine tapped my knee, "Put on your seatbelt, okay?"

Slowly leaving my sleepiness behind, and with a certain level of automaticity, I said, "Okay."

Elaine looked at me sideways, "Were you dreaming?"

"Ya."

"Was it a good one?"

"Ya, it was quite good."

She slipped the car into gear, released the hand brake, stepped on the accelerator, and we slowly rolled forward to disembark.

It's good to be back on the island.

Part Six

Rules of the Road
Dr. Randal Reilly

*Don't feel like you are under any pressure, you aren't.
Just get out there and do it.*

~ Wayne Alfred Anderson (1950 – 2018)

Rules of the Road

Many, many years ago, when I was a *young* psychologist, the rules of the mental health highway were so much simpler. Traffic was lighter. The lanes were wider, seldom saw sideswipes. The business management angle was ancillary to theory and applied practice.

Personal computers were yet to be invented. How did we survive without personal tech? No email or websites back then. My first cellular phone wasn't dialled until 1992. It was a brick size device with an imitation leather case. Analogue versus digital, everything was changing, quickly.

"Try and keep up, okay."

Back in the old days, appointments, meetings and case conferences with patients were all made by landline telephones. Secretaries took messages and wrote them on small pink notepads.

"I called back, twice." Cassette taped message machines were in their infancy. "At the tone, leave a message."

Sure, shrinks had sex with patients in the old days. It was wrong then, and it's wrong now. Still happens too often. "We fell in *love*," is a frequent yet ineffective defence. *Both* male and female psychologists get caught having sex with patients. I remember a few years ago when a prison psychologist got caught having sex with an inmate. "They have cameras everywhere. What were you thinking?"

Ethics and legal principles have evolved. Something may be legal, but it's an unethical practice. Big difference don't do it. Patient confidentiality and privileged relationships have their limitations. Malpractice insurance costs lots more nowadays. Now it's called errors and omissions. Same thing though. Mistakes.

Nowadays it is much harder for young graduates to get a psychologist's license. It is also *easier* to have it taken away, too. Don't screw up. Stay in your lane. If you don't know what you are doing, don't do it.

Angus Sutherland, my old friend from psychology graduate school, screwed up his practice massively. He was a clinical psychologist hypnotist. Things went south when he could not keep his hands to himself. Gus lost his license. An open and shut situation. More than *three* complainants said he touched them inappropriately.

"Why'd you do that?" I asked Angus. "You can't touch your patient's private parts!"

He shrugged and said, "Yup, I fucked up."

Shaking my head, I said, "That's an understatement."

I couldn't understand why or what Gus was thinking, but best guess was – clearly, Gus wasn't thinking. It's hard when a good friend fails. I wish I could have helped him before it was too late.

My main mentor, Dr. Harold Swanson, always emphasized, "Randal, clinically, as long as you can explain 1) what you did; 2) why you did it; and 3) how you were trying to *help* resolve the patient's problem(s). No one could ask more." He should know, Dr. Swanson is listed as a University of California, Distinguished Scholar!

When I was writing my doctoral dissertation, Dr. Swanson and I met every Thursday morning at seven. These meetings were important to maintain momentum and motivation. If one faltered the other picked up the slack.

In addition to being a distinguished scholar. Dr Swanson is a marvellous man, he's patient Jand kind. He taught me a lot. Although those school days were mathematically many miles back in the distant past, in my memory it still seems like it was yesterday. Strange how long-term memory works. I can remember all sorts of stuff from way back when, but sometimes I can't remember why I came into the kitchen. "That's the difference between long-term memory, short-term memory, and *working* memory. Each one is unique."

*

Urban and rural relationships between psychologists and patients differ. My colleague, Diana Penney, learned this principle quickly when she moved her practice to the small town of Cumberland on Vancouver Island.

Deindividuation is common in the urban milieu. Not so much in a small town. In the big city it is easier to follow the rules about psychology dual relationships with patients. No therapy with your neighbours and acquaintances. More than an arm's length distance is demanded between shrinks and patients. You can't do an assessment and then do therapy. That's a clear conflict. Its self-serving.

In a small town, or a little island, everyone knows everyone. You bump into each other at the grocery store, gas station and post office. That's how small towns work. Consequently, it is not unreasonable to accept patients whom you know. Neighbours need therapy too. These are things the licensing board concedes. Urban conventions are different.

*

So, back on Mayne Island, I bumped into Earl Porter shopping at the Farm Gate Store, out of verbal automaticity, or typical small talk, I asked, "How you doing Mr. Porter?"

"Please, call me Earl," he said as we awkwardly shook hands. COVID carryover concerns never seem to leave us. "I'm not doing well at all. I'll call you later," he grimaced and walked out of the store.

Sean, one of the proprietors, looked my way, shook her head, "Earl's been going through a bit of a rough patch these days."

I nodded in agreement, "Yes, that's the truth."

Sean is such a lovely lady. She's a farmer. Sean titled her head, sighed and whispered, "Couldn't help overhearing you and Earl talking. I hope he calls you. Earl's a good man. Help him out if you can."

There was no need for me to explain psychology's rules to Sean because it didn't really matter, I simply said, "For sure, I will do whatever it takes."

Saying that, of course, I've already broken the rule where a psychologist does not acknowledge whether a patient is or is not on the caseload. Confidentiality breached before we began. Oh well, there will be days like that.

Earl called my cellular phone two days later, at six in the morning. I didn't retrieve the voicemail message until after nine. That's when I check emails, voicemail, and the overnight computer headlines. It's my morning routine both at home and the clinic at the York Street office.

"Hello, this is Earl Porter calling. It's Tuesday morning. Further to our discussion the other day at the Farm Gate Store, I should get together with you to talk about some recent events that have occurred in our family. Frankly, the thing is, my daughters keep harassing me to *talk to someone*. The girls say, don't keep it all in your head, talk to someone. So, if I tell them we are meeting to talk, they will get off my case and move on to something else. Call me back at your convenience. Or you can email. Text message is fine, too. Whatever suits you best. I am available and open this week. Mornings are preferable, but whatever works for you is good with me. I will make space. Thanks."

*

Way, way back when I was a young psychologist, I did not hesitate to take on lots of files. Sometimes I was overextended. Maybe I worked too hard, but it seemed like everyone was working hard.

"Know your limit, stay within it."

Nowadays I try to not take on *any* new files. Rather than enter into a formal therapeutic relationship with Earl, I was going suggest an alternative route. That way we would not need to fill out formal intake consent agreements. That's where I explain confidentiality has limits. I must breach confidentiality if the patient discloses that they may hurt themselves *or* someone else.

In the Chapman case the patient told his therapist that after their session he intended to hunt down his estranged wife. The therapist did nothing. The patient went and murdered his estranged wife. The family sued the psychologist and won.

Thus, the rule where therapists have a legal *duty* to warn *possible* victim(s) was established. Malpractice insurance might not cover you for breaching those errors.

By not establishing a formal file, I would not need to discuss fee for service parametres. Appointment obligations, cancellation timelines or emergency contacts did not apply by holding a no file arrangement. Psychology's rules of the road would not require the professional attention. Therapeutic boundaries would not be required. Keep it simple.

I pulled out my phone, dialled up Earl's number, two rings and it went to voicemail. "Hello, leave a message at the tone."

I disconnected without leaving a message. Then I called back again, this time I left him a message.

"Hello Earl, it's Randal Reilly returning your call. Looks like we are playing telephone tag. I'm travelling from Vancouver tonight to the island. Tomorrow morning at ten I'm hiking up to Mount Parke. If you would like to join me, we can meet up at the Fernhill parking lot trailhead. Otherwise, we can catch up and talk some other time down the road. Okay, take care, bye."

These days I'm trying to make a concerted effort to not leave long rambling voicemail. Nobody likes them. I'm better with email. Although I am a professional talker, writing is a strong suit. I like to edit. Voicemail is always off the cuff stuff.

Whatever, telephone tag is like that. It's the nature of the modern communicating game. Snail mail is passé.

I guess.

Mount Parke's History

Rising up to 255 metres (840 feet) above sea level, Mount Parke is the highest point on Mayne Island.

Not Mount Kilimanjaro or anything, just a nice local climb.

Maybe the Sencoten speakers, Coast Salish indigenous people, who lived on the southern gulf islands archipelago for thousands of years before the settlers' arrival, had their own name for what is now known as Mount Parke. Settler history has no record of those names.

Guess it depends on who writes the history, and who records what.

One hundred and twenty-two acres (forty-nine hectares) is what was *staked out* and designated as Mount Parke territory.

*

"I've quit using the *stake holder* term."

"Why's that?"

"It's offensive."

"How so?"

"Americans started it. Although Canada never had a *Manifest Destiny,* we did adopt some of their tricks."

"Indigenous people probably didn't think the American settlers had a *manifest destiny.*"

"Yes, that's the point! The idea that you put a *stake* in the ground to mark your territory is preposterous. It's their territory. Putting a stake in the ground doesn't make it yours."

"Good point. I'll find another appropriate term to use to describe vested interest people."

"Gypsies. You should not use that term either?"

"Incorrect parlance, politically speaking, it's a no-no."

"Don't say you were *gypped?*"

"Correct. Racism is deplorable."

"Despicable."

"Bigots are bad."

*

European explorers began sailing the southern gulf islands archipelago in the 1700s. The Spanish named Galiano Island and the Strait of Juan de Fuca.

The British Captain George Vancouver landed on Mayne Island in 1794. They camped on what is now called Georgina Point. One century later settlers found an

English coin and a knife left behind by Vancouver's crew. Hard evidence confirming the British encampment.

The name Mount Parke comes from Lieutenant J.J. Parke who was an engineer on the American Army survey ship in 1854.

During the Gold Rush years many men stayed in Miners Bay on Mayne Island before rowing over to the mainland to seek gold.

Homesteaders arrived in the late 1800s and began staking claims on the island.

Nowadays a few thousand tourists flock to Mayne Island every summer.

Winter is always quiet.

Hiking, Therapy, and Theories

Summer is my most favourite time to hike to the top of Mount Parke. Although I march up there year-round, summer is the best. Warm and comfortable climbing.

Winter is doable, but sometimes the paths are slippery from the morning mildew and rain. I have taken a tumble, more than once because of mud. Besides, the view from the top can't be reliable in winter. Low cloud cover occurs too often, you can't see much. Snows sometimes up top.

It gets dark too soon in the winter. I've been caught racing dwindling light coming down from the top at four o'clock in the afternoon. Gets too cold in the winter. Not Edmonton cold, but still chilly enough to rate as unpleasant.

Summer is the best. The sun rises early, sets late, and the *heat dome* doesn't amount to much at my place beside the ocean. Winter is a different deal altogether. The winds come whistling off the water shaking the shack something fierce. Winter is not endearing.

Although I know, from an applied mental health perspective, one should try to find the beauty in each of the seasons, I still prefer summer. I like the sunshine.

When I worked at the hospital, as the low person on the totem pole with the least seniority, I had to do a lot of clinical psychology intake mental status interviews. Of course, I complied and asked all the requisite standard mental status questions. Do you know what day it is? What is your birthdate? Do you know why you are here?

Because it was accredited as a teaching and research hospital I felt fine augmenting and expanding intake interviews with projective questions like: what is your favourite colour? Salt or sweet tooth? Are you a morning person or night owl? What is your favourite season?

After some months of data collection, the tally showed as I hypothesized. Close to seven out of ten said *summers* were their favourite season. A few would say winter. When I asked why winter they would explain that they were a snowboarder, skiing enthusiast, skaters too. A few simply *liked* cold weather. They were always minority responders.

Every now and then I got a patient who would say they liked *all* the colours. "I can't pick *one* colour. I like them *all!*" These people often said they liked all the seasons the same amount. They could find the beauty in each season.

For a while, I also kept track of handedness. Left or right-handers personality preferences didn't add up to anything significant. Social science research is like that. Of course, statistical significance and clinical significance are another matter altogether.

Soft science stuff.

*

The Mount Parke entrance sign could be missed if you drive too fast, you have to pay attention. I have gone too far before, but not this time. As I drove my old truck into the parking lot, I could see Earl and his redheaded grandson had arrived early. They were playing catch with a bright neon yellow tennis ball.

We all waved to one another. I got out, started getting my hiking gear together in the back of the truck, Clifford yelled over to me, "Heads up Dr. R., because here it comes." He heaved the ball as hard as he could, yelling, "It's three-corner catch."

I caught the ball, one handed. Earl strolled over, giving me a salute style greeting wave, "Good morning, Randal, how you are doing?"

I tossed him the ball, "Great, nice day, eh?"

"Sorry, no choice, I had to bring Clifford with me this morning," Earl tilted his head, "we can't leave him home alone. The girls left for town early. They're doing errands."

I simply raised both palms in the air, "No problem at all." I waved over to Clifford, who was running full tilt towards us, "Nice to see you, Clifford."

He answered with a robot voice, "We're going mountain climbing!"

Earl raised his eyebrows, nodded, looking up the trail, "He's excited. The girls took him up the Grouse Mountain grind climb in Vancouver a few times. He likes the climb. Nine-year olds have lots of energy to let loose."

I signalled approval to Clifford, "Yes, that's terrific," I waved with a smile, "delighted you are able to join us, Clifford."

It was a perfect day for a hike. We got started going up the path. Earl frequently reminded Clifford to *not* go too far ahead of us and to stay *on the path* within earshot. "Don't get lost, you understand, right."

"Yes, Gramps," Clifford called back, "I understand, and no, I won't get lost."

I tapped Earl on the shoulder, "I was sorry to hear about your dog. You've probably done this hike many times with him. Must be hard now to be trudging along without him?"

"Yes, that's the truth," Earl said, kicking a rock off to the side. "Jaspar was a good dog. We miss him a lot. Especially Elaine, she was awfully fond of the old boy."

"Are you going to get another dog?" I asked.

"Maybe," Earl let out a heavy sigh, "if things start to settle down a bit we might be able to think about another dog. Right now, every-thing is complicated. Too difficult to try and train a puppy."

We strolled along at a slowish pace, discussing some the recent events and their implications. Earl explained that his daughters wanted him to talk to someone about his mental health. They are concerned about the cavalcade of catastrophes that seem unending and the difficulties facing the family.

I tried to clarify the professional therapeutic boundary rules psychologists are expected to follow. Rather than taking Earl on as a patient, formally, I preferred we meet regularly as friends to talk things over.

Earl agreed, but added, "I've got lots of money, tax deductions, and various benefits. There's no problem paying you a stipend."

"Naw, that's fine Earl, I'm more than solvent."

"Fine, whatever you say."

When we reached the top the view was spectacular. We could see for miles and miles. Clifford had found a spot where we would picnic for a while. He pointed out the nearby islands, and their names. "That's the USA on the horizon," Clifford waved his arm with punctuation. "Elaine is an American, but she holds dual citizenship."

"Best of both worlds," I said with a wink.

We sat for a while, eating, drinking, and enjoying the scenery before the descent. Earl emphasized to Clifford that he was not to go too fast. "Watch where you are going. No need for speed."

Personally, I find going downhill is sometimes harder on my legs than uphill. Earl agreed, explaining the biomechanics involved with descending steep terrain. "My knees are not what they used to be."

"You can say that again."

Clifford was patiently waiting for us at the bottom. He was busy working with his electronic devices. Earl had insisted no electronics on the hike.

"Leave them in the truck."

It had been a good day. Just before getting in our respective trucks to depart, I suggested, "Give me a call tomorrow Earl if you would like to go paddling."

"Will do, depending on the weather, and the girls' schedules."

"Or, coffee," I shrugged, "we can get together for coffee."

"Thanks, I'll give you a call."

Part Seven

OCD and Me

Finding a key on the ground is useless until you know which door it will unlock.

~Dr. Ronald F. Jarman (1941 – 1995)

No One is Normal

"There are a lot of things that I don't understand."

Elaine says, "Clifford, listen, don't worry about it, Einstein said he didn't understand it all."

"I'm not worried, or anything like that, sometimes it all seems so much to try to interpret. What's it all about anyway? What does it mean?"

"Yes, that's true," Elaine smiled, "but you said the same thing about algebra."

"Ya, that's true, at first calculus was harder to synthesize. I couldn't see the patterns."

"Some things take time."

"Music makes sense. I can hear the notes and transpose them."

*

In many ways life is much quieter now that we are back on the island. The city was fine by me, I liked being there well enough. It was okay. Lots of restaurants. I liked takeout and curb side pickups.

Gramps, on the other hand, seems so much more relaxed on the island. He doesn't go to face-to-face meetings on the island. He uses virtual software for meetings from the island.

Gramps wears casual clothes on the island. Brogans instead of brogue shoes.

Elaine designed four projects for me. I am running all four concurrently, it doesn't matter where we are staying for me to do the data processing. The net cloud doesn't care. Electricity is essential. Camping is nice, but there are limits. We went on an overnight kayak trip to Tumbo Island. It was nice. Gramps did campfire cooking. He's good at that stuff.

Gramps was really, really sad when my dad died, but now Elaine is saying Gramps is off the Richter sadness scale, now the dog has died. Although Gramps tries to not show too much on the outside, inside he's broken hearted.

"Dog deaths are a lot more difficult than most people realize."

Everyone worries about Gramps. Lately he's had a steady string of unhappy things, one after another. Mathematically, the straw that breaks the camel's back is an old adage. Katy doesn't get it. Elaine explains that too many psycho-social stressors are the same thing that breaks the camel's back. "The cumulative effect is the problem. It all adds up until the breaking point. And then it's broken."

I hasten to add, "Can't put toothpaste back in the tube once you squeezed it out."

*

Yesterday, Elaine had to go to Seattle. She's got stuff to do with her mum. It seems it could be health related, but maybe not. Either way, as they say, her health is none of my business. I offered to accompany her, as I'm a good supporter. Elaine thought it best to go solo, "Thanks Cliffie, I think you should stay here and hold down the fort. Besides, there's now a backlog of data to deal with."

Truth is, we can't leave Gramps home alone with Katy. She's too much to handle. So, I agreed to stay behind. Lately, I've been helping with Katy's daytime educational management. They told her that she's helping with me symbiotically. That makes Katy more amenable to the whole thing.

Gramps reports regularly to a bunch of people about Katy's educational progress. Even though Elaine does all the work, Gramps signs stuff, and shoulders the official responsibilities.

Yesterday Katy and me went through the normal curve's bell shaped distribution. "This math principle originated a couple hundred years ago with agriculture's advancement. Even though Galton was a racist, his math was good."

Katy raised her fist, "I hate racists."

"Ya, ya, agreed," I then explained, "So, Katy, here's the practical real-life situation. Some people are fast runners, their bio-mechanics assist and facilitate speed. Some people are slow runners, they are the human Clydesdales. Workhorses, they are not physically well suited for running, but push comes to shove they can do it. They don't run fast. The thing is, anyone can run, it's just some are better than others. Just like art. Some people can draw pictures in realistic detail. Some can only draw basic stick men."

Katy nodded her agreement, "I like drawing."

I explained how the mathematical normal curve's linear dimensions will go low to high on one level of a trajectory, but we can also plot a perpendicular path. Like the extrovert and introvert continuum. Or the high achiever and mediocre personality.

"So, Katy, you know how everyone complains that you are too impulsive."

She scrunches her face, and said, "Yes, I'm so sick of that silliness."

"Is it a trait or state?"

"What, dunno," Katy shrugged, "who cares? I don't think it matters much."

"Remember when I taught you the reverse alphabetical sequencing for anxiety management?"

"Yes," Katy quickly recited, "ZYXWVUTSRQPONMLKJIHG-FEDCBA."

"That's it," I signalled, "the same sort of strategy I use for anxiety can be used for your impulsivity."

"That's different," Katy scoffed, "you are more contained than I am. Everyone keeps saying I'm hyper."

"Maybe, I don't know that part. Elaine was showing me TED talks and YouTube videos about self-regulation and executive functioning. She got the lead from her interweb friend, Jeannie Lidgren. They are colleagues."

"Elaine's the bomb." Katy pantomimes something strange.

I just smiled and pulled out the alternate tablet, "You want to see the cartoon where there is this guy sitting all by himself in a lecture hall under a sign that says, Conference for Normal People."

"What does that mean?"

"No one is normal."

"Whatever, let's go e-biking."

"Okay."

Circadian Rhythms

"Gramps is sleeping," I whispered, raising my index finger up to my lips to signal quietness to Katy. "I checked on him."

"Was the door open or closed?"

"Open."

"That's a good sign."

"Ya."

Closed doors mean the person wants privacy. Don't disturb someone who has closed their door. Unless it is an emergency. A *real* emergency. Not we've run out of milk or what's for dinner type of thing.

Although Katy and me are free to do lots of things, there are rules and conditions, and some are non-negotiable. For example, if we are leaving the property, or even just going outside for some reason, checking in with Elaine or Gramps is required. They need to know what we are doing, and where we are. They say safety, but Katy says its more than that.

"Dunno, it doesn't matter to me," I reply with a shrug. "I have no complaints."

Another important rule, if you can see that they are in the middle of something and intruding would be rude, or disruptive, or inconsiderate, then you leave a note on the refrigerator. Katy interrupts too easily.

We left a legible printed piece of paper put onto the kitchen refrigerator attached with a magnet that said: "Gone For a Bike Ride @ 11:45." Then we wrote our names on the bottom.

Gramps is a paper person. When we use paper there are three kinds of writing. Today's note was with printing. Longer letter like things we use cursive writing where the letters *flow* and are joined together. We do ink calligraphy for fancy cards.

Elaine, on the other hand, is a digital screen person. She's okay with paper hard copies, but prefers electronic cyber copies like text messages, emails and electronic missives.

Gramps sleeps a lot these days in the afternoon. Elaine says it's no big thing. Don't worry about it. Gramps is old. He gets up quite early, before everyone else, makes phone calls and other stuff. Elaine says Gramps is depressed, but we are not to obsess about it. Our presence is helpful. He's happy we are here. Good company companions.

My dad's circadian rhythms were all jumbled up. Sometimes he'd be awake all night stumbling about in the kitchen, and then he'd sleep for hours during the day. Elaine says my dad was sleeping so much because he was *severely depressed*. His wife and daughter were senselessly killed in a car crash. So, of course, he was depressed. Moreover, his lawyering job was depressing, too. "When you think about the whole thing it's understandable."

"Well, if you say so," I shrugged, "but it is hard for me to understand."

"Yes, naturally," Elaine sighed, "you can't get bogged down with despair. We just keep going forward. That's the way it is."

Elaine is good at explaining. Katy is *not* good at explaining. No patience, I guess. Katy's is a ready, fire, aim, kinda person. Elaine says Katy is OTM. That means On The Mind and Out The Mouth. Katy doesn't filtre. And that can get her in trouble sometimes. We all have quirks to work on. Some more than others.

Don't get me wrong, or mislead you, I *love* Katy because she's funny, kind and caring. She's a good singer, too. Sandy was my first sister from my first family. And that will always be that. Cousin Katy is like a sister now, in this new family. I'm glad she's here. We're never lonely.

*

I don't like sudden noises. So, my pocket phone is kept on vibrate mode, unless Elaine is calling, and then it vibrates, pings, and flashes until the receive button is pushed. Elaine will not be ignored or summarily dismissed. Katy has lost her pocket phone a few times. Sometimes she forgets where it has been left. Any of us can find Katy's phone by pushing the phone finder button. We can find Katy too, if she has the phone with her.

Katy was e-text messaging me: Where are you? Bikes? Hurry up. Barn

I quickly messaged back: Coming straightaway.

Not to suggest I was dawdling, or anything, but Katy's patience is limited. I quickly got my biking clothes together and took off towards the back of the barn where the bikes are kept. It was a perfect day for riding.

On the island, we've got different bikes for different rides. The fat knobby tire bikes are for trails and gravel. Skinny tire bikes are for paved roads. Frame sizes and component weights are important for comfortable riding. A sturdy lightweight carbonfibre frame is good for climbing, but bad for bumps. Doing stunts, Katy has bent wheels, forks and frames.

Recently, we got some new electric bikes. Two are folding bikes that are kept at our condo in the city. These bikes are sorta like the folding bike Dr Reilly uses. They have little wheels with a folding frame. Gramps says they won't get stolen because you take them with you and don't leave them outside attached to a bike rack. Bike theft is a big problem in the city.

The other three hybrid electric bikes are heavier because of the big battery weight and drivetrain hub motor. We have an old motorcycle in the back corner from Gramps younger days. Elaine's the only one who can ride it these days. Katy knocked the motorcycle over while posing for pics no one was taking. The gas leaked out all over the floor. That wasn't good. We needed help to pick it up right.

Motorcycles – remember, the shiny side should stay face up, always.

At first Katy and me were not allowed to ride the new e-bikes. Katy's reputation for stunts was the main reason. "Why do I get blamed for *everything*?" Katy moaned.

"Your history hasn't helped," I suggested. "Gramps and Elaine are worried we'll get hurt or wreck the new machines. You must quit saying you have the need for speed. No one likes that." I pointed my index finger at her.

After a few tutorials and practical demos from Elaine on safe acceleration and basic e-bike riding skills, we were allowed limited access with conditions. We promised no stunts, no rough riding, or bad bike behaviours. "Trust is earned."

The e-bikes provide power and are mechanically well put together! Quite different from my old standard speed bike, that's for sure. Unlike Katy, I get tend to get a bit nervous with too much speed. Took me a while to get comfortable, but now I'm fine. We can cruise all over the island, quickly with little effort at all on the big hills.

By the time I got to the barn Katy was close to completing most of the pre-trip maintenance for the bikes. It's a safety-first type thing. Gramps says, "Unlike our truck with four wheels, the two wheels on the bike must have correct air pressure. That's important. Don't forget air pressure."

Made sense to me. Besides, unlike Katy, I'm not much for arguing. Go with the flow is how I roll.

"The e-bikes must be *fully* charged before taking off down the road," Gramps points the finger of doom to Katy and me.

One time, one of us, no names mentioned, did not push the charger all the way into the battery connector. Consequently, next time, when we went to use the e-bike, it was a no-go because the battery was *dead*.

"It's a learning curve, right."

Today Katy's plan was for us to e-bike all the way to the other side of the island. Mayne Island is not that big so it's not a difficult trip on smooth pavement. Recently, a tall sailing ship arrived with a crew. It's docked at the red government wharf at Miners Bay. Evidently, the ship is open and available for visitors to tour.

Fortunately, Katy is past her pirate phase. She still talks pirate lingo, but not obsessively. We are all grateful for her transition. Pirate songs all day long were a bit much to handle. "What do you do with a drunken sailor?"

I like Miners Bay. The bay's name came from back in the gold rush days when miners would come up from California to seek their fortunes. They would arrive in rowboats from Victoria to Mayne Island. They'd stay at the Springwater Inn overnight, or longer, and then row across the Salish Sea to the mainland for gold. The Springwater Inn has the *best* fish and chips. Miners ate *grub*.

Katy is not as fascinated by the principles of refrigeration as I am. Really, when you think about it, refrigeration is a big deal in terms of progress and power. "It's just as remarkable as electricity, you know."

Katy shrugged, "Whatever. You and Elaine are all about science. When I grow up I'm going to be an artist."

With an index finger point, I replied, "I'm a musician."

"Yes, you are. I love your tunes." Katy nodded her head, adding, "Elaine says genetics."

"Genetics?" I asked.

"Your mum was a musician."

"That's true. Maybe Mendel was right."

"Mendel?"

"Ya, Gregor Mendel, he's the scientific father of genetics."

Katy rolled her eyes, "Whatever, we better get rolling."

With that we shoved off, Katy leading the way. Road riding is quite different than the paths and trails that we traverse on our knobby tire bikes. No cars or big trucks on the paths or trails. The paved road has lots of speedsters. Although the locals always blame the tourists and weekenders as speedsters, I've seen plenty of resident Mayners blasting down the road to catch the ferry.

Theoretically, as a general rule, on the island, we are supposed to bike ride single file. Just like when we are walking down the island roads, Gramps demands, "You *always* walk facing the oncoming traffic. *Never* have your back to oncoming traffic." The idea is you can see what's coming towards you. Of course, you're trusting that the vehicles behind you behave properly.

In the city, Katy and me rode bikes all over everywhere. Seldom sharing the road with cars, trucks or giant trolley buses. The city has cycling paths protected with concrete barriers or weird white pylons bolted to the pavement. Consequently, city biking seems safer. No horns honking at us in the city.

Sharing the roads with cars is dangerous. Gramps said his dad said, in the old days rich people had cars and poor people had horses. Nowadays poor people have cars and rich people have horses.

We arrived at Miners Bay and toured through the tall ship. The sails were down, tied up, and the masts had signs saying, No Climbing. Katy wanted to scramble up the main mast to the crow's nest. That wasn't happening.

After we had toured stem to stern we decided to go up the street to the Trading Post store for ice cream. "Did you bring money?" Katy asked.

"I have my phone, and it has lots of money. All I do is tap the device to pay."

"How much money do you have?"

"Lots," I held up my palms, "my parents died, so I inherited their money. My dad was a baseball player. Also, Elaine's research business pays me money for the projects we work on, and my investments pay dividends to the trust account."

"All that is on your phone?"

"Yes, do you want me to explain the difference between liquid money and vested cash?"

"No, not really," Katy sighed, "I just want to get some ice cream."

"Does your phone have money on it?" I asked.

"Of course not," Katy snorted. "I'm lucky to have a phone in the first place. It is only thanks to Elaine that I have one now. My parents were strict they said no phone until I was older."

"How old?"

"They didn't say, but I knew what they meant."

I smiled, "Gramps and Elaine want you to have a phone. That way they can know where you are and can you send messages."

Katy scrunched her forehead into wrinkles, "Does your phone have parental controls installed?"

"No."

"Mine does, and I'm older than you."

"Probably set to factory default settings. Want me to show you how to circumvent and modify those controls?"

"You can do that?"

"Sure, nothing to it, we can do it."

"Well, I don't know," Katy pondered. "When Elaine gets back we can talk to her about it."

"Sure, good idea."

Katy threw her ice cream wrapper in the trash bin, "Times ticking, we best be heading home, eh?"

"Ya gotta be back by three for tea."

We got back on the bikes, started pedalling up the Campbell Bay Road hill, Katy was leading the way, setting the pace.

I like the e-bike for big hills.

Down doesn't matter.

Mayne's Fallow Deer

While we were pedalling up the steep hill, happily assisted by battery power, I remembered that, at first, moving to Mayne Island seemed like an awfully dumb idea to me. Of course, I'm nine years old, I have no say in nothing. My mum and sister were dead, dad was devastatedly depressed and hospitalized. Then dad was dead, too. So, they had to put me someplace. Gramps said he'd take me. Then he took Katy. Elaine was already here (coming and going).

Einstein said time stands as a difficult construct to understand. So, Elaine says if Einstein struggled with time as an abstract, we should feel less fussed about it all. I'm pretty good with numbers, coding (encoding), and data analyses, but some of this social stuff is confusing. So much has happened in the last while. It is awfully overwhelming. "Save your tears for something more monumental."

"I can't tell the difference. Big or small they get me all."

I was wrong. It was a good idea to move to Mayne Island. Ya, sure, it's in the middle of nowhere yet it's quite nice here. Maybe qualitative versus quantitative aspects are answers, but maybe it's all the animals. There are always lots of deer, squirrels, otters and raccoons roaming around. I am used to seeing them. However, yesterday morning all I was doing was eating breakfast when I looked out the window and saw, what I swear was a *cat,* swimming in front of our place.

I ran down the hall to get Gramps to come and look, but he was busy tele-porting. He simply waved and softly said, "Hold tight there lil' buddy, I will be there as soon as my call ends."

Darting back to the front window, armed with binoculars this time, I tried to find the cat. There she was. I spotted her again. She's an orangey colour, sorta skinny, and swimming towards the shore.

Gramps finally came clomping down the hall, "What's the ruckus, Cliffie?"

"There's a cat *swimming* in the ocean! Come and see." I handed Gramps the binoculars.

"That is a mink," Gramps reported, "not a cat. We see lots of them around here."

"We do?"

"Yes, they are like the otters. Mink swim and run around the shorelines."

"Looked like a cat to me."

"Yes, I can see how you would think that, but it's a mink, not a cat."

Katy was starting to pull farther away from me going uphill. She turned to look back and yelled something. I don't know what because the wind was blowing and I don't always understand stuff she says. So, I just waved and put more power into climbing the hill.

Sir Isaac Newton was the English physicist who first said, "What goes up must come down." Don't know about him climbing hills. He also invented calculus. I like calculus.

Darwin's mother was the daughter of Josiah Wedgewood, maker of fine plates, cups, and bowls.

Katy's not supposed to use the *good* china anymore. She's had more than one accident due to excitement, and arm waving while eating. Katy might be higher strung than most eleven-year-olds.

Finally, I made it to the top of the hill. Katy's bike was leaning against a giant cedar tree. I looked about the immediate zone but could not see her anywhere. So, I started to call her with a fairly soft, not too loud, because loudness might not be beneficial, "Katy, where are you?"

There was some rustling noises in the bushes. "I'm over here." Katy came bouncing out of the salal shrubs, "I had to pee."

"You couldn't wait?"

"Wait for what?"

"Wait until we got home."

"Nah, why wait," Katy shoulder shrugged, "do what you gotta do when you gotta do it. Besides, it's the island, no one cares. Gramps does it."

"Ya, dunno," I raised both palms in the air, "Elaine made me promise to try and keep you outa trouble while she's away."

"Really."

"Ya."

"She's so sweet!"

*

After our recent episode with the mink, not a cat, swimming in the ocean, Gramps began teaching us about the local wildlife. What is what is important to learn.

"There are two types of deer here on the island," Gramps said, pointing to the tablet screen pictures. "There's the black tail deer that are supposed to be here, and the *fallow deer* that escaped from the farm."

"Deer were farmed?" I didn't understand. "How does that work?"

Gramps made one of his harrumph noises, "Doesn't work, that's the point."

We've often gone over philosophical principles like government for the people, by the people, of the people, but we often wonder what the government was thinking at times. "Why'd they do that?"

Elaine says we must realize the science of the day sometimes seems silly with modern hindsight. Yet she adds, "The only people who fail are those that don't try."

Happily, we are meeting up with Elaine next week in the big city. She has finished the Seattle stuff and has to take Katy downtown Vancouver for a *meeting*. Gramps seems relieved, otherwise he'd have to do it. He yields to Elaine who doesn't try to intimidate anyone. Elaine is quite nice. "Everyone likes her."

Okay, back to the deer being bred on a Mayne Island farm gone wrong. Evidently, according to Gramps, the government gave a local farmer a permit to raise European fallow deer. The idea was to raise deer for their meat. The government's oversight failed to ensure the farm's fencing was *adequate*. The fallow deer broke out from their farm and spread all over the island. The island's deer population soon started to explode. That's because there are no predators on the island. No bears, cougars, coyotes or wolves to eat the fallow deer. Hence their numbers keep growing and growing. The fallow deer eat almost everything that gardeners grow.

"There was an open net fish farm outside Horton Bay. It got shut down. Didn't work out because the farm fish got sea lice and natural fish were in jeopardy. Fish farms cause more trouble than they are worth."

Katy is not really a clock person. Time doesn't much matter to Katy most of the time. Nevertheless, *my* wrist clock, which we use to collect biometric data, digitally reads military time as 1427 or 2:27 post meridian time. "Katy, should we get a wiggle on it to get home by teatime?"

"Yes, OMG," Katy shifted into a concerned status, "what time is it now?"

Rather than show her my wrist clock, which has a smaller display, I held up my cellular/satellite phone with the large display. "Military time is 1428."

Katy scoffed, "Whatever, how much time until three, when we have tea?"

"Thirty-two minutes."

Katy seemed pleased, "Okay, José, that's *plenty* of time," she pointed to the road, "its all downhill from here. Let's go!"

Although Katy has done her level best to abandon the need for speed mantra, certainly she doesn't scream it out so loud anymore, Elaine says it likely is a neurological etiology. Doesn't matter which lobe, frontal, temporal, amygdala, or thalamus, Katy has a sensory threshold thriving speed.

"Musicians must bop to the tunes in the same way artists paint. Katy is like that."

"Could be genetic?"

"True, could be a nature/nurture thing."

"Professor Zumbo says you can't reduce competitiveness to a single construct."

"Same with sensory thresholds."

"Analogous."

*

Again, back to all the deer on the island, they are everywhere. The deer just wander wherever they want. Today, however, as Katy and I flew the bikes down the Campbell Bay hill we could see a herd up ahead crossing the road. Although Katy is not one for using bike brakes, slowing down stuff, she did not want to try riding *through* the herd.

A Tesla appeared on the other side, or what we would think as the *wrong* side. The Tesla *hit* a deer square on in the middle or the road. The deer went flying up in the air. All the other ones scattered, except two little ones with spots. Those are fawns. They didn't know what to do, I guess.

The Tesla took off, didn't stop or anything, just hit the deer and then kept going. Katy cursed the Tesla driving by faster than the law allows. Then she biked up closer to the deer that was sprawled on the road. As Katy approached the two little ones took off into the bushes.

At that point I caught up to Katy, as I arrived on the scene, "Katy, hold back a moment, okay." I could see the deer was still alive. "We don't want to make things worse. Don't scare her."

She held up her hand to signal something, but I don't know what, "Hiya deer," Katy said softly, staying back a bit to survey the situation. Then the deer made a snorting sorta sound.

"She's stirring Katy, stay back." I knew the deer was a female because no antlers.

Katy, talking softly, said, "I think she got knocked out, or something."

"Maybe got the wind knocked out of her. That's happen to me."

The deer rose to her feet. She was wobbly stumbling into the woods. Katy followed her.

"Katy, what are you doing?" I asked as they both disappeared into the trees.

"Gotta make sure she's not dying," Katy shouted back over her shoulder as she ran after the deer. "Maybe I can help her."

So, there I was standing on the side of the road. I knew not to follow Katy. For sure I'd get lost because there's no path or such. Who knows which way they went? No panic attack per sé, but I was more anxious than needed. My cell phone seldom is used for *live* direct calling. I use it for everything else but direct conversations. I mostly text and direct message people. I use the email function for attachments.

I called Gramps, he's a phone person. I didn't know what else to do. He would know. Three rings and I got voicemail. "Gramps, I need help. This is Clifford calling!"

Now I was nervous. My phone's ringer, vibro-function, and pinger all start up because Gramps is on the other end. Elaine programmed it so that he wouldn't be ignored. Maybe she did that to his phone too if I called him. I wondered.

"Hello," I pushed the green icon.

"Clifford, you okay?" Gramps asked.

"No, do you want the short story or whole thing?"

"Are you safe?"

"Guess so," looking around I couldn't see direct danger, but couldn't see Katy, either.

"Where's Katy?"

"Chasing a deer that got hit by a car."

"I'm coming to get you. Stay put, don't *wander,* stay still, stay safe."

"Can you see me?"

"No, I can't see you. I have your GPS pin. You are on Campbell Bay Road."

"Yes, I think so."

Gramps was breathing heavy, "Look at your clock. I will be there in five minutes."

"Okay, I will click on your icon that shows where you are."

"Yes, do that. I am in the truck now. I'm coming."

"Okay."

Although everyone says my crying spells have improved, today was not one of them. I tried hard to keep it together. It was no use. This was not good.

"Clifford, can you hear me," Gramps called out through the speaker.

"Yes."

"Can you see me?"

"No, doesn't work that way," I tried to explain the tracking parameters. "I can't see you. All I see is a blue dot coming down the road. That's you."

"How far away am I?" Gramps asked.

"Do you want the metre measure?" I asked.

"Sure."

I started to input the calculator function to measure the distance between the two map dots which were me and Gramps, but before the number appeared I could *see* the truck roaring towards me.

Recently, Elaine wrote an academic paper on *Eyewitness Reliability Reports*. I proofread her work by running a separate spelling scanner, grammar checker. She says its *esoteric* stuff and I might not be interested, but she likes to have my eyes go over documents because I might catch things that might get overlooked. Elaine claims, "I do my best editing after I've hit the *send* button." That's her humour style.

Gramps jumped out of the truck, *ran* towards me, and hugged me hard. I explained the situation the best I could, save now that I'm a section in Elaine's eyewitness report.

Gramps shouted out for Katy, "WHERE ARE YOU KATY?" No response, of course. He wanted to try and use her GPS tracking locator. Unfortunately, all it showed was her device was in her backpack, which beside her bike on the side of the road, three metres from us.

Gramps wanted to know which way she went into the woods. I couldn't say because it happened so fast. I didn't know, "That way," I pointed. Wish we had our old dog Jaspar with us, but I didn't say so out loud because Elaine says *not* to bring that topic up at all! Gramps is sensitive.

Gramps told me to get in the truck and honk the horn a few times to try and get Katy's attention. "Do you want me to do dot, dot, dot, dash, dash, dash from the truck?"

Gramps went squinty eyed, "You know Morse code?"

With a shrug, I replied, "That's *all* I know."

Waving his arms, he said, "Go ahead, give it a try."

I climbed into the truck and started tapping on the horn.

It worked! After a couple minutes Katy emerged from the forest. She was dishevelled, some dirt on her clothes, leaves in her hair, yet she seemed okay. "I couldn't catch up to the deer," Katy said with a sigh. "Could be dead, could be alive, I don't know."

Gramps gave her a hug, "Well," he said softly, "you tried. That's the best you can do, that is good enough."

"Sure'd like to catch the car driver that hit the deer *and* didn't stop!"

"Yes, I know what you are saying."

"Wanna go to the ferry terminal and see if the Tesla's there?"

Gramps gave out a heavy exhale, "No, now that I know you two are safe, I just want to go home, have a cup of tea, put my feet up and relax."

Katy knows when the jig is up and it's time to think about what is best for Gramps. "Ya, okay, let's go home." Katy soft saluted.

Gramps heaved the bikes up into the back of the truck.

I was determined not to start crying again. I gave him a big hug, whispered, "Thanks for coming to get us."

Gramps squeezed out a smile, "Anytime," he winked at me, "you just call, and I will be there. I got you covered."

We all got in the truck and started to drive home.

Katy looked over at Gramps, "Can I turn on the radio for music."

"Yes, you may."

No grammar corrections today.

Part Eight

Resiliency Recipes

I was in my twenties during the 1970s. Now I'm in my seventies in the 2020s. Time flies fast.

~Earl Porter

Confident of my Competence

Wouldn't you know it – three rings and my call goes to his voicemail. I left a message.

"Hello Earl, it's Randal calling you back. Telephone tag time. From the sounds of your message this morning, you have been having some excitement lately. Let's get together and have a brew, or two. I'm running some errands this morning. Home all afternoon, so give me a shout."

Earl and I have become fast friends. These days we get together often whether we are in the city or the island for coffee, hikes or a paddle. Sometimes we have a beer, or two. We have much in common. In particular, we are old! Seniors forging ahead one way or another. Mind you, we hold significant differences, too. Earl is raising his grandchildren. That makes him a single parent. All three grandchildren are unique.

As Earl quite correctly points out, Elaine, at seventeen, the oldest, looks after everyone, including Earl. She's an incredibly bright, engaging young lady. In addition to her academic studies, Elaine runs Earl's homes. She keeps all the moving parts synced with those that need to stay stationary. She's gifted.

Eleven-year-old Katy and I first met when I had been retained to do an applied cognitive capacity psychological assessment for the justice system. Impulsively, Katy shot her father, with *his* firearm, after learning of her family's dissolution. Katy's mother had been having an affair and Katy's father announced he was leaving. Katy shot him with a pistol he had left lying in his bedroom nightstand. Fortunately, the injuries were not fatal.

Katy's mother moved in with her new man. Katy's father returned to London to recuperate. Katy moved in with Earl.

Earl is most concerned about his nine-year-old grandson, Clifford. "He's already endured so much trauma," Earl shakes his head with a grimace and shrugs. "Cliffie is exceptional is so many ways. He's neurodivergent and he's different, but in a remarkable way. Sometimes a savant, sometimes I don't know what. But, you know, he's a good kid. And now I'm looking after him. Well, I'm trying."

Clifford's mother and sister recently died in a car crash. His father could not cope with the tragedy, went into a deep depression, and eventually took his own life. After which Clifford continued to live full time with Earl, Elaine, and Katy.

Earl is the first to admit that at his senior age of seventy, suddenly, abruptly, undertaking the task of raising *three* kids is daunting. On the other hand, Earl also said he thought it was rewarding, too. He held up his hand, "See how each one of these fingers is different. Same with these kids, each one is different."

I nodded in agreement, "Yes, no doubt, each one is unique."

Earl asked if I would do him a favour and take Clifford on a couple of one-on-one jaunts. Just the two of you. Earl wanted my nonbiased opinion on how Clifford was doing, "Do you think he's going to be okay? Is he coping with everything? You know he still cries quite a bit."

My sister, the lawyer, often asks for a *favour*. It's her strategy with a calculated agenda. Earl's the antithesis. I'm happy to help Earl with Clifford, despite the fact that I know it's not a simple situation. They have *all* endured a lot lately. Some seem more resilient than others. It's all relative. Stressors and their impacts are more difficult than we can understand. Latent or blatant they can take a mental health toll.

*

Many, many years ago, back when I was a young psychologist working at the provincial hospital for children, I was awfully confident of my competence. I graduated from UBC. I knew what was going on with psychometric test bias, Eurocentric measurement validity concerns, halo effects and sample size problems. Nevertheless, those measurement issues notwithstanding, I was not deterred, diagnosing was my *job*. Although some pundits alleged we were pigeon-holing people with labels and pejorative stereotypes, we countered with the *value* of problem identification, intervention strategies, and clinical recommendations.

We were all about *everything* being above board and transparency. We were not hiding behind white lab coats with clipboards. My written reports were readable, without too much jargon, technical terms, and yet could also stand peer review.

Although the convention was parents could *not* accompany their child into the testing room, for all sorts of assessment reasons, I was always quite accommodating to let parents, advocates, agents and authorized family members (some stepmothers) observe my assessment of the child through the one-way mirrors of what my colleagues called the fishbowl testing room. I did not mind observers – provided they did not thump the mirror when the kid got a question wrong or, when the kid responded with, "I don't know," when the observer thought they knew, or at least *should* know.

*

Earl told me he was worried about Clifford's mental health and general well-being.

Meanwhile, everyone else was worried about Earl. "He's been through a lot lately, one catastrophe after another."

For the past while, Clifford, Earl and I have gone on a number of excursions as a trio. "The girls are overly occupied and we can't leave Clifford home alone," Earl said with a smile.

Consequently, Clifford had become quite comfortable jaunting around with me. The morning I arrived to take Cliffie out for lunch and a visit to the Deaconvale farm to see newborn baby lambs he was not the least fazed going as a duo. Earl simply told him that he had to stay home and wait for a video zoom meeting. It's normal, Cliffie is used to it. Business from home.

When we arrived at the Deaconvale farm, after driving over their swerving bumpy road, farmer Daryl greeted us and took us down to the barn where the ewes and baby lambs were in their stalls. Clifford was awfully impressed with how cute the babies were and their bleating noises were amusing.

Farmer Daryl said, "Well, if you think these lambs are cute you should come up to the house and see our baby Labrador retriever puppies. The mother, we call her Socks, just had a litter of *eight* puppies."

Clifford needed Daryl to explain why lambs are born in a barn and puppies in the basement. "Dogs are different, they are like family members. Lambs are farm animals. There's a big difference between the two."

I could tell Clifford found Daryl's explanation falling short, as soon as he saw the puppies he was *mesmerized*. They were so young that their eyes were still closed. We explained the weaning process to Clifford. "After eight weeks these puppies will be ready to go to their new homes."

Clifford looked up to Daryl and said, "We had a black lab. His name was Jaspar. He got old and died."

Daryl shook his head, "Yes, that's too bad. We all get old. Maybe you can have one of these pups. Ask your grandfather. See what he says."

Clifford got all wide eyed, "Yes, I will ask him as soon as we get home."

"Sure, get Earl to come over and take a look. These pups aren't leaving their mother for another eight weeks. You got time."

Clifford was extremely excited. When I took him back home, he leaped out of the truck to go ask Earl about permission for the pups. Guess a can of worms was opened now.

Earl seemed to take things in stride. He was happy to hear that we had a good outing. He was even more relieved to hear that I thought Clifford was doing well – all things considered.

"Dr. Reilly says that black labs are great therapy dogs. A new puppy would likely be helpful around here. We could use some help."

Earl smiled, "Well, we'll see about how Elaine feels about it next week when we meet up in the big city."

"May I give her an advanced organizer now?" Clifford asked enthusiastically.

"What's an *advanced organizer*?" Earl inquired.

"Ausabel's psychometric preparatory term from the 1960s."

"Yes, that's fine with me."

"Katy?"

"She's visiting at her mother's new home. You might call her?"

"No, thanks," Clifford held up his palms, "Old people call, we message."

"Communicate as you wish," Earl emphasized, "But remember, no promises."

"Okay, I'll tell Katy, *no promises*."

Schadenfreude and Sigmund

I've never had a puppy, or a cat, for that matter. My dad had allergies. Dog hair and dog dander were the reasons. Same thing with cats. I got over it. My mum got me a turtle.

The puppies at the Deconvale farm are extremely cute. We definitely need one. It's my current goal. I'm working on creating a coalition.

*

Katy said the best day of her life was when she was told that she could come and live with us. The authorities and both parents approved. She stayed awake all night because she didn't want the best day to end. When I got up next morning, she was still going on strong. Katy's not much of a sleeper.

I knew Katy wasn't going to jail for shooting Uncle Julian. Everyone told me so. She's only eleven with diminished capacity. Katy doesn't know what she's doing most of the time. But she was in big trouble, nonetheless. Still some repercussions yet I don't know the whole thing. It's complicated.

I don't know much about the ins and outs of business, capitalism and free enterprise, but you always hear people saying *mind your own business.* Historically, as I understand it, tend your own fire preceded the business bit. Either way I got the message. Less said the better sometimes. Dry wood works the best. Green gets smoky.

Katy really did not want to go and spend the week with her mother but she had to go because Gramps said he had agreed to the visit. Non-negotiable means don't argue because it's a blind alley. I had offered to go with her but my attendance was not an option. Reconciliation is aspirational – according to Elaine.

I definitely miss Elaine because she is patient and explains these things well. Elaine is in Seattle *helping* her mother. Although we all have a number of microcomputers, tablets and such, Elaine and I both use the big computer with powerful co-processors. We share it because two of the same would be duplication, and that's not what we want. We have our own respective password protection and biometric scans for our portions of the drives and the shared system storage. Elaine guarantees those things as a secure responsible researcher. She says accountability must be documented.

It's our shared system CPU where calendars and schedules are synchronized that I knew Elaine went to Seattle because her mother is having a hysterectomy. Never had I heard of hysterectomies. So, of course, I had to search out what was with that thing. And it was not good. Medical treatments are highly minding your own business stuff. Our grandmother died from cancer so we seldom talk about that because it makes Gramps very sad. I didn't know her, but Elaine says Grandma was wonderful!

I love Katy, I do, but she knows nothing. Katy has absolutely no filtres. She's an OTM person – on the mind, out the mouth. I'm *not* telling Katy about Auntie Emily's hysterectomy. She'll get me in trouble, but I will need Katy's alliance with the puppy proposition. I already sent Katy messages and puppy pictures. No words returned yet so I suspect Katy's cellphone has been confiscated or in a timeout period. This happens to Katy all the time with her mum.

Likely getting Elaine on my side is much more important than Katy as far as influencing Gramps about the potential puppy acquisition. Before I message Elaine, I'm going to work on a few files she left behind. That way I lead the convo with something other than my personal desires. I'm not manipulative, far from smooth, yet I'm learning some social skills. YouTube has social skills videos.

While packing and giving me final departure instructions, Elaine explained, "It's unethical, maybe illegal, crossing the American border with Canadian data on the hard drives. It's a sovereignty security situation." Elaine is sensitive to some stuff I would never know otherwise.

Lance the Labrador sounded like a good name to me. Although I am of course open to alternative name suggestions, Lance the Labrador is my preference. I'm full speed ahead adopting a Deconvale farm puppy. As soon as everyone sees how sweet these puppies are I am sure they will agree.

We *need* a puppy.

COVID-19

The applied clinical practice of psychology will *never* be the same, I explained to Earl on our hike to the Edith Point Park peninsula. COVID-19 has changed *everything*. In 2020 when COVID descended, the government shut everything down fast, trying to flatten the COVID curve. Patient numbers escalated too fast. The hospitals were under siege. People were dying.

Lock downs were the government's best attempt to try and turn the tide with the virus spreading so fast. At first we all made cloth masks at home because they said medical grade masks must be reserved for first responders and medical personnel.

I had a bunch of homemade masks for grocery shopping and other *essential* tasks.

Psychologists are seldom first responders. Nevertheless, all face-to-face therapy sessions were cancelled. No more appointments in offices.

At our homes, everyone was expected to have enough food to last two weeks. Toilet paper got sold out everywhere. Hoarding was a new thing. Supply chains were broken. Flour and butter were rationed.

Everything went virtual. Everyone sat in front of computer screens. I had never heard of Zoom before, but that was the new direction forward. Therapy was conducted this way, or not at all. People adjusted. The patients met with their therapists from home computers.

Certainly, does not look like *normal* will be the same as we were familiar with practicing. Sure, some psychologists these days have gone back to office visits, but many still continue with virtual sessions. Many patients prefer virtual sessions. They can meet with their shrink wherever they are located. No commuting, or parking problems, patients are happy because they are not confined to being in the same city, province or country as their therapists. The Internet allows for long distance therapy.

Earl scoffed and explained the same phenomenon has happened with the current practice of law. When COVID started spreading quickly, law offices shut down. Lawyers worked from home. No one wanted to ride in elevators to the thirty-fourth floor for a meeting. Mediations, negotiations, and settlements were *all* done virtually. And to this day most mediations are still done virtually. Not much chance of it changing.

"How many COVID shots have you had?" Earl asked.

I thought about it for a moment or two, "Don't really know anymore, lost count," I held up my palm with four fingers wobbling. "I've had boosters with flu shots, the omicron bivalents shot, and recently got the shingles shot. They'll send me an email when I'm due."

Earl nodded, "True, you don't want shingles. My colleague, Ronnie Zimmer had shingles and he was all messed up."

"Do you remember your first COVID shot?" I asked.

Earl grunted, "No, not really, other than it was a while ago."

"Oh man, I remember my first shot." I gave out a soft whistle. "We were in the first wave for health professions vaccines. We all got emails telling us to go a big tent at the Vancouver Community College parking lot. They said bring your driver's license, bring your psych license, wear a *good* mask. Freaked me out when I got there. A big line with weird looking people. Cops guarding the entrance with guns."

Earl snorted, "Cops with guns, why?"

"Yes, that's what I wondered. Why were there cops with long guns held chest high?"

"That's bizarre."

"Yes, well, I was in line with the local dentists, optometrists, physiotherapists, and assorted other folks who had their offices shut down due to the virus. We were all getting our documents checked by minions. People without *correct* paperwork were turned away summarily. One of the dentists in my line said the cops were there to protect the vaccines."

"Really?" Earl chuckled.

"Yes, some officials from somewhere up high thought it would be bad optics if the vaccines were stolen."

"No one knew what was happening big-picture stuff. The hospitals ran out of ventilators."

"Remember the travel ban?"

"Yes, that was another covid calamity!"

"You going to Vantown tomorrow?" I asked.

"No, not until Tuesday. We're meeting up with my granddaughters, Elaine and Katy."

"What's the word on the puppy?"

Earl moaned, "We're getting a puppy. Everyone *promises* they will train, look after the puppy, and I will not regret it."

I tapped him on the shoulder, "That's great, enjoy the ride."

"He's their *therapy dog*."

"Cool, because therapy is expensive."

"I'm insured."

"Even better."

"I'll call you tomorrow."

"Okay."

Laurie or Lance

Katy has gone underground – she's incommunicado. Who knows what is going on with her? Sometimes Katy's mum takes away all of her electronics. Sometimes while in the middle of something Katy gets distracted – squirrel.

"Hey Katy, I have sent you six text messages, three emails, and now here's a voicemail to pile on the list. Time to surface. I have good news. Socks the Deaconvale farm Labrador had a litter of eight puppies – four females and four males. I first saw them when they were so little, they still had their eyes closed. We *need* a puppy! Gramps said he would *think* about it, but everyone has to be on board. Everyone has to take care of the puppy. If you help me get a puppy, I will owe you a favour. Google black lab pups and you will see."

Elaine, on the other hand, is the opposite, she's hyper-vigilant. In everyday life, Elaine looks at everything through a wide-angle lens. She catches stuff that most people miss. Gramps told me to watch for that. On the virtual cyber level Elaine also pays attention with a wide net. I'm not like that because sometimes the forest from the trees is hard to see when I am focused.

Next to my sister, Sandy, Elaine's the smartest person I've ever known. Gramps says same thing – except he didn't really know Sandy so well. He and dad were in between us. Elaine says some family stuff gets complicated, "Don't get fussed about it."

Elaine is always quick to respond to *anything* I send. She's sorta like Gramps in some ways. First, Elaine acknowledges the message, but caveats with, "I will get back to you shortly." That could mean she's busy, in the middle of something else, or wants to *think* about it. Digestion of data doesn't happen simultaneously.

I forwarded Elaine the same puppy pictures that I sent Katy. She responded with a smiley face emoji. So, of course, I am assuming that means she'll side with me. Male or female puppy is a discussion that I know nothing about but expect some advice from those who do know more about it than me. I've never had a dog before.

Early this morning I called farmer Daryl's landline to check on the puppies. Daryl said that they are all doing well, growing bigger every day. Then he said, "Clifford, you are certainly welcome over to the farm for a visit."

I asked Gramps if he'd like to go with me over to the farm to meet the puppies. He said he couldn't because "I'm waiting on a call," but "Clifford, you can ride one of the bikes over to the farm for a puppy progress update."

"Alright, thanks."

Gramps pointed his index finger at me, "Remember, no promises."

"Yes, Elaine said the same thing," I said placatingly.

✻

Rather than riding on the main roads, which would take longer, I took the overland shortcut Katy had shown me. It's the one where you go over the ditch, under the fence, and through the hay field path to get to the farm. When I got there, Farmer Daryl was working on a massive machine by the big barn. They have one big barn, another smaller barn, chicken coops, and a bunch of glass green houses. "Good morning, Clifford," he called out with a wave, "Give me a minute and I'll be right with you. We can go up to the house and check on Socks and her puppies."

"Okay, thanks."

We walked up to the main house and went in through the basement door. The puppies were so cute. Some were sleeping, some were sucking on Socks, and a couple of them were rolling around on the rug. It was awesome.

Farmer Daryl knows lots about dogs, cats, farm animals, and politics. I asked him whether we should get a male or female puppy. "Which sex would work best for us, you think?"

Daryl just smiled, "See my left hand," he asked.

"Yes." I wondered where he was going with the hand analogy, but I paid close attention anyway.

"Four fingers, each one is different, I like them all. Same thing with my right hand, four fingers, each one is different."

"What's that got to do with *dogs*?"

"This is Socks' third litter. Labs usually have litters with five to ten pups. So, this one with eight pups is normal. We don't always get an even-Steven split with four males and four females, but that's what we got this go-round. They all seem pretty healthy, even the runt seems fine. So far so good, I think they will all make it."

"What does that mean?" I asked.

"Mother Nature can be cruel," Farmer Daryl shook his head, "often times only the strongest puppies survive."

"That's Darwinistic."

"Dunno, but that's how it works with litters on the farm."

I shrugged, "So, you have no advice on whether we should get a male or female?"

"Nah, not really," Daryl smiled, "ying or yang, girls and boys, alpha or runt, they all have their own personalities. It's good to get one that suits you."

"Well, that's the hitch," I sighed, "it's not just me but also Elaine, Katy, and Gramps."

"True, sometimes you just get a good feeling for a particular puppy, and that's what you should go with."

"If we get a male, his name will be Lance the Lab. If the girls *and* gramps want a female we will call her Laurie."

"Picking out a name is a good start, but you better get your family on board."

With a smile I said, "Ya, that's true."

A Hard Day's Night

Earl gestured to me, "You know Randal, I was a barrister for some time. Sometimes it seems like I'm still always talking to a jury. Bad habits die hard, I guess."

We were walking up the Campbell Point trail while Earl started this morning's narrative by explaining, "Did you know, originally the Beatles 1964 movie's working title was going to be called, *The Beatles*, then they changed it to, *Beatlemania*" until an exhausted Ringo came up with the title, *A Hard Day's Night*."

"Ringo always was quick with a good quip," I snickered. "Sixty years ago, I saw the movie in the theatre, bought the album, and sang the songs. Can't buy me love."

Earl smiled, "Yes, health is the first wealth. Can't buy love *or* health. "

*

Four years ago, Earl's wife, Ellen, died from ovarian cancer. So, of course, when his daughter sent Earl and Elaine a message indicating that at age 45 she was going to have a hysterectomy, their level of anxiety skyrocketed. Elaine returned to Seattle to provide support for her mother.

The surgery went well. No cancer. Everyone heaved a big sigh of relief.

Elaine was scheduled to arrive back in Vancouver tomorrow. Katy was scheduled to conclude her visit with her mother. The plan was for Earl and Clifford to rendezvous with them and then they would all return to Mayne Island together.

*

"Earl, are you taking the new puppy to Vancouver?" I asked. "If you want to leave her behind, I can dog sit while you are away."

Earl sighed and smiled, "Thanks Randal, but I'm afraid the puppy is coming to town. I'm sure she'll pee and poop all over the floors and my Indian carpets. Clifford, however, insists he will cleanup."

"OCD, eh."

"Something like that."

Feeling Good Again

Robert Earl Keen's 1998 song, "Feels so good feeling good again," was playing loudly in the kitchen. The speakers weren't rattling, but it was quite loud. Woofers are designed to produce low frequency sounds. Speaker size is relative. Gramps is the expert.

*

You know Gramps is in a good mood when he's singing, whistling and barefoot dancing around the kitchen. Strolling into Gramps's galley, "Whatcha cooking?" I asked.

"Hashbrowns, bacon and eggs for the two of us," he replied with a smile.

"Great," I was happy to see him doing what he calls the *two step* while pivoting from the refrigerator to the cooking stove. Gramps will use the micro cooker, but he's not big on it other than warming up coffee.

Gramps has been worried about the hysterectomy and the health implications. Particularly cancer. Soon as he got word everything was okay it seemed like a large lift of worry was taken off his shoulders. Even his face seemed brighter. Yesterday he came clomping down to my room and announced, "Cliffie, I just got off the phone with Deaconvale Daryl. Got good news and bad news. What'd want first?"

Seemed as though Gramps had a gleam in his eye, but I'm not as good reading these things as Elaine. Nevertheless, I knew to play it through, "Bad new first," I said, "because good news can soften the blow."

He scrunched up his forehead and squinted at me, "Okay, bad news Daryl's going to some farmer's co-op get together up island in Courtenay and he'll be gone for a few days."

"Okay," I knew a hitch was coming.

"Good news is we have to go over to the farm this morning before he leaves to pick up the puppy you've been ogling."

Although I didn't know what he meant by *ogling,* I understood what was going on. This *was* happening. We were going to get a puppy. I liked *all* the puppies in the litter but there was one very sweet female pup that seemed to really like me. She's the one.

We ate breakfast, washed up and climbed into the truck. All the way over driving to the farm Gramps kept reviewing rules to be followed with the puppy. Didn't matter to me, I was agreeing to everything anyway.

"Does Elaine know about the puppy?" I asked.

Gramps grunted, "Yes, spoke with her last night." He gave me the index finger pointer, "Elaine agrees, the puppy is *your* responsibility."

"Yes, no problem," I gave him the thumbs up signal, "I understand."

"Big responsibility training a puppy, you know." Gramps was trying to show some level of something, but I knew he was happy, really happy. He kept humming, and under his breath singing, "Feels so good feeling good again."

Part Nine

The Therapy Dog

Sometimes just talking about the problem can help.

~Donna Greenstreet (1948 – 2023)

Leopards Spots Assessments

The definition of Predictive Validity – When psychologists are paid to predict future behaviours with accuracy.

*

Over the years I've testified in a number of courtrooms, responding to the question, "Dr. Reilly, in your professional opinion, what is the likelihood of the accused reoffending, committing additional violence, and acting lawfully?"

The answer is not always straightforward or easy, however, to the best of my ability, my job is to put the puzzle pieces together trying to predict a person's future behaviours.

"It is my clinical opinion, based on our interviews, evidence collected, that the likelihood is…". I complete the statement with what seems valid.

*

All my professional life I've been making clinical recommendations and psychological suggestions for patients. That's the nature of this job. Training, experience, and evidence-based social science research form the basis of my recommendations. Some patients pick up and follow through, some interpret their own perspective, and some ignore them altogether discounting any therapeutic value. Psychologists have long understood the old adage about leading a horse to water but remember you can't make the horse drink.

People are complicated. Some are simple. No one ever leaves me voicemail saying they are doing well and need an appointment right away. It's the opposite.

*

Voicemail and the Call Display shows – BC Crown Prosecutor .

"Hello Dr. Reilly, this is James Rooney from the Vancouver Crown Prosecutor's Office calling you regarding Katherine Angelita Porter. I note in her file your recent report states the likelihood of Katherine committing further violence is low. We would like to discuss this with you at your earliest convenience. Please call 604-822-4639. Thank you."

After listening to the prosecutor's voicemail, twice, my first call was to Earl. He didn't answer. I got his voicemail. I didn't leave a message.

Katy is, at best, unpredictable, but I didn't say that out loud.

Other than the validity of an opinion.

Socks the Dog

"We got a puppy!" I messaged Katy and Elaine. "She's the most beautiful being I've ever seen. She's so soft *and* cuddly. Can't wait for you to meet her." I was quite excited to say the least.

Gramps waved his hand at me and told me he was going up to the house with Daryl because there was paperwork and dickering to do and I should not wander far from the barn. "This won't take too long."

Evidently, because this is a farm the local veterinarian has been visiting regularly for some of the other animals in addition to the Labrador puppies. Gramps thinks that's a good thing. Shots or something are an issue for their discussion.

I didn't know anything about paperwork or what was with *dickering,* yet I was moon-dancing with the puppy. "Yes, Gramps, no problem," I acknowledged his instructions with a big smile, all while the puppy was nibbling me all over with her tiny teeth.

Jaspar, our old black lab, who recently died was eleven calendar years old. Katy insists *dog years* are a different deal. Labrador retrievers often live up to twelve calendar years or more as a life span index. I guess Jaspar was typical in that sense. Elaine said Jaspar died from old age, not cancer or anything like that. Of course, Katy said, "What does it matter, dead is dead. The reason doesn't change the outcome."

For me, lately, the whole death thing has been awfully difficult to digest. My mum, Sandy, dad, are all dead now. If I start thinking about it, sadness seeps over everything and I'll get overwhelmed. Dr. Reilly says that's normal, and I need to learn to live with the reality. The dead don't come back. Although some of his sayings sound silly, overall Dr. Reilly has been helping Gramps and that, in turn, helps me.

Elaine gets all academic and explains our anthropomorphic feelings for Jaspar are reasonable because we all loved him, but we need to remember Jaspar was a dog. These days Katy and me are pretty good with things we don't really understand. We make like we do so we won't have to sit through a complicated explanation because Katy often slips up and says silly stuff that makes others angry. Although, seriously, just a dog, doesn't seem to suit Jaspar's memory in my mind. Nonetheless, it's not an argument or discussion.

Gramps clomped down to the barn, holding some papers in his hand, "Okay," he waved us over to the truck, "we've settled things up here. Time to go home."

When we got back home Gramps suggested firmly that I should pack all my stuff tonight because we are catching the early morning ferry tomorrow. "What should I pack for the puppy?" I asked.

Gramps wrinkled his forehead, "Don't worry about it, I got things covered. Just make sure you have the things you need for Vancouver."

"Okay, no problem." I saluted.

Tomorrow, after we get to Vancouver, the plan is to pick up Katy from her mum's new place. Katy has been staying with her mum and Bryan Petersen – her mum's new guy. Katy didn't want to go, but Gramps and Elaine explained that there was no negotiation on the deal. She had to go. It was a prearranged agreement.

"Contract law?" I asked.

"No, family law," Elaine said with some tone to her voice.

Previously we had learned, according to Gramps, contract law was the most important kind of law existing. "If contracts are not honoured, then everything else is subverted. And we don't want that."

We were previously concerned with criminal law because Katy shot her father, but she's only eleven years old and can't be charged with a crime until she is twelve. That's the Canadian Criminal Code definition.

While I was organizing my electronics for the trip, Katy beeped with an incoming video message. I answered putting her on the wall's big screen. "Hi, how you doing?" I asked.

"Terrible, I *hate* it here," Katy said with a scowl. "Where's the puppy?"

"Over here in her box?"

"Why's she in a box?"

"That's her bed. She'll get into trouble if I let her roam around."

"That's good, glad things worked out with the puppy. Dr. Reilly came through for you."

He did?" I asked with a puzzled look.

"Ya, Gramps said no more dogs after Jassie died, but Dr. Reilly told him Clifford's mental health would benefit from a *therapy dog*. Elaine told him he should do it, so he did. Now you got a dog, but Elaine says we are all supposed to help with the training."

"I didn't know that. Elaine told you?"

"Ya, she's been coaching me about visiting my mum and Bryan."

"Family law."

"Ya, I guess, sorta." Katy rolled her eyes, "So, you know that *Laura the Lab* is a dumb name, right?"

"Why?"

"Just is dumb that's why. I think we should call her Socks because those white patches on her front paws."

"Daryl says that white markings might not stay when she matures."

"Ya, same with you, when you *mature*."

"Very funny," I raised my clenched fist at her.

"Uh oh, gotta go, my mum's coming down the hall. I can hear her clickety shoes. She took my phone away because I was rude, but I stole it back from her desk drawer."

"Okay, Socks says, good night, Katy."

Katy laughed, "Good night Socks, see you tomorrow. Love you Cliffie."

Her screen went black.

I kissed Socks soft head, "You are going to love Katy. She's quite crazy, but very lovable."

Accidents are Awful

We got back to Vancouver in time for lunch. That's important. Then after a few phone calls back and forth, Katy got delivered to the condo. After which Auntie E and Gramps had a heated discussion in the kitchen. So, Socks, Katy and me retreated to the west deck patio to goof around. Serious stuff wasn't for us, we just want to have fun.

"There's tempers flying and speech spittle, too," Katy whispered to Socks and me. "Probably money, poor decisions and property problems, I suppose, but I'm not involved in the discussions. I'm eleven."

Tomorrow Gramps has a summit meeting with Katy's parents at his favourite restaurant. Neutral restaurant territory is needed to ensure tempers are kept in check. Uncle Julian is angry with Katy's mum for all sorts of reasons that I'm not privy to, and Gramps is mad at both of them because they must consider *Katy's best interests*. They disagree with everything.

The truth is Katy doesn't want to live with *either* her mum or dad. They are all terribly estranged. Katy wants to live with us on the island. However, Elaine says, Katy's wishes are ancillary to the big picture. Eleven-year-olds don't dictate to elder's agendas.

"We don't want this to go to court," is what they're all saying, according to Elaine.

"Why's that?" I asked.

"Looks bad on everyone," Elaine grimaced, "Who knows which way a judge would rule. It's a crap shoot all way round."

"Okay, if you say so."

"Good thing Gramps is Katy's advocate, yet he has limitations," Elaine explained, family law can get complicated.

It appears that Elaine will still be delayed in Seattle so Gramps friend, Mrs. Moriarty, is going to have Katy, me and Socks over for the afternoon. Katy and me can't be left home alone and we certainly can't leave Socks home alone because she's going to constantly cry and cry. And we don't want that! Sometimes Gramps seems concerned with disturbing the neighbours below us, but it's a thick concrete floor that's soundproof.

For another day, or so, Elaine is staying in Seattle so she can help her mum with more medical concerns. And those things are private. So, she called to tell *me* to be *cooperative* and make sure Katy is cool. I didn't even know that I've ever been seen as uncooperative, but everyone knows Katy can be a bit much when she gets wound up. A pedal to the metal person – according to Gramps.

I've only ever met Mrs. Moriarty three times before today. Once at Gramps favourite French restaurant, and twice at two soirées at our condo. She seems like a nice lady. She's more of a listener than a talker. A quiet person.

Gramps is dropping us off at her house at Kitsilano Beach before he goes to the big restaurant meeting. We know he's already in a mood by his breathing pattern and under breath mutterings. Socks, Katy and me are all sitting in the back seat because the law says kids under twelve can't sit in the front seat because if the airbags deploy we will die. Elaine doesn't care, I sit up front with her.

At the red light Gramps turned around to face us, pointing his finger, "Now, I don't need to remind you two that best behaviour is expected. Mrs. Moriarty is doing me a big favour by looking after you two today."

In unison we say, softly, "Yes Gramps."

"Pardon."

So, again, in unison, with more intensity, we say louder, "Yes Gramps," and then Socks gives out a woof woof woof. Gramps just shook his head and mutters something.

Of course, as soon as we arrived at the Moriarty's house, Gramps pivoted his mood to smiles and happy hugs. "Hello Peggy, you look lovely today." He stood back a bit and puts his hands on her shoulders, "Again, I must thank you for looking after my grandchildren this afternoon."

She blushed, and gushed, "Oh Earl, you old flatterer," then she kisses me and Katy on the top of our heads, "It's my pleasure to spend some time with Katy and Clifford. Too bad Joe is working, he is missing out on all the fun!"

Gramps gave her a smirk, "Oh Joe knows which way the wind blows." He waves goodbye, "I will be back as soon as I can."

"Take the time that is required," Mrs. M said sternly, "Get the job done right."

They are cryptic talking, like it's an inside joke type thing, but we don't care because Mrs. M has laid out a large spread of lunch goodies on the dining room table.

Katy scans the table and sees one of the big bowls, looks at me, raised her eyebrows, "Whoa-oh, cheese puffs."

Mrs. M smiled, "Yes, yes, please help yourself. I have hotdogs cooking in the kitchen, French fries, too. I will be right back straight away."

Katy and I look at each other, "Thanks Mrs. Moriarty, everything looks fabulous, but at our place the rule is for a table sit down meal we must wait for everyone to be seated before we start eating," I explained.

She waved both hands in the air, "Oh that's nonsense, besides you are at my house where there are no rules. Go ahead, dig in, start eating, and I will be right back." And with that said, she darted off to the kitchen where we could hear her banging stuff around.

Socks is in her box, sleeping, again. She's growing. Farmer Daryl gave me strict instructions to *not* feed Socks junky food. "A small amount when she's older, as a treat, is okay. But not as a puppy."

Katy *loves* junky food! Her mum insists Katy should eat healthy food and believes junky food makes Katy hyperactive. When I told that to Mrs Moriarty, she got all excited, "Oh my goodness, that's just *rubbish*! Katy, dear, you eat as much as you want of whatever you want. And after lunch we will walk down to the beach confectionery for some ice cream. I particularly enjoy their waffle cones."

We had a fabulous time, just a tonne of fun. Mrs. M told us stories about when she was a little girl living on a farm in Alberta. They had horses, cows, pigs and chickens. It's called *mixed* farming. "We must go riding horses at Southlands soon," Mrs. M said, while clearing dishes. "They have some nice gentle horses there that we can ride. I will make the arrangements with you grandfather."

"Great," Katy and I looked at each other with smiles. "I'd love to go horseback riding with you Mrs. M!"

"Very well then, it's a deal," Mrs. M took a quick drink of whatever she was drinking, tapped her crystal glass down on the table with a clank, and said, "Ahh, okay, let's stroll down to the beach and get some ice cream."

We took Socks out of her box and put her into a cool pouch carrier that Mrs. M had in storage. The straps went over my shoulders like a reverse backpack. Socks liked it. She poked her head out the hole and could see the sights as we walked down to the beach.

Katy and Mrs. M went inside the ice cream shop. There was a bit of a lineup because it was a hot day, and the place is popular. Socks and I waited outside because dogs are not allowed inside. We didn't care. We were happy to watch the world walk by us. Socks let out a yip, yip. She's still too small for full force barking.

While we were waiting two boys approached Socks and me. The one boy said, "Nice dog, let me pat him."

I said, "Okay," and let him touch Socks on her head.

The other boy said, "Take off the carrier and give me the dog."

I said, "I can't do that."

He pulled out a knife and said, "Listen geek, I'm not asking. I'm telling you to give me the dog."

I backed up and started screaming, "KATY, KATY, KATY."

The boy tried to wrestle the carrier pack off of me when Katy came flying out of the shop with fists flying yelling, "MOTHER-FUCKERS leave my brother alone!"

She kicked the knife out of the one boy's hand, pivoted, and hit him hard in the face. I had forgotten that Katy had taken karate lessons. One of her parents thought it would be good for Katy's self discipline skills. It wasn't.

The boy who Katy hit in the face, fell down hard. He hit his head on the concrete. The other boy ran away. By this time Mrs. M was now outside the ice cream shop. She was calling 911 emergency services. Then she started tending to the boy on the concrete.

A middle-aged lady stepped forward saying, "I'm a *witness*. I saw the whole thing. It was self-defence. That boy who had the knife got what he deserved!"

Mrs. M looked up at the lady and said, "Well, yes, self-defence is one thing, but this young man is unconscious, and that's not good."

Before I knew anything, an ambulance arrived, a police car, *and* a fire truck pulled up to the ice cream shop. It was loud. Sirens and screaming. Socks and me were sorta freaking out. Katy seemed to be calming down now that things seemed under control. However, little did I realize, at that time, things were far from under control.

The ambulance had a man and a woman. They put the boy on a stretcher and roared away with loud sirens. More police cars came. One of them was yelling something at me and Socks, but we didn't know what he was saying because Mrs. M started screaming at him, pointing her finger and arm waving.

Katy came over to me, where I was leaning on the wall. She hugged me hard, saying stuff like, "Take deep breaths, we're okay, I'm here. I gotcha."

I wasn't full force crying, or anything, just low-level whimpering. I was confused. "What happened Katy?"

She seemed to sigh or something, "It was an *accident*." Katy shook her head, "Accidents are awful."

"Ya, I know," I squeezed her hand, "my mum and Sandy died in an accident."

Katy turned around and I could see she had blood on her shirt. I pointed it out to her. She was startled and said, "That's not *my* blood Cliffie. It's yours. You got stabbed!"

I didn't even know that the guy stabbed me until Katy gave me the hard hug. The blood wasn't gushing out because my clothes and the dog carrier pouch had been soaking up the blood.

Guess I was starting to slide down the wall. Katy broke my fall. I could hear her yelling, "Get my brother to the hospital! He needs help!"

I Will Be Okay

Didn't know where I was or what was happening when I woke up. Sometimes I will wake up in Vancouver and think I am on Mayne Island and vice versa. Today I knew I was neither. Who knew where I was, I didn't. I looked around the room and saw Elaine sleeping on a chair in the corner. Seeing her always makes things better.

"Yo, Elaine," I called out croakily, "are you sleeping, or just eyes closed?"

She didn't stir, so for sure she's sleeping. Deep sleeping. I thought, maybe I'm dreaming, but maybe not. Something is not right here wherever we are. I was wired up with tubes or something strange. My moving around in the bed made a machine make some beeping noises. And I also made some groaning unhappy sounds. Those noises roused Elaine.

She got up, wobbled over to me, and kissed me on my forehead. "Hi, how you doing?"

"Dunno," I whimpered.

"You are going to be okay."

"That's good to know."

"The doctors have you loaded up on pain medications, antibiotics, and this is an intravenous tube," she said pointing to the machinery. "This is a good hospital. You are getting good care."

"Okay."

"Do you remember what went on yesterday?"

I tried to think, but came up empty, "Not really, can you give me a hint?"

"Do you remember going for ice cream with Katy?"

I closed my eyes, and everything came flooding back. "Socks," I gasped, "is she okay?"

"Yes, she's fine," Elaine smiled, "My Ma is looking after Socks."

"Socks went to Seattle?" I asked with confusion.

"No, we flew up last night. Ma's going to stay with us for a while."

"What about your Pops?"

Elaine brushed my hair with her hand, "He stayed in Seattle. He's got a project. He'll visit later."

"Katy?"

Elaine pursed her lips, wrinkled her forehead, "Katy is going to be okay."

"What happened to the boy that tried to take Socks from me? Katy hit him hard. She knows karate."

"Yes she does," Elaine got glassy eyed. "The boy's name was Adam Landy ." She shook her head, "He died last night."

"He died?"

"Yes," Elaine sighed, "he hit his head on the concrete, and that's what killed him."

I gasped, "First, Katy shot her father. Now Katy killed the kid who tried to steal Socks. This is bad!"

Elaine nodded, "Not to mention Katy stabbing a boy with scissors in grade three because he pulled her hair."

"Ya, I heard about that one. Is Katy in trouble now?"

"No, not really, she'll be fine. Adam pulled a knife and stabbed you twice. One wound is not too serious, and the other hit your kidney. Katy's punch, legally, will be considered self-defence. Also, there's a bunch of witnesses, and the store's security camera captured everything."

"I feel bad about the boy dying."

"I know," Elaine gently touched my cheek, "Me too."

"Am I going to die because he stabbed my kidney?"

"No, no, no," she reassured me, "you are going to be okay."

Figuring it Out

Earl returned my call, however, there's no cell phone service available because I was on the BC Ferry in the middle of the Salish Sea heading to Vancouver. He left me voicemails.

"Hi Randal, it's Earl calling, Thursday afternoon. The doctors say Clifford's surgery yesterday was successful. Looks like he's going to be okay with some healing time and rehab. We'd appreciate it if you could visit him at the hospital. He's confused about the situation. Clifford likes you. Maybe you can help him figure things out. You know more about talking to nine-year-old boys than me. Okay, I have to go, so call me when you get a chance. Thanks."

Next message:

"Oh, it's me again, I forgot to say in my first messages, your name is included on the hospital's visitors list. So, you will not have any access difficulties."

I could clearly hear the stress in Earl's voice. He's got a grandson recovering in the hospital from knife wounds. The Crown Prosecutor, James Rooney, has been suggesting man slaughter charges against Katy. Even though Rooney fully knows self-defence surpasses his efforts to appear to exercise due diligence on behalf of the office. And to top things off, Earl's youngest daughter from Seattle has arrived to recover from some undisclosed surgery. Talking to myself, "Earl's got a lot on his plate."

*

It's been so many years since I last worked at the hospital for children. Some things change, others remain the same. Twenty-five years ago, parking wasn't a problem. These days it's a different story. I had thought about riding my bike, but then different clothes would be required. I wanted to look good for Clifford and whoever else was supervising on his floor. Definitely, a professional appearance seemed like a good idea despite the fact that, technically, Cliffie isn't my patient. I'm a friend of the family – so to speak.

This hospital has categories: sick kids, injured kids (who are different from sick kids), and those kids that need assessment diagnostic evaluations for categorizing. When I worked here, at the hospital's Child Development and Diagnostic Centre, the mental health world was different. The categories were different.

*

Without a doubt, Clifford is a special kid in so many ways. Yet, on the other hand, kids are kids, neurodivergent thinking and behaviours notwithstanding. As a nine-year-old he's already endured too much trauma and death. Now he's in the hospital recovering from stab wounds. I promised his grandfather I would do what I could to try and help Cliffie make sense of the situation.

He was sleeping when I got through the hallway maze to his room. Sleep is good, no need to wake him unnecessarily. I'm in no hurry, so I pulled up in the bedside chair, sat down, closed my eyes, and relaxed. Of course, I fell asleep. A deep sleep.

Who knows how long I had been sleeping, must have been at least an hour or so. Generally, I'm a fairly light sleeper most of the time, except when I'm too tired and fatigued from ferry travel and all the stress of being a bystander in these recent events.

A nurse came into the room and started banging stuff around. I was almost awake enough to hear her talking to Clifford. "Who's your guest," the nurse asked, banging more equipment, "At least he quit snoring."

"That's the famous Dr. Randal Reilly," Clifford replied, "He's a government shrink, a private shrink, *and* a professor."

"You don't say," the nurse seemed less than impressed. "Nice shoes."

"Ya, he has lots of shoes. That's his thing, I guess."

"Shoes?"

"Ya, shoes, and folding bicycles."

"Folding bikes," the nurse asked, rolling her eyes, "Interesting."

"Ya, they're harder to steal," Clifford explained. "Lots of thieves and bad guys in the big city."

I was starting to wake and come to my senses enough now to contribute to the conversation, "There's good guys, too." Sitting up straight, shaking out the sleepy cobwebs, I waved, "How you doing Cliffie? Sorry, guess I fell asleep."

"Ya, you've been snoring for a while."

The nurse softly chuckled, gave us a smile, and said, "I will be back in a little while. Do you need anything before I leave?"

"Dunno," Clifford turned, pointed over to me, "You need anything doc?"

I gave the thumbs up signal, "No, thanks, I'm good."

The nurse nodded and left the room.

"Gramps told me you were coming," Clifford seemed chirpy. "I talked to him on the old-fashioned hospital phone. The other lady, not the nurse that left, brings the hospital landline phone into the room when I get calls."

"That's good."

"Ya, my phone, my clothes, and my dog, Socks," Clifford heaved a deep sigh, "They're all gone."

"Yes that's true, but don't worry," I said reassuringly, "we'll get you new ones."

"Socks?"

"She's good, back home now with your family, her family. She's doing just fine."

"Katy?"

"She's good, too."

"Really."

"Yes, everything is copacetic."

"The guy who stabbed me, he's dead."

"Yes, Adam Landy, didn't make it, he died." I exhaled and began the explanation of events. "The other boy, Grant Wilson, turned himself into the police today. His father brought him in."

"Is he in trouble?"

"Not too much, really. Grant didn't actually assault anyone or steal anything. He was going to assist with stealing Socks, but it all fell through when Katy's punch knocked Adam down."

"Ya, I remember that part now."

"Grant told the police that their plan was to steal Socks and try to sell her to someone."

"Who?"

"Oh, they didn't have any buyers lined up. It was just a hair-brained impulsive plot that they hadn't thought out very well. Grant said that they watched a thing on Facebook where someone stole Lady Gaga's dogs. That's where they got the idea."

"Facebook?"

"Yes, Facebook."

Clifford winced, made a scowling face, "I feel bad about the boy who died."

"Me too."

"His name was Adam?"

"Yes, Adam."

Stage Six Sleep

I was deep in stage six sleep, or somewhere thereabouts. Medication mixes up sleep cycle signals.

*

Both Dr. Reilly and Elaine, explained at great lengths, that these hospital doctors are pumping various medications, painkillers and antibiotics into my arm through a transparent tube. "It's an intravenous infusion drip."

I understand, more or less, it's because I got stabbed when those boys tried to steal my dog, Socks. Additionally, I've had some sort of surgery and, consequently, my recovery requires infection fighting. I do, however, still feel numb and fuzzy. Dr. Reilly says that I'm not sick, I'm injured. There's evidently an important distinction, but I don't know what it is anyway. Seems an issue for him.

"You might have some strange dreams," Elaine said, as she examined the hospital's equipment, "and that's perfectly normal considering these medications you are receiving. So don't worry about it, right?"

I just smiled, "Sure, I am not worried, but I think you have me confused with Katy. She always has the weirdest nightmares, and she's not on anything, I don't think. Too many comic books likely cause some of her strange dream stuff."

"That's true," Elaine shook her head. "Gramps has been looking after her since the incident."

"Just wondering, is the *incident* the same thing as the boys who tried to steal Socks?"

"Yes, same."

"Okay, good to know."

For most of us, the whole dreaming part of the sleep cycle is mind blowing at best. Elaine says that the basic principles are not that complicated, neuropsychologically speaking. "Everyone dreams," she raises her finger, "Some people are not aware of their dreams. It's the brain's self-sanitizing procedure. When you sleep your body rejuvenates, relaxes and repairs. Dreams are different. That's the brain *not* the body."

Some people are light sleepers, they wake easy. Some people can sleep through loud noises and not wake up. I'm in between, in the middle section.

Tonight, I don't know what I was dreaming about exactly, but I could hear my name being whispered and some shoulder shaking. I woke up, and there was Katy, whispering my name, and rubbing my shoulder.

"Shhhush, you have to keep quiet," Katy said, putting her index finger perpendicular to her lips. That's the universal signal for silence.

"Okay," I whispered back, "why do we have to be quiet?"

"Because it's 2:00 in the morning and the hospital doesn't want any noise at this time. People are sleeping."

"How did you get here?"

"Rode my bike."

"Gramps or Elaine know you are here?"

"No, they would get angry."

"That's true, you snuck out."

"Yes, but you have to be quiet, okay," Katy pointed her finger at me with meaning.

"I am being quiet," I whispered back, with emphasis.

"Okay, stay that way." Katy took off her backpack, "I've brought someone here to see you." She reached into the backpack and pulled out our puppy, Socks. Again, she did the finger to the mouth thing to signal quietness.

Socks and I were so happy to see each other. Socks let out some little yip, yip noises of happiness. She's so soft. Of course, I couldn't help but think, "Oh geez Katy, you are really going to be in trouble when Gramps and Elaine realize you smuggled Socks out to see me."

She scoffed, "Ya, well, I'm already in trouble. So, what's a little more going to do anyway."

"How much trouble are you in?"

"Dunno exactly, but I killed a kid."

"It was an accident."

"Ya, I guess so."

We whispered back and forth for a while about the situation, and the authorities' reactions to Katy killing a kid. Before you know it the three of us had fallen asleep on my hospital bed. Katy on one side, me on the other, with Socks in the middle.

There was sunlight coming through the windows, but otherwise I don't know what time it was in the early morning when Gramps and Elaine showed up. Elaine took pictures of the three of us sleeping. All in all, they were not angry with Katy. It was easy to find her because the bike has a GPS tag embedded.

Gramps took Katy and Socks home. Elaine stayed with me because all the hospital people started coming and going in the room. The hospital people make lots of noise. It's their place so I guess that's how it goes. One nurse changed the plastic fluid thing that put stuff in my arm. Another nurse came and took blood samples from my other arm. I hate the blood stuff. Elaine seemed to be supervising and told me, "Everything is going to be okay."

"When?" I asked.

She kissed me on the forehead, "Right now, everything is okay right now." Elaine smiled, tussled my hair, "Just hang in here for a while longer. We are all going to be okay. You will be back home soon."

"Okay."

Epilogue

So, Sandy, finally, I made it back to Julsons Bay on Mayne Island. It wasn't easy getting back here. Don't know how many days altogether I was in the hospital. The first time I was in for surgery, and recovery from the surgery. Then Katy and Elaine insisted that Gramps get me out of the hospital and bring me back home to the condo to finish recovering.

Bad decision, it didn't work out, something went wrong, and I left the condo in an ambulance in the middle of the night. I don't remember much about it. Elaine says that's just as well. The brain's coping mechanism functions to help compensate for those instances. Same sort of thing happens in an accident when the brain sends a person into *shock*.

One of the Woofers (Worldwide Opportunities on Organic Farms) on Farmer Daryl's farm was cutting fallen logs with a chainsaw. The chainsaw hit a knot, bounced back, and cut a big gash in her arm. Her brain sent her into shock. Elaine says that's helpful because otherwise if she was flailing her arm around, *more* damage would occur. Shock puts you down in place.

Gramps seems good with a chainsaw. No one is allowed to touch his chainsaw. No one is allowed to touch his computer, either. Katy touches too many things that she shouldn't, but she's doing well these days. Elaine's Ma, Emily, has taken over as Katy's home school teacher. They work well together. Ma's with us for a while. I don't know the whole deal, yet I know when to mind my own business (despite the irony of business versus science).

Socks, the therapy dog, has grown a lot. She's still got some puppy clumsiness because her big paws are uncoordinated with her legs. She thinks she can do stuff that she can't. Just like when Gramps tells Katy, "Your eyes are bigger than your stomach."

Dr. Reilly comes over all the time to chum around with Gramps. Old guys are peculiar. They like to hike. They look at the world differently. Whatever, who cares, they seem happy.

"Every generation blames the one before."

I still think about mum and dad from time to time. I don't obsess about things so much because everyone emphasizes that obsessing is not so good. Did you know mum was a singer and dancer? I didn't. Gramps got me a new Cowichan Lone Tree guitar made from north island cedar and south island oak. I'm getting good singing mum's songs. I still miss her all the time. But don't worry it's okay, it's just the way it is. I'm keeping my head above the water line.

I have to sign off now because they are taking turns calling me for lunch. I like lunch. Elaine's Ma makes the best grilled cheese sandwiches with bacon. They've called from the bottom of the stairs twice and buzzed my phone. It's rude of me to not respond, so I'm going now. Social skills supersede everything.

Elaine keeps reminding me, "You are a work *in progress.*"

Sandy, I like to think you sit on my shoulder. I still hear you whispering suggestions in my ear. It's good. I'll be fine.

Cousin Katy says, "Life goes on – one way or another."

Okay, I gotta go. Lunchtime.

Acknowledgments

Richard Wagamese (1955 - 2017) wrote, "It's not easy bringing a book into this world."

"Same thing, I know what you mean," that's what I'd say to Richard Wagamese.

A number of people helped me put this book together. Here's where I acknowledge and note my appreciation to those who helped bring this book into the printed world.

First, this book is a work of fiction. I made up this story, however, having said that, there are a number of incidents, influencers, family, and friends who should be acknowledged in this section for their assistance in how this story came together.

1973 – I worked for four months at the Cassiar Asbestos Mine. It was *only* a four-month summer job in between Mount Royal College and WSU. Seemed like a long four months altogether considering how the time ticked slowly. Fifty miles south of the Yukon border, it never got dark – land of the midnight sun.

"Stay in school, son," said the Mine Manager, Mr. Rupert MacKenzie. He was quite nice to me because the townsite swimming pool was his personal project. One night the man who looked after the swimming pool got drunk, called it quits, and took the morning bus out from Cassiar to Watson Lake in the Yukon.

Fortunately, I was working on a novel in between mining shifts. I had my *portable* Smith Corona typewriter with me. When word got out that the swimming pool would close because they needed a lifeguard with a license to operate the place, I ran back to the bunkhouse after my shift. Typed out a fresh resumé, and a cover letter, put them in an envelope, jogged over to the mine's admin building, slid the envelope under Mr. MacKenzie's door.

The next day I was in a tunnel shovelling rocks that fell off the conveyor belt in a curve of the tunnel. It was like the famous *I Love Lucy* episode. I was assigned the spot, and no one thought it was funny. Some summer jobs suck – rich people don't do this stuff, was my thinking.

Long story made short, there I was, shovelling away when Mr. Rupert MacKenzie came stomping down the tunnel towards me holding my envelope, "You John Carter," he asked. I nodded, yes (the tunnels are loud). "Put your shovel down, come with me."

It was snowing when we emerged from the tunnel. His pickup truck was off to the side, but not out of the way, everyone knew that was a big deal truck. We climbed into the cab and the job interview began, as we descended to the townsite. Snow turned to rain; it was May.

"You know how to run a swimming pool?"

"No, not everything," I explained. "I can clean filtres, do backwashes, adjust chlorine to the manufacturer's specifications. I can't do repairs."

"You have a Red Cross Lifeguard Certificate."

"Yes."

"Okay," he nodded, "you work for me now."

Although my thoughts were, "Who was I working for before?" I said nothing. It was a union job, he was management. Going forward, I did mine maintenance in the morning, pool work in afternoon and evening. A type of split shift. Rupert knew I was leaving in late August for university. He had time to get someone from Edmonton replace me at the pool.

Asbestos was called *white gold*, fifty years ago (half a century). Now we know better. Asbestos is bad. I was *only* there for four months. The mine opened in 1952 and shutdown in 1992. It's ghost town now.

In this novel, Randal Reilly explains to the hospital's psychology department director, Dr. Andrea Kovanski, "Working here is way easier than the asbestos mine."

1990 – close to twenty years after leaving the mine, I landed a summer job at the Child Development Diagnostic Program at Sunny Hill Health Centre (subsequently amalgamated with BC Children's Hospital). Dr. Linda Eaves, director of the psychology department hired me. Dr. Eaves is a scholar and an autism expert. Although I did not claim much expertise in autism in 1990, I certainly claimed expertise in psychometric omnibus intelligence measurements, sustained attention assessment, and learning difficulties. Linda said that would be adequate and we would work from there. Psychology was different back then, but better than mining.

1997 – Dr. Truman Spring, City University, Director, was the first person to talk to me about therapy dogs. I think Truman's was named Teddy. We worked at Winslow Centre back then and that always brings a smile. I thank Truman for planting the therapy dog seed so many years ago.

People often ask: How did you end up on Mayne Island?

2001 – I worked as a psychology consultant for Warner Brothers on the film *Dreamcatcher*. Stephen King sold them his novel's film rights for one dollar. The film's director, Academy Award nominee, Lawrence Kasdan, hired me. I received film credits and BCPA scale pay. My dad's friend, Dr. Stanley Blank, gave the production company my name and number.

On a nice early December day, I drove out to the large film studio in Burnaby. Previously, the various assistants had already couriered three updated colour coded versions of the script and screenplay. An armed guard met me at the gate, radioed my name to someone, and pointed to where I should park. A couple of well-dressed young ladies came out to ask if I needed help with the equipment. All I had was a backpack full of books, VHS tapes, and the last package of the colour coded script, and documents they had sent via courier.

Inside the massive studio I was introduced to one of the production assistants who said it will be ten minutes before Larry can meet with me. Meanwhile, she suggested, "Maybe I could get prepared for the meeting." I replied, I was prepared, but maybe she could explain more about the format expectations. She said, never mind, just follow me to a conference room.

We started walking down the hall when a young man popped his head out of a doorway and asked, "Is that Dr. Carter? Larry is ready."

Larry and a group of guys were huddled in front of a large monitor on wheels. I was introduced to Larry, then we went through a series of greetings with the various producers and their assistants. After which we got down to the business of discussing the Dreamcatcher Duddits character.

Larry announced that they had selected Donnie Wahlberg for the role of adult Duddits. My job was to advise and coach Donnie in preparation for the role. In Stephen King's novel *Dreamcatcher*, the Duddits character had Down's syndrome. We watched some of the video clips that I brought, talked about the new script and how the screen adaptation could be presented. In the end they decided the film version Duddits would present as moderately mentally challenged. With that concluded the meeting adjourned, we shook hands, Larry said, "See you in Prince George."

I hadn't planned on going to Prince George in January. Too cold for me. I thought Burnaby was adequate. However, I was getting paid well *and* film credits. So, of course, I caught the airplane. It was raining in Vancouver when we left, but snowing and cold landing in Prince George.

Disembarking and strolling into the Prince George airport there were a lot of people with placards and various signs. I saw a young lady who was holding a sign with my name. I waved hello, approached, set my luggage down, and said, "Hi, I'm John Carter."

"Fabulous, welcome to Prince George, Dr. Carter," she grabbed my luggage, quickly introduced herself, smiled, and said, "Follow me."

We went outside where a long row of black SUVs were lined up and waiting. We climbed inside and took off down the road. The airport was not close to town. "First, I'll take you to the hotel to check in. I'm taking Tom Sizemore to the dentist, after which I will come and get you to meet with Donnie."

"Okay," I smiled, "I'll be ready." That's when I learned there is a lot of waiting around time in the making of a movie.

I met with Donnie Wahlberg (New Kids on the Block, Sixth Sense, Blue Bloods) in the afternoon while he was in the makeup trailer getting ready for some shots. We discussed the Duddits character, practiced gaits, and inflections. That was it, I was done for day one.

Day two, the big black SUV picked me up and took me to the production centre. All the drivers are Teamsters. He asked, "Are you talent or tech?" I said, neither I'm a psychologist. But I *was* in the Steel Workers Union when I worked in the mine. The driver chuckled, he said he always enjoyed driving comedians.

Inside the production place I met Morgan Freeman, Damian Lewis, Timothy Olyphant, and Donnie. Quite an all star cast. We waited around for the table reading to begin and then I went back to the hotel. Down time in Prince George I spent surfing the internet looking at Southern Gulf Islands real estate listings.

The following weekend we took the ferry to Mayne Island, met with the real estate agent I had been corresponding with and toured the listings. A couple places were duds, a couple were too much, and we finally settled on an old cottage on the beach with a giant Arbutus tree looking out to Mount Baker.

And that's how we ended up on Mayne Island. It is a small island (eight square miles), a quiet place, where I like to sit and watch the tide roll in and out while writing stories. Summer is the best season.

2023 – In this story Cliff goes to lunch at the French restaurant where he explains to Dr. Joe Moriarty why batting is more important than pitching in baseball. "You need runs to win the game."

I'm indebted to John Dinning for that discussion. It evolved from a quality versus quantity explanation where "One home run is worth more than two doubles."

2024 – Susan Wagner is the nicest Australian I have ever met. Ever. Thirty-four years ago, Sue and I shared an intelligence test kit (budgets were tight and resources were limited). We met Wednesdays at the Whitespot Restaurant in POCO to exchange that kit and other assorted psychological things. Sue was a proofreader for my previous novel, Shane's Coma. And she agreed to do it again for this one (of course, needless to say *all remaining errors are mine*. Sue is such a good friend. I appreciate her enormously!

2012 to 2024 – Special thanks to Vladimir Verano. This is the *sixth* novel that Vlad has created the cover and block design. Vlad is best in the business. I certainly appreciate his work.

Harbans says, just do what makes you happy (within reason and not too loud).

www.ingramcontent.com/pod-product-compliance
Lightning Source LLC
Chambersburg PA
CBHW051140190726
48290CB00006B/1930